Connor's gaze swerved to her, his eyes intense and focused. It was difficult not to reach out and touch him, to complete that connection that burned hot.

"Did you see anyone?" His hand covered hers, no doubt to get her attention, but the gesture turned primal. She laced their fingers as she shook her head.

Connor didn't drag his hand away. He brought his free hand to the back of her neck and pulled her close. "What are you doing?" Darkness danced in his eyes, and she sensed a danger that lay in wait in him.

"What do you mean? I'm holding your hand...and waiting for you to kiss me. I want you. I want to know what it's like to kiss a man like you."

He traced his finger over her lip. "You are a complicated woman, and I haven't begun to figure you out."

Her mind swam with thoughts, but her body ached for more. "You have all night."

His eyes blazed. "You're playing with a fire you can't control."

She pressed against him. "Don't underestimate me."

Dear Reader,

Connor West made a brief appearance in *Shielding the Suspect* as Brady Truman's landlord. A former spy who could be called paranoid if it weren't for the fact that "they" really are after him, he is an intriguing character and I immediately knew he would have his own story. Connor has met his match in Kate, a talented intelligence analyst who works best behind a computer. Connor prefers the outdoors, but when his brother goes missing, finding him will require both of their skills and all their cunning.

When I was growing up, my father and my brothers spent a lot of time outdoors: camping, hiking and exploring. I was never much for dirt and bugs, but I always loved their stories. I don't know how many were fictionalized, but here's an outdoor adventure of my own.

Happy reading!

C.J. Miller

TRAITOROUS ATTRACTION

—

C.J. Miller

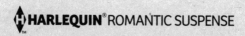
HARLEQUIN® ROMANTIC SUSPENSE

Recycling programs
for this product may
not exist in your area.

ISBN-13: 978-0-373-27871-8

TRAITOROUS ATTRACTION

Copyright © 2014 by C.J. Miller

HARLEQUIN®
www.Harlequin.com

Printed in U.S.A.

Books by C.J. Miller

Harlequin Romantic Suspense

Hiding His Witness #1722
Shielding the Suspect #1770
Protecting His Princess #1777
Traitorous Attraction #1801

C.J. MILLER

loves to hear from her readers and can be contacted through her website, www.cj-miller.com. She lives in Maryland with her husband, son and daughter. C.J. believes in first loves, second chances and happily ever after.

Part I: America

Chapter 1

Connor West had an eight-second warning before the knockout blonde with a too-serious expression showed up in front of his house. His perimeter security alarm beeped and her newer-model luxury sedan displayed on his smartphone screen. A camera situated along the driveway scanned her car's tags and ran a DMV lookup. Another camera snapped a picture of her face and ran it through facial-recognition software.

Nothing popped up immediately on his computer, which checked his watch list first: federal and local law enforcement, known special operatives, and convicted and released felons. The woman in his driveway must be lost. Connor lived in the woods, far away from civilization, and it was how he liked it. He didn't often get surprise visitors, and when he did, their arrival was either a mistake or delivered a problem.

Connor hoped she'd take one look at his cabin, spin her car around and hightail it off his property. He gave it an 80 percent likelihood she wouldn't stop to ask for directions. Didn't most people have GPS on their cars and their mobile phones? Why would she turn onto his private road? Had to be a mistake.

To his surprise, she climbed out of her car, one long, shapely leg followed by the other. She was wearing a pair of bright green shorts and a white tank top. In her hand, she grasped a small piece of paper. She looked between it and his cabin and back to the paper.

Yes, she was definitely lost.

He mentally urged her to get back in her car and not look back. He wasn't in the mood to deal with her. Connor hadn't seen another human being in a week and he was happy to have it that way.

To his annoyance, she walked up the stairs to his front door. Guess she wasn't a woman who was easily put off. Connor hadn't gone so far as to put no-trespassing signs everywhere. He didn't think he needed them. The location spoke for itself.

The curvy blonde knocked on his door. He could either slip out of the back or pretend not to be home. She would get back in her car and he'd never see her again. He could return his attention to the book he was reading and forget this interruption to his day.

At her second knock, his curiosity overtook his annoyance. What if she needed help? If she didn't turn and run at the sight of him, telling her she was at the wrong location and sending her down the road would take five seconds. Not difficult. She was a beautiful woman and Connor rarely had the opportunity to speak to a woman who looked like her. It would be his one social interaction for the month.

If her looks didn't cinch it, her worried expression and terse mannerisms drew him to his feet. Leaving a woman lost and concerned didn't sit right with him.

Connor opened the front door, expecting a startled reaction. A few months of forgoing shaves and haircuts in combination with his worn jeans and battered, holey T-shirt made for a distressingly poor appearance. She got courage points for not immediately fleeing at the sight of him.

The woman smiled. "Connor? Connor West?"

He instinctually reached for the gun tucked in the holster at his side and unsnapped the strap, letting his hand linger on the handle. Pretty face, short shorts and a tight shirt wouldn't distract him. He was too smart to be taken out by a female assassin. He was a survivor and this woman wouldn't get the best of him. Perhaps this visit would be more exciting than he'd first believed. "Hands where I can see them. I want your name and why you're here. You get ten seconds and then I start shooting."

Her hands went into the air, and unless she was a great actress, the shaking of her arms and trembling of her lips gave away her fright. She was missing the hard edge and the precise and skilled movements of a Sphere assassin. Perhaps not an assassin, then. "My name is Kate Squire. I have information about Aiden. He was a…friend of mine."

Another surprise…and Connor hated surprises. His brother had been a friend of hers? She'd paused before that word. A friend? Or his brother's former lover? Given Aiden's track record, it was believable that he had been sleeping with this woman. She was his type. Tall, fit and blonde, with a smooth, sexy voice.

A stream of jealousy shot through him and Connor batted it away. What was the point of being envious of a situation he couldn't change and that had been true all their lives? Aiden had been the handsome, fun brother. Nothing had gotten him down. Connor had wanted Aiden to be happy, had worked to make it the case, and Connor liked to believe that Aiden had been.

Aiden hadn't mentioned this woman by name during any of their late-night conversations. Not unexpected, since Aiden had grown increasingly secretive and distant in the months before he'd died. Their last conversation had been in anger, a reality Connor deeply regretted. It made it harder to cope with losing Aiden.

"How did you find me?" Connor asked. He kept his home address off the radar. It wouldn't be found using a typical internet search.

The blonde's arms dropped a few inches. "Aiden gave me your address for emergencies."

If Aiden had told her where to find his brother, they had to have been good friends. Why hadn't Aiden mentioned he'd shared Connor's information with someone? Why hadn't Aiden mentioned this woman? His distrust was heightened.

"What's your emergency?" Connor asked. This woman was at his home, claiming to have information and an emergency. How dramatic. Maybe it would feel good for her to get something off her chest, but in all likelihood, whatever she told him, Connor would already know or would find insignificant, as most everything was compared to his brother being dead.

Connor also wasn't sure he believed her story. If

they didn't plan to outright kill him, it would be like Sphere to send an attractive woman and launch upsetting information at him to get him off guard. Sphere hadn't given up on bringing him back in, and psychological games were their specialty. Connor wouldn't fall for tricks. Aiden had been gone for seven months and Connor had made his peace with his brother's death. He wasn't getting taken in by a beautiful woman. Whatever this Kate Squire needed to say, he wouldn't let it affect him.

"Could you please take your hand off your gun? You're making me nervous," Kate said.

He hadn't realized he was clasping the handle. He removed his hand from his gun and put it at his side. If she gave him any reason to think she was reaching for a weapon, he could get to his gun before she could get to hers. "Answer my question. What is your emergency?" Connor didn't take his eyes off her hands. A difficult task given that she had a lot of features worth a second and third long look.

She lowered her hands and he allowed it. "I heard you were tough but, wow, I didn't expect this."

What *had* she expected? If Aiden had told her about him, he would have told her Connor was a hermit who lived alone, who didn't like visitors and who preferred the company of his books to people.

"I have something to tell you that might be upsetting for you. Do you want to sit down? Or do you want to get a drink first?" she asked.

No and no. "I don't need to sit. I don't need to drink. There's nothing you can tell me about Aiden that will upset me." Both he and his brother had worked for Sphere. They had completed missions and tasks that were difficult and dangerous. They had walked the line just shy of immoral at times, they had lived fast and loose, and they had loved the adrenaline high of working rogue missions all over the world in the name of liberty and justice. Whatever this woman had to say about his brother, whatever story she would tell, it didn't change that Aiden was a good man with a good heart. Nothing would sully Connor's memory or change his deep respect for his younger brother.

The woman folded her arms over her chest. "I'm the one who needs a drink." She laughed, a nervous jitter. The sound was light and tingled in his ears. Kate took a deep breath. "I don't want to get your hopes up and I don't want to make trouble for you, but I believe Aiden is alive."

Unrealistic hope flared at the word *alive* but realism tamped it down. "My brother is dead." It was a fact. If his brother was alive, Connor would have heard from him. If Aiden's lover had convinced herself Aiden was alive, perhaps it was a coping technique or the denial phase of her grief. Connor worked firmly in reality and the reality was that Aiden was dead.

The woman looked at the ground, and when she lifted her head, tears shone in her eyes. "I think he is very much alive and he might need your help. I think he was captured in Tumara and is being held by the Armed Revolutionaries in one of their prisons."

Connor's denial skidded to a stop. How had this woman known his brother was working in Tumara for *el presidente* and against the revolutionaries? *El presidente* was fighting to stay in power despite a burgeoning lower class who was demanding higher wages and better living conditions. Bruno Feliz was their outspoken leader. Armando Lopes, or *el presidente,* as the dictator was known, had assistance from Sphere to keep the revolutionaries down. Keeping Lopes in power would prevent upheaval, but Sphere only cared about the money.

Aiden's involvement in the region was classified. He hadn't spoken about his mission or the work he'd completed for Sphere. Connor knew what he had done from keeping his finger on the pulse of Aiden's work, a task he'd found more difficult the deeper Aiden had gone with Sphere. "Where are you getting your information?"

Kate stepped closer to him. As she neared, the light scent of vanilla wafted over him. "I could get in trouble for this. For telling you anything about Aiden and his work. But I feel like I have to tell someone. I work for the same company you and Aiden did. I analyzed some intelligence we received from our overseas allies and I have reason to believe your brother is alive. My cover—that is, my work with the State Department— puts me in touch with important people." She shoved a hand through her hair as if frustrated with her explanation. "I know this sounds crazy, but I need you to believe me."

Connor's thoughts shifted into overdrive. She worked for Sphere, the organization responsible for his brother's death. Sphere's agenda was buried beneath a flurry of excuses and stories and rationalizations. It was one of the reasons Connor didn't work for them anymore. "You work for Sphere?"

Kate looked around as if someone could overhear them. At least she had the paranoid-operative part down pat. Not that he had room to judge.

"Yes. I work there," she whispered.

"Let me tell you something, Kate." If that was her name. "I know how Sphere operates. They told me he was dead. Now you are telling me he is alive. If someone gave you that false hope, I'm sorry." They could be manipulating Kate into seeking him out. This could be another attempt to coerce Connor to work a mission for them. "If my brother was alive, he would have contacted me. You're being played."

Kate shook her head. "This isn't a game. Aiden needs you. I have a picture in my smartphone that might change your mind. Can I get it out and show it to you?"

Connor nodded his assent, and Kate reached into her back pocket and withdrew a slim phone. She typed on it and then turned it to face him. Connor closed the distance between them, poised to react to any sudden movements. Sphere would take out a target by any means necessary: deception, surprise, full-on attack. If Kate pulled out a weapon, he'd disarm or kill her.

The picture on the screen startled him. Aiden was sitting on a dirt floor, a bamboo fence behind him. It was too small for Connor to notice any photo editing. She could have gotten a picture of Aiden and inserted it into the setting. A phony picture to tear at his resistance was a simple lie for Sphere to manufacture.

Connor should have told her to leave the moment she mentioned knowing Aiden. He should have forbidden the slim ray of hope that his brother was alive from shining on his thoughts. But the thinness of his brother's face, the bruises, the worn and tattered clothes spooked Connor. Could Aiden be incapacitated and unable to send a message to Connor for help?

Thinking of his brother in desperate straits took hold

of his core and shook him. If the picture was real, and if it was recent, it wouldn't help him locate his brother. Unless Kate had more, Connor would have to mount his own operation to search for his brother. It would take time and resources.

Growing up, it had been he and Aiden against the world. To know the only person he'd ever trusted could be hurt, in need and alive changed everything. Kate might be lying, but was he willing to stake his brother's life on it?

"Did you check if the picture was edited?" he asked.

"The picture is legit. I obtained it, with great difficulty I might add, from work. A contact of mine in Tumara believes I work for the State Department and that I have a streak of goodwill in my blood. He sent the picture to me in case it developed into an international incident. You know, American held against his will by the Armed Revolutionaries," Kate said.

When someone lied to him, Connor usually knew it. He sensed it. Nothing about Kate screamed liar. What was her angle? "What do you want?" Connor asked, cutting to the chase.

"What do I want?" she repeated, her eyes wide and confused. "I want you to help Aiden."

Was Connor ready to believe that this woman was telling the truth and his brother was alive? That he was already thinking about how to find Aiden told him that he'd bought Kate's story. "Tell me what you know and I'll take care of the rest." He'd fill in or locate the missing information. If Aiden was alive, Connor would find him.

Kate blinked at him, her bright blue eyes giving away nothing. "If I tell you everything, you'll take off and I'll never hear from you or Aiden again. You're taking me with you and I'll tell you what you need to know as you need to know it."

Gutsy. She'd shown up on his property, asked for his help and then set the terms of their arrangement. "Tell me everything and we'll go from there." She was right in deducing his intention. Once she spilled the information he needed, he'd ditch her. He preferred his work how he preferred his personal life: solitary.

"Nice try. We work together on this."

"If you work for the agency, why not find him yourself?" It was as much a challenge as it was a test.

"I'm a computer analyst, not a field operative. I've completed the mandatory cross-training, but I am not foolish enough to attempt this alone."

Sphere recruited two types of people: highly skilled assassins with unique talents, like him and his brother, and überintelligent supergeeks who excelled in their areas of technical expertise. Connor couldn't envision Kate rapidly typing at a computer. Most attractive people used their looks to their advantage and she couldn't do that behind a computer. Sphere liked attractive operatives to work the field. A good-looking woman could pull information easily from a smitten man.

Kate set her hands on her hips, bringing his attention momentarily to the dip in her slender waist and the roundness of her hips. "I know the odds are stacked against me. If you won't help me, you've taken away my best option. But I can't let this go. I won't let this go."

Connor glanced at her smartphone again. "This might be a setup. You might be too late. You could lose your life trying to save his when he's already dead. They could be using you to find and tie off loose ends." As he spoke the words, his doubts whispered less loudly. *What if Aiden is alive?*

"I don't believe he's dead. I won't give up," Kate said, her voice quiet and determined.

Connor would never forgive himself if Kate was right and he did nothing about it. She'd trapped him, as perhaps she'd planned. He had to take action. "Aiden is my brother. I'll search for him until he is either home safe or I know this is a lie."

Relief rushed across her face. "Thank you, Connor. You won't regret this." She reached for his hand and he jerked away. He wasn't agreeing to an alliance with Kate. He'd search alone. Having another person along would bungle the operation.

He stepped back from the door and gestured for her to come inside. "Stand here," he said, pointing to a location next to the entryway.

Watching her in his peripheral vision, he pulled his travel pack out of the closet. "I work faster and better alone," Connor said.

Kate's eyes narrowed. "You can work faster with information. Information I have. I speak Portuguese— the most common language spoken in Tumara—plus Italian, Spanish and Arabic. I know the area and the culture. I know the political climate."

She was bound and determined to search for Aiden. He'd accept it. For now. He opened his bag to check his supplies. "I speak a number of languages myself. I have boundaries. I have lots of them. Respect them or I'll leave you wherever we are without notice and I won't look back." He glanced at her in the mirror.

Kate's eyes widened. "That's fair." She seemed unsure. "Spell them out."

He waited a beat and she stared at him. She was serious. She wanted him to give her a list of rules, the dos and don'ts of spending time with him. Most people who met him quickly understood he didn't like idle prattle, he didn't like people being close to him and he preferred to be alone. The most comfortable path was to give him as much leeway as possible. He could be harsh and direct and didn't hesitate to be blunt. What was it about Kate that made him censor and soften his words? "You want boundaries? Don't talk except when you have relevant information. I'm jumpy and don't like surprises. Give me space." He composed a mental list of supplies he'd need for the trip.

She was looking around his cabin, seemingly eager to snoop around. He didn't keep sensitive information here, so there was nothing to find. Even so, she hadn't moved from the spot in the room where he could watch her most closely. She wasn't seeing any more of his place. He didn't give tours. "Aiden mentioned you could be grumpy. But I'll do my best to respect your boundaries so long as you understand that I'm a woman who likes to talk sometimes, I don't mean to surprise you, but given the nature of this situation, we'll be surprised at times, and if we're traveling together, you won't be alone."

Connor suppressed a smile. She gave as good as she got. He liked that. It had taken courage for her to come to him. He liked that, too. But he didn't trust her. Trust was hard-won and easily lost. She hadn't given him the whole truth about why she was here and he didn't care for that in the least. He would find out what she was hiding, and if she double-crossed him, she would regret it.

Kate had seen Connor West only once before in person when he'd attended his brother's memorial service seven months before. Connor looked remarkably different today. His dark beard was scraggly and unkempt, his hair in disarray and his clothes in need of mending, stain treating, heavy-duty washing and ironing. Or maybe they were too far gone and should be scrapped for cleaning rags. She should be disgusted by his appearance, but stress and guilt were making her feel strange things. Kate was still attracted to Connor. Maybe it was his confidence or the stories Aiden had told her about him, but the crush she'd had on him took hold of her and morphed into something more potent. She felt a little dizzy and wanted to get closer to him.

Kate shouldn't have feelings for a man she'd seen only twice, including today, and hadn't spoken to the first time. Connor had slipped into the somber room and had blended with the other mourners. His dark suit had fit him well, the jacket sitting across his broad shoulders and the tailored pants showing off his athletic build. His short hair was neat and trim, giving him an almost schoolboy appearance. A slight arch in his nose indicated it had been broken in the past, marring what would otherwise be considered model good looks. Kate had fought the attraction that sprang up. She'd learned her lesson about getting involved with special-operations men. That he was Aiden's brother made her attraction even more unfortunate.

Kate wouldn't have seen him at all, except she'd been waiting for him at the service. She'd owed him an explanation, something to help give him closure. To her dismay, she hadn't gotten the opportunity to speak to him. Connor had stridden directly to the front of the room where a portrait of Aiden in a golden frame sat on an easel among the floral arrangements. He'd looked at the picture and bowed his head, bringing his hand across his face.

She'd averted her eyes, feeling she was intruding on a deeply private moment. When she'd finally looked back, Connor was gone. She'd searched the crowd for him but she'd had no luck locating him. Kate wasn't entirely sure why he'd come. Perhaps he'd felt a sense of obligation to make an appearance.

Outside his home, even when he'd had his hand poised near his gun, Kate wasn't afraid of him. She knew too much from Aiden about his older brother. Connor might be abrasive on the outside, but he was a good man who wouldn't hurt anyone without a compelling reason. Male special-operations agents were a different breed of man. They could be chillingly cold and insensitively direct. Kate had learned not to let their words and tone intimidate her when she worked with them.

Kate reached into her handbag and withdrew two plane tickets. "I'll tell you more when we arrive. You ready?"

"Are we traveling as ourselves or have you made other arrangements?" Connor asked.

Other arrangements, of course. Members of Sphere never traveled under their real names for business or pleasure. It was easier to cover tracks when using pseudonyms and fake documents. "We'll be traveling undercover."

Connor shook his head. "If you're using an identity

Sphere provided you, they'll know exactly where you are and what you're doing."

Kate knew how the system worked. The tickets she had purchased and the identifications she carried had been generated using her personal resources. "Give me a little credit. No one knows I came here to talk to you and no one knows what I'm planning."

Connor folded his arms. It was an improvement on his waiting-to-pounce stance. "Don't underestimate Sphere. They know everything. It's their business to keep everyone on their payroll under their control."

Kate shivered. She didn't like to think about the privacy she'd given up when she went to work for Sphere. Her financials, her personal life and her business life were open and available to Sphere for review at their discretion. But she had been careful about approaching Connor and creating their covers. She hadn't made her plans at work or on any Sphere network or device. "They don't know about this."

Connor shot her a look of disbelief. "I'll provide our travel documents."

Kate suppressed an eye roll. That was another trait of special-ops men. They always thought they were right. "If you think it's safer, then fine." He was willing to come to Tumara. She was willing to make compromises to get what she wanted.

She had to make amends for what she had done and for the mistake she had made. Her guilt was severe and she was willing to risk her life to see Aiden safe.

Part II: Tumara,
South America

Chapter 2

"When we land, are you planning to tell me more or do you need to keep me in the dark?"

Kate looked up from her ebook reader. It was the first time Connor had spoken to her on the long flight. His silence had stopped bothering her hours ago. He'd asked her not to make idle chatter and she'd respected the request. If he was angry at how she'd gone about convincing him to help her, she could accept that. "I'll tell you what you need to know as you need to know it." If she told him everything, he would ditch her. Maybe ditch her with enough resources to get home, but maybe not.

Her answer came out sharper than she'd intended. To her surprise, Connor appeared amused. "That's the unofficial motto of the company where you work. Don't believe it. It's always better to know more."

Was it? Kate had been happier before she'd uncovered one of Sphere's secrets: they'd knowingly left a man behind enemy lines with no intention of rescuing him. If her contact in the Tumaran government hadn't secretly passed on a rumor he'd heard and a picture of what looked like Aiden, she would have believed Aiden was dead. If she wasn't successful in finding and liberating him, Aiden would die alone in a dirty cage. Now that she knew what Sphere had done, she couldn't forget it and she couldn't walk away from the situation. "Knowledge is power, but knowledge can also destroy someone."

Connor's smile faded and his eyes turned darker. "The job you've chosen isn't an easy one."

"I never expected it to be." Although when she had been recruited by Sphere, she had been an idealist, expecting the agency to have pure and noble intentions. She had never heard of Sphere prior to them approaching her. Most people outside the organization had never heard of them. It was how they preferred it. When she accepted the job, she had viewed the agency as a superheroes-slash-secret-spies organization. Their resources had seemed infinite and their power unending. When they talked about the conflicts they had resolved and the potential disasters they had avoided, she had thought of them as the good guys.

Since then, she had developed a different view of her job and a much different view of the organization.

Connor studied her face, and his gaze dropped down for a second and then back up to meet her eyes. "I wouldn't have pegged you as working there," Connor said.

A mixture of insult and annoyance streamed through

her. Kate had worked against the assumptions people drew about her from the time she was a teenager. Her blond hair, slim—which she used to think of as scrawny—figure and long legs brought to mind a woman with little brain activity who was overly preoccupied with her looks. It wasn't the case. Her intelligence was her greatest strength. Either that, or the way people underestimated her. Pride lifted her chin. "I am good at my job."

"No doubt. You wouldn't have been hired if you were anything less than exceptional."

No trace of sarcasm touched his words and they stunned her. He thought more highly of her than she'd first believed. Whenever she made an assumption about him, she was wrong. He hadn't been happy to hear about his brother; he had been on edge and anxious. He hadn't believed her proof that Aiden was alive; he'd questioned her extensively. He hadn't wanted her help in locating Aiden; he'd wanted to work alone.

She'd be smart to remember not to rush to judgment about Connor. He kept his thoughts private and concealed, and might have been trained on intentionally misleading people. "If you know I'm competent, then have a little faith in me and trust that I'm doing the right thing."

"We both know it's unlikely I'll trust you. When it comes to my brother's safety and well-being, I'd rather not put a stranger in charge."

Harsh, but honest. Most undercover operatives for Sphere weren't known for their social graces. Those who were gifted with a silver tongue were often sent on missions that used their ability to con a target to meet their objectives. "Then at least recognize I will be useful in this mission," Kate said.

His eyes traced down her body again. "Having you along will cause more distractions for me. I'll need to watch over you."

Distractions had a heated overtone to it. Was he flirting with her in his own Connor-esque way? Acknowledging the basic human attraction between the two of them? He could have picked up on her crush on him. Despite his borderline rudeness, her interest in him hadn't diminished. The strange attraction was textbook. Her father had been a firefighter. Kate had adored him. He was strong, smart and successful with an edge of danger. It was the type of man Kate chased, perhaps wanting to have the deep, exciting relationship her parents had. "I can watch over myself."

"If we're a team, we should watch out for each other."

Which was it? They were a team or she was an impediment to him? He was impossible. "You want us to work together."

"I didn't say that."

Regardless of what he said or how he tried to confuse her, she'd act like a team the best she knew how. "I'll look out for you and me, okay?" It was how she operated on a mission even if she was behind a computer. She could take care of herself. She'd had training from Sphere, including weapons handling, hand-to-hand combat and survival techniques. If she couldn't handle this mission, she wouldn't have insisted on coming. She had limitations, but she would rise to the challenge. She always did.

Connor shrugged, though not dismissively. "Working at a desk won't give you the skills you need out here. I'll do whatever I can so when I find my brother, he won't be pissed that I let his girlfriend get hurt."

"I'm not his girlfriend," Kate said. Where had Connor gotten that idea?

Connor lifted a brow. "I don't believe you."

Kate sighed. His unwillingness to trust her was a problem. She had been forthcoming about the fact that she was withholding information about Aiden. Why couldn't he accept she was telling the truth about her relationship with Aiden? "I'm getting accustomed to that response from you."

Connor let the conversation lapse into silence. He liked doing things his way and he didn't let anyone into his private thoughts. Fine. She could deal with that. She had enough on her mind. Her most pressing concerns were Aiden and ignoring the fact that she was in an airplane thousands of feet from the ground. Sitting on the aisle seat lessened her phobia of heights slightly.

Her e-reader was her diversion. She returned to her book. It didn't hold her attention despite being the latest release by her favorite author. Kate's thoughts switched to the captivating man in the seat next to her. Connor and Aiden looked very much alike. Both brothers were tall, broad and dark, though Aiden's hair was a shade lighter. Connor had shaved his beard and cut his hair shorter, giving him an appearance more like his brother. The similarities ended there. Their personalities were acutely different. Aiden, though businesslike in the field, was warm in person. Ten seconds with him, and he had people eating out of his hand. He had never questioned her or Sphere. He did as he was told and he did it well.

Connor, on the other hand, was icy and distrusting.

His distrust had cost them a full day. He had gone out of his way to organize transportation when she had made careful arrangements. He still thought she might be setting him up. Maybe he'd picked up on her nervousness and had assumed she was leading him into a trap, not suffering from guilt.

When the captain of the airplane announced they would be descending, Kate turned off her e-reader and closed her eyes, pressing her head against the seat. In a few minutes, they would be on the ground. A mild headache pulsed at the fringes of her mind and her stomach turned over.

"You look pale. Are you going to be sick?" Connor asked.

"No. I'm fine," she said, her stomach dropping. She didn't want to admit to him her fear of heights.

He swore under his breath. "Are you afraid of airplanes? Or heights?"

No point in lying. He'd already noticed her body language. "Just the latter and only when it's high enough that I know falling will kill me." A perfectly reasonable fear: falling to her death with nothing to stop her.

"Great. That's great. Phobias in the field will get us both offed." Connor was whispering, but the irritation in his voice was clear.

"I'll be fine in the field." She'd been authorized to work for Sphere and they had an extensive screening process. They didn't think her height phobia made her a danger to anyone. Her primary job function was performed from behind a computer, but if her fear had been debilitating, she would have been eliminated as a candidate.

Connor didn't let up. "You should have told me. Full disclosure. You're playing a dangerous game."

She rolled her head to look at him and opened one eye. "First, you asked for no such thing. Second, you haven't told me any of *your* fears. Third, I wasn't about to give you more reasons to want to ditch me."

"One, fair enough. Two, I don't fear anything happening to me and, three, I've already tried to ditch you. You're a pit bull when you want something."

A pit bull? He was comparing her to a dog. She chose to take his words as a compliment. "Thank you. Perseverance is one of my best qualities."

"Your perseverance will get you killed. You've got to know when to back down and back away."

That got him a full-on stare, eyes wide-open. "I'm not backing down on this. I will find Aiden."

"We'll see."

Dismissive words. Anger gripped her. She would prove him wrong. "Yes, we will. And when I return to the States with him, I won't invite you to the welcome-home party."

"Just like a woman to worry about inconsequential things like having an exclusive party for someone."

Her mouth opened. What a jerk! Her crush on him waned to almost nothing. Despite her frustration, she kept her voice low. "How can you say that to me like that's all I care about? I sought you out to help your brother, and it wasn't exactly easy to find you nor have you been particularly pleasant to work with."

Connor shrugged. "I don't know what you care about, but I'd wager most of your intentions are self-serving. Just like a typical, shallow woman. Do me a favor. When we're looking for my brother, try to keep the whining to a minimum. I can't stand to hear a woman jabber on about her nails and her hair and her clothes, especially when I have something important to do."

She sputtered. Was asking Connor for his help a mistake? She wanted to help Aiden, but could there be another way? How could this be the amazing, considerate man whom Aiden had spoken of? Aiden had made his brother sound like a hero. But the Connor she was seeing was a self-centered, misogynistic—

The plane jarred against the tarmac and the pilot's voice announced their arrival.

Connor grinned. "Look at that. We're on the ground and you didn't throw up on me or pass out. Nice job."

Realization flooded into her. "You were antagonizing me on purpose?"

He winked at her. "Not hard to do and it distracted you, didn't it?"

It had. Her anger lessened. "You didn't mean any of that?"

"Not the insulting stuff, no."

She wondered what he considered insulting. She didn't question every word he'd said, though certain phrases replayed in her mind. *Dangerous game.* Would her perseverance get them killed? Kate didn't thank him for the distraction, though she'd seen yet another side of Connor. He'd seen her need and had taken action.

When they debarked the plane in Carvalo City, the capital of Tumara, Connor said nothing to her. He gathered his carry-on from the overhead compartment, murmured his gratitude to the flight attendants as they passed and strode down the hallway into the main airport. He blended into the crowd around him. Connor didn't turn around to see if she was following. Maybe he didn't care. He disappeared around a corner and mild panic shook her. A man like Connor could vanish and she wouldn't find him. He'd been trained by the best in the world in evasion and disappearance techniques.

A hand came around her forearm and pulled her into an alcove. Kate started. Connor's grip on her arm was strong as he held her against his body. The tension in his muscles tightened his hard body and his eyes burned with red-hot emotion. "We were followed."

The words were accusatory. "What? How?" She struggled to step away from him. He didn't release her.

"I don't know how. I thought you might."

Her jaw slackened. He was quick to imply she was lying and trying to screw him over. "I was careful. We traveled under your arrangements, remember?"

He pulled her bag from her hand. "This has to go."

She wasn't an amateur. "I checked my things. They're clean."

His eyes narrowed. "Then it's something on you." He dropped her bag to the ground and his hands moved to her shoulders, inspecting the fabric of her clothes. As he moved his hands lower, Kate shrugged off his touch. His intentions were to find a bug or tracker on her, but the contact was igniting her desire for him, making her hot and bothered. "I don't know if you've been living in the woods for too long and you've forgotten basic social decency, but you can't feel me up in an airport. I don't have any tracking devices on me."

"I'm not feeling you up. This isn't about a cheap grope in a public place. This is about keeping us safe and finding my brother. Take off all your clothes and change into mine. They could have sewn something into the fabric of yours. It's not safe. They track every employee every moment of the day. The sooner you realize that, the safer you'll be."

Kate didn't believe him. Her movements at work were monitored and her use of the computer equipment restricted, but Connor made it sound as if Sphere tracked her everywhere. They could request access to her personal financial documents or talk to her friends and family about her leisure-time activities, but she would have been alerted if she was under investigation. "You've lost it. They don't know I'm here and they certainly don't know I'm with you." Aiden had mentioned his brother was paranoid about security and she had witnessed plenty to support it, but this was ridiculous.

"Change. Your. Clothes."

A man and a woman walked past them, their heads bent together in conversation. Connor tensed and lowered his head, tucking it into the nape of Kate's neck. The closeness and his hands on her shoulders sent lust spiraling through her. It was the wrong time to get turned on, but Connor did something to her. He had the confidence and the moves and just enough daring to make him dangerous.

"They've been following us," Connor said.

Kate had noticed the couple on the plane, but it didn't qualify the man and woman as stalkers or Sphere agents. They didn't approach, and aside from a casual glance at them, neither seemed interested in her and Connor. Their disinterest was the most curious part. Not even a second glance at the couple lingering in a dark alcove in an airport?

What reason did anyone from Sphere have to follow her? Her boss had been clear he wouldn't search for Aiden. Kate hadn't told him she'd planned to do so because Sphere would have discouraged her or outright forbidden it. Instead, she had pretended to accept what he'd said and had made her plans to find Connor.

Kate hadn't given a reason for her leave of absence, except to say she needed a break after months and months of long hours and high stress. Lots of her colleagues took sabbaticals from work. Vacations were encouraged to keep stress from causing mistakes. Her work leave shouldn't have been a big deal or raised any red flags. Was Connor right? How closely did Sphere track her activities?

Connor took off in the direction from which they'd come.

Kate grabbed her bag from the ground and chased him. "Where are you going?"

"Getting out of this airport. You need to ditch your clothes and that bag," Connor said. He tore the bag from her hand and shoved it inside a nearby trash can.

Kate looked at it and then him, confusion and fear overwhelming her. Her clothes and supplies were in that bag. He was making fast, impulsive decisions as she knew field operatives were trained to do. Indecision cost precious time that was sometimes in short supply. On her training missions, she'd had time to think and plan. Connor was moving in the opposite direction of the exit signs. With a final look at her bag, Kate left it in the trash can and followed him. Connor glanced over his shoulder.

"They know I made them," he said.

Glancing behind her, Kate felt her heart rate escalate. The same man and woman from the airplane and the hallway were following them. Though they weren't running, they were closing the distance and moving quickly. Could it be a coincidence that the couple had changed their direction soon after Kate and Connor had?

She wasn't that naive. Not anymore. "What should we do?" Kate asked, accepting that Connor was the expert on this mission and they were safest following his directions.

Connor didn't say anything. He'd quickened his pace. He pushed at doors as they passed, perhaps searching for an open one to duck inside. After several tries, a door popped open. They slipped inside an office with a window to the outside. She assessed their options. The L-shaped desk and bookcase were cheap particle board covered with laminate and the file cabinet was made of scratched and dented mental. Connor grabbed the desk and pushed it across the carpet. He slid the file cabinet in front of it, angling it against the wall to barricade the door.

He unlocked and opened the window. "It's a ten-foot drop. Can you make it?"

Kate looked between the door and the window. Ten feet? That didn't seem high.

The door opened partially before slamming against the desk Connor had used to block it.

"Open the door. Kate, please be reasonable. We're worried about you."

They'd used her name. She tossed away the final remnants of her flimsy theory that she and Connor had misread their intent. They were agents from Sphere.

"I'll go out first and break your fall," Connor said.

Break her fall? Running to the window, she looked down and her vision blurred. She'd told Connor her fear of heights only included life-threatening falls. Faced with one that might only injure her, dizziness washed over her and fear threatened to freeze her in her tracks. The desk moved across the carpet, and the file cabinet ground into the drywall and slid along the wall as the agents forced open the door.

Connor disappeared over the ledge, his backpack strapped to him. With a final look back, Kate mimicked his actions. She slipped through the window onto the ledge, refused to look down, wobbled at the edge and jumped. Several seconds later, she was pressed to Connor, his strong arms around her. He'd caught her fall as he'd said he would. As far as she could tell, nothing had been broken.

Her stomach was against his face. As she slid down his big body to get her feet on the ground, the friction between their bodies burned through her. She wove her arms around his neck to gain her balance. He set her down and his arms lingered around her. "Are you injured?" he asked.

The eye contact set off a tiny shower of sparks between them. "I'm fine. I think I lost my job, though."

"Those are the stakes. The moment you pursued this course of action, you put your job on the line. Smart woman like you, you must have considered that."

He'd worked for Sphere. He knew what it took to separate from them and the consequences if the separation was not amicable.

Kate's stomach knotted with worry. She had considered it, but facing the reality was harder than she'd expected. Her home, her car, her bills and her reputation were at risk because of one decision she'd made. Refusing to turn back now, she forced the negative thoughts away. Her career wasn't as important as a man's life, and for the next several days or weeks, however long it took to find Aiden, she would stick to their plan.

Connor released her and Kate grasped his upper arms to steady herself. "Would you have left me behind if I'd been caught?" she asked.

"Would you have stayed behind if you knew it could save your career?" he asked.

"I jumped, didn't I?" She'd made a clear choice.

His brow lifted. Had she earned a sliver of his respect? "Let's move. They'll get through the barricade soon enough."

He hadn't answered her question. He'd made it clear he didn't trust her, but could she trust him?

The airfield encircled the terminal. With the openness of the layout, she and Connor had few places to hide. The garden surrounding the building was filled with drab green bushes, sparse in some areas, overgrown in others.

"Stay close to me," Connor said.

At the moment, it was the safest place to be. Kate wasn't trained to avoid Sphere agents or survive an altercation with them.

They crept along the side of the building. Though Connor tried to hold them from her, bush branches scraped at her face, arms and legs as they hurried. "This can't be just about Aiden," Connor said.

Kate took the branch he was holding and slipped past it. "If we find him, it would look bad for them, like they left a man in danger."

"They have enough staff working to keep their name out of the media through threats or force. I don't think they'd go through this trouble to stop us from finding one man. Aiden knows something or Aiden did something that they want kept quiet. Maybe they have tried to find him and failed. Maybe they want us to lead them to him."

Connor was a conspiracy theorist and shades of doubt entered Kate's mind. Kate had witnessed Sphere taking extreme actions to further their agenda, but she had been on the team that had worked the mission when Aiden disappeared and she'd never heard or read anything to indicate Aiden had displeased Sphere. If Aiden was alive and Sphere knew it, why the charade of a memorial service? Why not list him as missing in action?

Where the building ended and opened to the airfield, they had a choice. They could continue to race along the perimeter of the building or break away from the building, leaving them in the open until they reached the fence encircling the airfield.

If two agents from Sphere had been sent to track her or return her to the United States, would they have been working alone? Sphere assessed the difficulty and the importance of a mission before assigning operatives. Would they have spent the resources to send teams of agents after her? They knew she'd teamed up with Connor, his reputation legendary and his skill renowned.

"What's the plan?" Kate asked, checking over her shoulder to see how close the Sphere agents were. She didn't see them. Were they circling around another way? Would they trap her and Connor in a dead end? Kate wiped at her forehead, the sun and her fear overheating her. The Sphere agents couldn't shoot at them, not out in the open in a foreign country with a complicated relationship with the United States. Not much comfort, since Sphere agents were taught plenty of ways to kill a person discreetly.

"The plan? Get away from the airport without being shot," Connor said.

Kate inwardly sighed at his obvious statement. Connor wasn't big on sharing details. According to what she knew of him, while at Sphere, he'd frequently worked alone. She could see why. At least he had a dry sense of humor that charmed her. "You need to give me more than that."

"I don't need to do anything," Connor said, "except find my brother. You forced this partnership. You'll have to deal with me as I am."

"Are you trying to be difficult?" Kate asked.

The pause before he answered told her he was considering her question. "No. I am difficult. I don't try to be. Didn't my file tell you I don't play nice with others?"

How had he known she'd read his file? It was a fair assumption. "You'll have to learn."

"You're withholding information, too," Connor said. "When you give me what I need, I'll tell you more about my plan."

Give him what he needed? He needed to relax a bit and trust her a smidgen.

"You want to trade information?" she asked.

"Tell me what you know about my brother and I'll tell you how we'll find him," Connor said. He grabbed her hand. "But later. We've been found. Come on," Connor said, turning the corner of the building.

Kate didn't have time to see how close the Sphere agents were. They faced more open space and they ran across the tarmac. A baggage handler en route to a plane shouted at them in Portuguese to stop. They continued to run. When they reached the narrow strip of grass on the far side of the airport, a fence topped with barbed wire prevented them from leaving the airport grounds. "What do we do now?" Kate asked. She wasn't climbing into the barbed wire. She'd heard of Sphere agents doing extreme things, but she wasn't an agent. Her threshold for pain was minuscule.

"Look for another way out," Connor said.

At least he hadn't suggested taking their chances with the barbed wire.

Cutting through the grass, they followed the fence until it opened into an oncoming stream of cars, buses and taxis moving slowly toward the airport's departures terminal. Kate felt better being among people. The more people around them, the safer they were. Sphere liked to work in secret.

If the Sphere agents had no other choice, how aggressive would they become to meet their agenda?

Connor's gaze was sharp as he searched the scene, but his posture was relaxed. She was taking her cues from him. Going up against Sphere alone was a risky, and some would say foolish, decision. Having Connor on her side leveled the playing field.

"How will we avoid them?" Kate asked. The Sphere agents had disappeared from view, meaning they could be anywhere. "Maybe we should go back and explain."

Connor whirled on her. "Go back?" He brought his face close to hers. "Do you have a death wish? Because we're beyond playing nice and talking things over. Do you think you can reason with them? They know you've betrayed them. Sorry, sweetheart, but you've passed the point of return. We've got to forge ahead."

Chapter 3

Connor knelt and dug through his bag. Removing a knife in a sheath, he slid it into the pocket of his pants.

A knife? "How did you get that on the plane?" Kate asked.

"Greased a few palms," he said.

Unbelievable. He was full of surprises.

"No time to change now. You'll have to change in the taxi," Connor said, lifting his hand to hail a cab. When one stopped, he practically lifted Kate inside. He climbed in after her and barked the name of the closest city to the airport in perfect Portuguese with a hint of a Tumaran accent. The driver didn't turn around to look at them, just jammed the gas and pulled away from the airport.

"Are we being followed?" Kate asked, turning to look out the back window and searching for any cars that were too close. In the distance, she could see *el presidente*'s palace set high on a hill overlooking the city. The white and gold of the building reflected the sun in a blinding glare.

"I'm not sure yet," Connor said in Portuguese. He withdrew a pair of jeans and a white T-shirt from his backpack. "Take off your clothes and put this on."

That earned a glance in the rearview mirror from the driver.

"Now? In a cab?" Kate asked. The road was congested with cars and trucks filled with people in plain view. Connor expected her to strip?

"Yes. Now."

Kate watched to see if he would break into a grin. Was he joking around with her? If he was, she didn't find him funny.

She had been careful about what she wore and, although Sphere had tracking devices as thin as thread that could be sewn into clothing, she gave it a low probability that she was being tracked. She'd buy other clothes when she could find a shop. Couldn't it wait?

"I don't want to be followed again," Connor said.

"That wasn't my fault," Kate said. "We used your arrangements to get here. If you're giving out blame, take some for yourself."

Connor tossed the clothes at her. "Change. This isn't a negotiation. I don't see anyone on our tail and I'd like to keep it that way."

She didn't like being ordered around. But if he was right about Sphere tracking her, she couldn't behave foolishly. Were they far behind them? The large white T-shirt and sturdy jeans didn't leave her many options for modesty. She draped the white shirt over her lap and struggled out of her own.

Connor turned away. At least he was giving her what privacy was available in the backseat of a cab. His shoulders shook, making an effort to hide that he was laughing. Though he couldn't see her, she glared at him. "What is so funny about this?"

"You. You're what's funny. I don't appreciate the company, but I do appreciate the humor you bring to the situation."

"I'm glad you're entertained," she muttered. Kate fought to pull the white shirt over her head without flashing Connor and the cabdriver. "I am trying not to get arrested for exposing myself."

"Relax. You're fine. Based on what we have planned, you should get used to me seeing you naked."

Both her and the driver's reactions were the same. Wide eyes, open mouths followed by an attempt to hide their shock. "Why do you do that?" she asked, getting the shirt on and pulling it as low as possible over her legs. At least Connor was tall and his shirt covered her to midthigh.

"Do what?" he asked.

"You say really rude, off-the-wall things. It's like you're trying to make me nervous or get a reaction out of me."

"I'm not trying to do anything. This is who I am." He turned and looked at her point-blank.

Was he waiting for her to remove her pants? She felt the challenge in his stare. If she was venturing out into the jungle with him, he would see her change clothes, assuming she managed to acquire more. Was this another test? To see if she had the nerve? She unfastened her pants and slid them down her legs. Heat flamed up her cheeks. She would prove she was capable of doing whatever came at her on this mission.

"All your clothes, Kate."

Meaning her underwear, as well. Her mother had raised her to be a lady and that included wearing the appropriate undergarments. Even her sister, Elise, the A-list movie star, was known around Hollywood for her modesty and relatively conservative dress.

Kate strove for indifference. Her attempt was hindered by the look in Connor's eyes. It wasn't indifference written on his face. It was interest. His gaze trekked down her legs to her toes and back up again. By that time, she had removed her underwear and was pulling on his jeans. Kate pinched the waist. How would she get them to stay on? "Happy now?"

"Immensely. You have nice legs and it's less likely we'll be followed."

His compliment both pleased and annoyed her. Most of the time, she downplayed her looks in an attempt to force the people around her to notice she was smart. Men found her attractive, but she wanted to be known as the smart girl, the resourceful one…not the hot one. Kate didn't use her looks to get what she wanted. At least, not often and never when she was working. "I stay in shape." She worked out at the gym before work two or three times a week and had for years.

"I can see that."

His clothes smelled of him. Being in the small taxi, it was impossible to escape him or to ignore her attraction to him. He was Aiden's brother, he was emotionally unavailable and he was dangerous. Though he didn't make her feel threatened, he was a trained assassin. Such rationalizations didn't destroy her attraction to him. Perhaps stress was making her crazy. "How do you suggest I keep the pants up?" Especially because she wasn't wearing anything beneath them, she hated how they gapped.

Connor reached into his bag and withdrew a long piece of rope and pulled his knife from his pocket. He leaned across the seat and wrapped the rope around her waist. His hands slid around her back, guiding the rope through the belt loops. Where his hands brushed her bare skin, heat flared across her body. He cut the rope and then knotted it. The result was a belt she could tighten and loosen.

"Thank you," she said and adjusted the rope.

"You're welcome."

Just when she thought she could use his rude behavior to demolish the crush she had on him, he did something kind. He was looking out for her. She didn't appreciate how he spoke to her at times, but he was doing what he knew to keep her safe, and that counted for something.

Kate rolled the legs of the pants and sleeves of the shirt. At Connor's pointed look, she removed her bra from under the shirt and pulled it out through the shirt's sleeve. Being naked beneath ill-fitting clothes was not a feeling she enjoyed. She was far, far outside her comfort zone.

"What about my shoes?" she asked, meaning the question to be sarcastic and then regretting it because Connor might tell her to get rid of them, too.

"Keep them. It will be too hard to find replacements and you can't run if you can hardly walk."

She looked ridiculous in the oversize clothes, but

it would have to do until she could get her hands on other clothes. When their car drew to a stop at a traffic light, Connor jumped out, jogged to a nearby trash can and shoved in her outfit. Getting back into the cab, he didn't apologize. "If they're tracking you by your clothes, best if they don't know where we're going."

Her superiors at Sphere knew she believed Aiden was alive. She hadn't shared the specifics her contact had told her, not wanting to endanger Marcus or his job. Sphere hadn't pressed her for information. Now she wondered if they'd already known Aiden was being held by the Armed Revolutionaries. They'd gone to the effort to stop her and yet they hadn't used those same resources to rescue Aiden. Curious. "They may know where we're going. They could have the same intel," she said.

Connor stabbed a hand through his hair. "Then we've got to get to Aiden first."

"You know what the worst part about this is? To put this effort into tracking me when they could have put that same effort into finding Aiden."

Connor snorted. "Whatever their agenda, it involves Aiden not being found. Tell me what else you know about my brother."

A challenge. Kate wanted his trust. To get it, she would have to tell him what she could and trust in return that he wouldn't ditch her.

Kate took a deep breath and switched to Italian. Smart. The driver wouldn't likely speak the language and Connor did. "Your brother was hunting members of the Armed Revolution, trying to capture key players and to prevent a large-scale insurgency against the

Tumaran government. His last verbal check-in was at a bar in Mangrove."

Connor wasn't familiar with either location. "What's the population of Mangrove?"

"Hard to say. It's a rural town in the middle of the jungle. Ballpark, maybe two hundred people."

Depending on how friendly the residents of the town were with each other, gossip could spread quickly. They might find someone who remembered his brother and who could clue them in to the last moments before he disappeared. "Which bar? Do you have more details?" Connor wanted every piece of information that could lead to his brother. Connor looked around them. Traffic was tight and they could be boxed in. He wanted to be able to get out of the car and flee. He liked having options in case they needed to escape.

Kate shook her head. "I don't know much about the bar. I wasn't on shift when he disappeared. I don't have access to the raw recording of that final conversation. If he named the bar, it wasn't in the transcript I read. After I told my superiors about my belief that Aiden is alive, they revoked my security privileges on the files pertaining to that mission."

Sphere was hiding something from her, but they were always hiding something. As the cab lurched forward, Connor felt his edginess move up a notch. He wanted to get to his brother quickly. "How many bars can there be in Mangrove? A town with two hundred people may only have one or two."

Connor had considered the terrain, wildlife, weather and disease-carrying insects that they might encounter in Tumara before they'd left the States. "Do you have experience navigating in the jungle?" He guessed her answer was no.

"I've studied the region extensively. I can identify the types of vegetation we might encounter, those that are safe to eat and those that are poisonous. I know the—"

She'd done research. That wouldn't cut it. "Actual experience, meaning, have you been to this jungle or any other?" Knowledge of an area was good. Being able to survive in the elements was better.

Kate lifted her chin proudly. "Don't discount my knowledge, but no, I have not spent time in the jungle."

"This is our stop," Connor said to the driver. He tossed some cash over the seat and climbed out.

Kate scrambled out of the taxi and followed him. "Where are you going? Are you ditching me just because I don't have experience?"

"I'm not ditching you. If I were, I would tell you first and then disappear. We need to change taxis. The driver's already heard too much. We didn't start speaking in Italian until later."

His clothes hung on her, far too large for her thin frame. Baggy wasn't a look he usually liked on a woman, but Kate wearing his clothes did something for him. It had been too long since he'd looked at and enjoyed a sexy woman. Kate fit the bill of sexy. Add to it smart and courageous, and it was hard not to admire the whole package.

A package that belonged to his brother and that was the rub. Why else would Kate insist on coming along? Connor would make another attempt to dissuade her from traveling with him into the jungle. He didn't want to see his brother's lover killed. "You should let me handle this. Aiden is my brother and I won't give up looking for him. When I bring him back to the United States, the two of you can have a glorious reunion." When he thought of her in Aiden's arms, it bothered him more than it should. Aiden deserved happiness, and a woman like Kate—beautiful, smart and caring—could give it to him.

Kate threw up her hands. "You can stop playing that same, sad song. I'm not turning around and going home. I'm not leaving you alone to venture into the jungle. What if something happens to you? Who would know? I would never forgive myself for bringing you this far and then abandoning you."

She was concerned about him. What about her job, her future and her life? She had obliterated her chances of returning to Sphere when she'd run from the agents at the airport. If she was involved with Aiden and Sphere knew about it, her position might have been tenuous anyway. A carefully constructed lie might save her—like claiming Connor had forced her to come along—but that was dicey. Sphere had zero tolerance for disobedience. "Most missions I've worked, I've worked them alone. You are not responsible for me or my decisions. You could return to the U.S. and your job. Tell them I forced you to help me. Say what you can to save your career."

Kate's mouth dropped open. "We've been over this. I can help you. I won't lie to save my job at the risk of hurting someone else."

Noble, but foolish. It was her funeral. He'd given her opportunities to change her mind. Connor could handle this alone. If she wanted to risk her life, so be it.

* * *

They found another cab, and Connor and Kate climbed inside. Connor had been walking as if his soles were on fire, and she was glad to sit again. Not that she'd utter one word of complaint. Hiking in the jungle would be more difficult and she was up to the task. Letting on she might not be able to keep up with him was unacceptable.

"Mangrove," Connor instructed as the driver pulled away from the curb.

The driver hit the brakes, almost tossing her and Connor into the backs of the front seats. Only Connor's hand across her chest stopped her from hitting her head. Between his arm and her bare skin was a thin layer of cotton. Her body responded and her breasts felt heavier and achy.

"No way, man. I don't drive there," the driver said.

Kate moved out of Connor's reach. Was the driver refusing because of the distance or the location itself? Kate had read towns in the jungle could be lawless, and in the current political environment, with Bruno Feliz and the Armed Revolutionaries working to overthrow the government, jungle towns were havens for the AR, and skirmishes between the two sides broke out occasionally.

"That place is trouble, man. If you're looking for sights to see, I'll take you somewhere better. Cleaner. Safer for tourists. No cabbie in his right mind will drive you into the jungle. Not anymore."

They didn't want somewhere better or cleaner or safer. They wanted to follow in Aiden's footsteps and find him.

Connor thanked their driver and they got out of the cab. They went through five more drivers and had to promise a hefty tip to convince someone to take them to Rosario, the jungle border town nearest to Mangrove. From there, the driver told them they could take a bus to Mangrove that would leave the next day.

It took thirty-five minutes to reach Rosario. As they drove, the landscape changed. Streets became less crowded, fewer cars were on the road, and houses and buildings became more run-down. Spray paint tagged the area as belonging to one gang or another. Few legitimate establishments operated from Rosario. The local economy was driven by gangs pushing drugs, prostitution and the sale of illegal goods. The gangs competed violently for turf, resources and money. The two most active gangs were the Snake Slayers, identifiable by the snake tattoos that covered their right arms, and the Blue Devils, who wore their group color prominently. Neither was directly tied to the AR, but Kate guessed there was some overlap in membership.

The cabdriver looked nervous as he let them out of the car. Connor paid him his fare and the sizable tip. The driver turned his car around in less than ten seconds, tires spinning in the dirt street and kicking up dust. Kate pasted on a look of what she hoped was confidence. With Connor at her side, she wasn't as likely to be mugged, but she made him more of a mark. Her clothing brought stares, which she ignored.

"Gangs are active in this area. Be careful looking at anyone the wrong way," Kate said.

"I'll be careful," Connor said, sounding unworried. "Tell me what you know about this town." Connor was earning long looks from women who passed him on the street and—unlike the ones she was receiving, thanks to her ridiculous, ill-fitting outfit—they weren't looks of disdain. Connor stood out as a foreigner and as a man. He was throwing off an approach-if-you-dare vibe, which both put people off and drew their attention.

"We need to locate the bus depot and find out when the next trip to Mangrove is scheduled." Two women passed and gave Connor matching long, beckoning looks. He appeared unfazed and Kate was insulted. What if she were Connor's wife? Didn't she deserve some respect and not the open ogling these women were engaged in? "We also need a place to stay for the night. Based on what I can see, you'll have your choice of beds," Kate said.

Connor laughed. "You almost sound jealous."

Not jealous. Justifiably insulted. "It's not jealousy you hear in my voice. It's disgust."

Connor adjusted his backpack on his shoulders. "I'm not looking for a woman to warm my sheets. Places like this always have rooms for rent. We'll pick the least dicey place we can find."

Kate hid her revulsion. *Least dicey place* was still likely a downright dirty place to sleep. This town wouldn't have chain hotels, just one-room rentals by the hour and by the night trafficked primarily by prostitutes. Though they could try to find transportation to take them elsewhere, they'd have similar options at any nearby town. Jungle border towns were notoriously dangerous, run-down and lawless.

"What's the matter? You look mad," Connor said.

"You're not good at reading me. This isn't mad. This is worry about contracting a disease from one of these places and concern that I won't find a decent change of clothes."

Connor patted her shoulder in a friendly gesture that bothered her. "I won't let you contract a disease, and we'll find you something that fits and some supplies." He was treating her like one of the guys, which was a position she usually preferred to be in around the office and while working a mission. With Connor, it bothered her.

Despite her reservations, Connor had an easy time locating a place to stay. He knew where to look and how to negotiate on a price. If she were alone, Kate wouldn't have known how to find a room to rent and would likely have had to sleep outside.

Their rented room was situated above a liquor store and was accessible from the back of the building via a splintering, wooden staircase. Based on the clientele and the women loitering around the entrance to the store, Kate guessed liquor wasn't all they sold. Their room was in the middle of two others. It didn't have working air-conditioning, but it did have a window fan, and with the lights off and the fan on the highest setting, the heat wasn't suffocating. The wood-paneled walls were outdated and the vinyl yellow floor worn with age. The tiny bathroom had a shower that would be a tight fit for her. Connor might need to hang a leg out of it while showering. The room had a single bed and a fold-out green canvas cot. The whole place smelled of stale smoke, as if a chain-smoker had spent the night inside it.

"Were you hoping for something nicer?" Connor asked, tossing his bag on the ground.

Kate schooled her expression. She hadn't expected five-star luxuries. "I didn't have high expectations for this town. I'm glad we found a place."

Connor opened his bag and withdrew a plastic tarp. "You can sleep on this if you prefer."

She did prefer. She didn't want to think about the bugs living in the mattress, on the floor and in the walls. "What about you? Where will you sleep?"

"Our sleeping arrangements don't matter to me, but we should avoid the bed. I'll crash on the floor. Before it gets too late, I need to head out for supplies and to check the bus schedule. Do you want to come? We might find a place to buy you something else to wear."

Staying in this room and attempting to sleep had a certain draw to it. But what if Connor decided to take off on his own? What if he left her here? What if she were approached by a local? The wood door to the room had a lock, although she wouldn't trust it to stand up to any force. As it was, sunlight shone through the cracks between the door and the frame. "I'll come with you."

"Because you don't trust me or because you feel safer when I'm with you?" Connor asked.

"Both." An honest answer. "I know the local language, but I don't know who might decide I make a good mark to rob."

"They'd be disappointed. We don't have anything of worth to steal."

Kate didn't mention she had been carrying items of worth in her bag, the bag he had insisted she throw away at the airport. Mentioning it would shake the fragile, temporary trust between them. She had to prove she trusted his judgment and that hers, in turn, could be trusted. "Do you have money to pay for new clothes? I can pay you back." She plucked at the overly large shirt, self-conscious about being bare beneath it. "I'll be more comfortable hiking in clothes that fit."

"I have ways to pay. I never leave the States without financial preparations. We'll see what we can find," Connor said.

They left the small room and walked through the town. Her shopping choices were limited. The town didn't have a dedicated women's clothing store and the outfits she could find were borderline indecent. She needed clothes suitable for a trek across the jungle, not a night of dancing in a hot club. Backless dress with miniskirt? Useless. Faux leather, skintight pants? Uncomfortable. Obviously, the stores catered to clubbers and prostitutes. On the plus side, they located a store carrying women's lingerie. On the negative side, she could forget about comfortable cotton. Silk, lace and leather were the most bountiful choices.

Kate finally settled on a pair of men's jeans, size small, a few tank tops and a pair of men's boots. She would wear the tanks under the flannel shirt she'd purchased and over the ridiculous lingerie. She exchanged her shoes for the boots. They purchased a sturdy nylon waterproof pack and supplies: rope, first-aid kit, a lighter, a knife, a water canteen, rechargeable flashlight, a local map and some nonperishable food. Beef jerky and granola bars would be the main course for the next couple of days. Kate reassured herself she could do this. Her father had taught her to be strong and to roll with the punches.

The bus station was several blocks from the main shopping area. The schedule was written in chalk on a dirty slate board. Posted around the board were flyers with *el presidente*'s face with black *X*'s over it and sheets of propaganda both for and against the AR. Kate had read of the government raiding towns like Rosario and capturing people for questioning. Those people often disappeared.

The next scheduled trip to Mangrove was the following day, leaving late afternoon.

"I was hoping for something sooner," Connor said, echoing her thoughts. "My brother is out there. Every second that passes grates at me."

Guilt threatened to force the truth from her about her involvement. The hurt she had caused Connor and his brother was unacceptable. She had made a mistake, and because of it, Aiden had been captured. Now Connor was involved and putting himself in danger for a rescue op. Telling him about her mistake wouldn't change what had happened and might make things worse between them. "I'm sorry. I wish I could do more to help."

His head swerved like a laser in her direction. "You can do more. Tell me everything you know about my brother and what he was doing in Mangrove."

Kate stuttered over her next words. She finally took a deep breath and started over. "I've told you almost everything I think is relevant to finding him at this point."

"Tell me something about my brother that might not be relevant to finding him. What you think is unimportant might be critical."

He was worried about his brother, so Kate ignored the implication that she didn't know the difference. "Aiden adored you. You were his hero."

Connor inclined his head. "He said that?"

"Yes. He used those words." *Hero. Courageous.*

Brave. Selfless. Every story Aiden told of his brother echoed those sentiments.

Connor ran his hand across his jaw. "Funny. I'm no one's hero. Never have been. Aiden and I have always looked out for each other."

That wasn't the picture Aiden had painted. "He told me you had a difficult childhood."

Connor's back went ramrod straight. She knew immediately she had crossed a line. "I'm sorry. I didn't mean to tread on a sore subject," she said.

"I don't like to talk about the past. Our childhood has nothing to do with the present," he said.

She disagreed. Perhaps Connor had put bad memories behind him, but it still affected him. His problems trusting were deep-seated. "It doesn't have to do with the mission," she said, striving for neutral. Aiden had told her that he'd implored his brother not to live alone, not to shut out the world, but Connor didn't listen. He had his own thoughts and feelings about life and he clung to them.

"I shouldn't have said anything. I was just telling you what I knew about Aiden," Kate said.

"Aiden's perspective isn't always accurate. We'll get our tickets tomorrow." He'd moved the conversation along. "I don't want to let on to anyone about our plans. Let's see what we can find to eat around here," Connor said. He slipped his arm around her shoulder in a proprietary gesture. Heat crackled between them. Or was this one-sided? Completely in her head? Kate had never before been this self-doubting about a man. Most of the time, a man's attention on her was take it or leave it. Whenever she'd had strong chemistry with someone in the past, they had felt the same. With

Connor, she didn't know where she stood. Some moments, it was as if he couldn't have cared less about her. Other times, they behaved as a united team. The polarity confused her, and confusion wasn't an emotion she embraced.

When she tried to shrug him off, he repositioned his arm and pulled her closer. Lowering his face to her ear, he whispered, "Interested people are watching. I want to make it clear to everyone that you are mine. Otherwise, you'll have visitors."

She'd read too much into his casual gesture. Kate turned to look at him. "I think it's obvious we're together."

"It's not obvious what our relationship is."

"That's because we don't know what our relationship is. How can anyone else?" Kate asked, hearing the heat in her voice and throwing some ice on it.

"I wasn't aware we had a relationship that needed defining. Our reasons for being together are clear. We have to find my brother and you're holding the information hostage. I need to keep you, and therefore the information, safe."

Kate mentally shook herself. Imagining an innocent touch was a hint of smoldering emotion just below the surface was ridiculous. "You make it sound like I have a choice. You're not easy to work with. I had to make sure you brought me along."

"Now that you're here, do you regret it?"

Kate looked around her. She had never been to a place like this and she hoped to never be again. "I don't regret it. I want to find Aiden. Besides, I have a feeling Rosario isn't the most difficult part of this trip. The worst is yet to come."

Connor laughed and slapped her on the back. "That's the spirit, Kate. Now you're thinking like a Sphere agent."

Their food options were slim. A nearby tavern served meals, the scent of greasy meat and peppers carrying across the street. In the heat, it was borderline nauseating.

"We'll try there," Connor said.

It was better than eating nothing or foraging in the jungle for food. Crossing to the one-story wood building, they stepped inside, the door brushing against a bell hanging over it. Every eye in the room turned to them. Connor appeared not to notice, though she knew otherwise. Kate's nerves jangled and heat fanned up her back. Her boots stuck to the floor as they walked.

Connor took a seat at the bar, his back to the wall. Nailed in the center of the dartboard posted on the wall was a picture of *el presidente,* his face pocked with dart punctures. The people of the town weren't hiding whom they supported, though Kate would be careful not to openly take anyone's side. *El presidente* could have moles planted everywhere, and she and Connor didn't want to invite attention.

Kate sat next to Connor and ignored the stickiness of the seat. She'd probably have to burn these clothes after this trip and she wouldn't worry about cleanliness now.

They ordered from a whiteboard posted behind the bar where two options were scrawled: enchiladas spicy and enchiladas fire. Kate chose the first and Connor the latter. With a side of beer, Connor seemed as though he was perfectly relaxed on the hard stool, his back propped against a wall that Kate wouldn't have touched. Everything in the bar looked smeared with grease, booze or sweat.

"Enjoying your food?" Connor asked.

Though it was greasier than she would have preferred, she was hungry. "It's good." Her voice carried and she had no intention of insulting the owner. She reached to her side to check the time on her phone and frowned when she remembered Connor had made her throw away everything.

"Missing it?" Connor asked.

Not as much as she would have expected. It provided security in knowing help was a phone call away. Now help was next to her in the form of a good-looking, but slightly crabby, operative. "Habit. It's useful."

"I don't know how you can stand to be plugged in all day. I see people staring at those things like it's their whole world. What about interacting with the people around you?"

He was one to talk. "The man who lives like a hermit has a criticism about socializing electronically?" Kate asked.

He shrugged. "Carrying those things around and staring at them will get you killed. You've got to be aware of what's happening around you."

No sympathy, then, from him. Her email and text messages would have to wait until they found Aiden. Would her boss have tried to contact her to let her know she was fired? She pressed away the anxiety that threatened to wrap around her. What difference did it make to read an email or listen to a voice mail? Her career with Sphere was over. Period.

The door to the bar opened and a man strolled in. He wore a black bandanna around his heavily tattooed neck. Her instincts told her he was dangerous and Kate watched him from the corner of her eye. After looking around the room, the man strutted to the bar and leaned over it. "How much?" he asked in a low voice, his mouth close to her ear.

Kate turned to him in surprise. He had a snake tattoo that ran from his neck, disappeared under his black sleeveless T-shirt and reappeared on both arms. "The lunch? It was six—"

"No," the man said, a faint hint of indignation crossing his face. "How much for an hour with you?"

Kate stared for a long moment before she processed his question. She waited for Connor to say something and glanced at him. He had an amused look on his face, but he hadn't moved to interfere.

"I am not for sale," she said, the words coming out in a stutter. Did she look like a prostitute? The clothes she had purchased in town and had changed into weren't anything close to advertising sex. They were men's clothes.

"I'll make it worth your while," the Snake Man said. He ran his finger along her hand.

Kate snatched her hand away. Worth her while? There wasn't enough money in the world to make her sell herself to someone. She narrowed her gaze and lifted her chin. "I am not for sale," she repeated. She had never encountered anything as overtly insulting as this man's suggestion.

The Snake Man looked at Connor. "Tell your woman to watch her mouth."

As though Connor was her pimp? The idea of it disgusted her.

Connor took a long pull of his beer. "She's not interested. Move on."

The Snake Man grabbed a chunk of Kate's hair, and Connor was on his feet in a split second. Kate cringed, and Snake Man released her and retreated a step. "You don't want to fight here. My crew runs this town."

Connor's nostrils flared. His posture had shifted from calm to aggressive. "You might run the town, but you don't run me or her. I'm protecting what's mine. Walk away and we'll keep this from turning into a very ugly incident."

The other patrons in the tavern were suddenly focused on their food and drinks, though Kate pictured their ears pricked up, listening to every word. No one wanted to get involved in a brawl, but everyone wanted to eavesdrop.

The Snake Man glared at Connor. "Don't start something with me."

"I don't want to have to hurt you. But I will."

Cold and unyielding. The man narrowed his gaze and took a swing at Connor. Connor caught the flying fist and squeezed, twisting the man's arm behind his back. Connor kicked his legs out from under him and the man slammed to the ground. A sickening crack made Kate wince.

The man groaned. "You broke my arm! My shoulder!"

Connor released him and stood over him until the man rose to his feet and limped to the door, rubbing his arm. He stopped at the door and looked back. "You'll regret this."

"No. I won't," Connor said.

"Did you break his arm?" Kate asked.

"Probably fractured it. Some people don't listen and have to be shown what is and isn't acceptable," Connor said, returning to his seat. "Sorry about that chauvinist, possessive act."

Kate wasn't upset by Connor's macho overture toward the Snake Man. Connor had said and done what was needed to protect her. The quick switch from calm to violent had surprised her. "Thank you for stepping in. I can't believe he thought I was a prostitute."

"Don't take it personally. I assume a fair number of women in this town work as drug runners or prostitutes."

"Do I look like a prostitute?" she asked, her discomfort taking on an edge of irritation.

He didn't answer right away. His gaze traveled down her body.

"Connor!"

His eyes met hers. "What? You asked a question and I was trying to imagine you as one just to see if he somehow misunderstood. Attacking me certainly didn't give him points for intelligence."

"And?" she asked. He had better give an answer firmly in the negative.

"Nope, I can't see it. You're too classy."

She took pleasure in his response. Too much pleasure. It shouldn't matter what Connor thought of her, and thinking she didn't look like a prostitute was a far cry from saying he found her appealing. "Most men find me attractive." She was fishing for a compliment and it pained her to admit it, even to herself.

"I know. It's why I thought Sphere sent you to draw me out. I have a thing for beautiful, smart blondes with killer smiles."

A thing for her? "You couldn't have been less friendly when we met. If that's your technique when you're flirting, it needs tuning."

"I wasn't flirting with you."

Her heart fell a little. "What were you doing?"

"Chasing you away. Hoping you would change your mind about coming on this trip. Hoping you would admit you were lying."

"I didn't run away, I won't change my mind and I wasn't lying," she said.

"We'll see if that holds."

Kate had the feeling his statement was about more than this mission. How would Connor react when he learned the role she'd played in his brother's disappearance?

him to sleep. He expected rough conditions in the jungle. Would Kate handle it? She'd have taken the mandatory Sphere training, but the real experience was more intense.

From the moment she'd shown up at his door, he'd been sizing her up—smart and capable. Connor had never met a woman with a smoking-hot body who didn't use it to her benefit. Kate was the first. He was almost anticipating the day that she would.

"I don't know if I can sleep here. I hear things scurrying on the floor," Kate said.

They had both dismissed the idea of sleeping on the stained mattress. Connor adjusted his posture, looking for a comfortable sleeping position. "Try not to think about that. Think about the roof over your head, the non-muddy floor beneath you and that we don't have to worry about nocturnal predators hunting us. At least, none of the four-legged variety." The sound of people entering and leaving the twenty-four-hour liquor store echoed through the room. Every time the door slammed shut, it rattled the window in their room. Those things didn't bother him. What did bother him was the hot blonde sleeping close enough to touch and knowing he couldn't and shouldn't touch her.

Kate was lying on the plastic tarp he'd given her. "Are you sure your legs have enough room?"

They'd arranged themselves on the floor, head to head, forming an L shape around the bed. They couldn't shut out the light from the single window in the room. Kate had one of his shirts rolled under her head. Her eyes were closed and Connor watched her.

She was a gorgeous woman. Intelligent, too. Why would she want to work for a place like Sphere? The pay was great, but plenty of private contractors would love to have a woman like Kate on their team and pay well for the privilege. Sphere had too many hidden agendas and made too many politically motivated decisions. He had wanted to work for them before he'd known they were always working an angle, and that angle was always to their benefit. Their employees were expendable, as was evidenced by his brother.

Connor's legs were only slightly bent. "It's best to sleep with my legs braced against the door. If anyone tries to open it, they'll wake me." Connor intended the display in the bar to set the tone for their stay in Rosario and leave no question as to Connor's commitment to protect Kate. Anyone who entered this room was making a grave error and would be treated as roughly as the gang member had, possibly more so since Connor hated to be woken.

"Too bad about the mattress," she said, sleep heavy in her words. When she was tired, her voice took on a throatier quality he found sexy.

"I prefer the ground. If I never get too comfortable, I start to forget what a warm, soft bed feels like." Luxuries spoiled him. He roughed it when possible. Sleeping next to a woman was a luxury he hadn't indulged in in years. A warm, soft bed with silky sheets and inviting blankets sprang to mind. Kate appeared in his imaginary bed wearing one of his blue T-shirts and beckoning to him, her long legs curled under her and the scent of vanilla invading his senses. Connor stamped out the image.

"I prefer to sleep where things aren't crawling on me," Kate said.

In the jungle, it would be near impossible to keep her

creature-free. Would she rise to the challenge or have a total meltdown? She had shown courage so far, but he didn't know her well enough to guess. Exhaustion, uncertainty and fear could break a person.

"Why are you staring at me?" Kate asked, opening one eye.

She had sensed him watching. "I can't figure you out."

She smiled. "Then we're on equal footing because you're a mystery to me."

He wasn't a mystery. Everything he did was for his survival and to protect himself and the people he cared about. Nothing about him was contradictory. "I saw you at Aiden's memorial service."

"You did? You didn't speak to me. I didn't think you knew who I was," she said.

"I didn't realize who you were at the time. I didn't speak to anyone at the service. I was too angry. My brother was dead." He had told Aiden to leave Sphere when he'd quit. He had given Aiden a list of reasons to walk away. Connor had begged him to see Sphere for what they were: an agency that did whatever was necessary to accomplish their goals. They worked without a moral code, hidden from the public and without consequences for their actions.

Sphere operated in a legal gray area and, over the years, they had let their motivations and actions slip firmly into a dark, unscrupulous area. They unquestioningly took the assignments that most government agencies wouldn't—or couldn't—go near. Too many scandals in the government had led to their very existence.

"I'm sorry you were lied to about your brother. If

you were so angry, why did you come to the service? There wasn't a body," Kate said.

Connor almost hadn't attended the service. He'd been aware that their father had been in attendance, but Connor hadn't spoken to him. If he'd spoken to anyone, he would have lost it. "I thought it would give me closure." He had thought it would allow him to move on and let go of his hurt and anger. God knew he didn't need to harbor more rage at life's inequities than he already did.

"Did you feel better until I showed up on your doorstep?" Kate asked carefully.

He hadn't felt better. He had only his guilt over his relationship with Aiden and anger for Sphere that had sharpened to a fine point. "No. The grief was almost intolerable." He blamed Sphere for his brother's death. They'd put their plan before the lives of their agents. Unforgivable. "Aiden is everything to me." It had never been clearer until he'd thought he'd lost him. To have another chance to make things right between them was priceless.

"I'm s-s-sorry."

She sounded genuinely shaken. Why? She had done what no one else in Sphere had. She had cared enough to look for Aiden. Was he giving her too much credit? Connor wanted to believe Kate was looking out for Aiden, that perhaps his brother meant enough to her to put her life on the line. The idea that Sphere was pulling the strings tugged at him and cast distrust over her intentions. What if Sphere was using her to manipulate him? Had they known all along Aiden was alive? Whose side was she on? Anger lit in his blood, hot and fierce. "Kate." Kate rolled onto her stomach to look at him.

"If you're lying to me, if you're using me, if my brother is dead and this is a game, then you will regret the day you met me. You'll wish you had never heard of Sphere. Do you understand?"

Kate's mouth fell open and shame immediately swarmed over him. Connor wasn't accustomed to threatening people. Especially not attractive females who had bright, innocent eyes and tempting, full mouths begging to be kissed. He'd felt he needed to say something to drive home the seriousness of his feelings about a betrayal. He couldn't openly accept that Aiden was alive based on her words and a picture and let the hope that his brother was alive spring too high. If Kate was wrong, if she was misleading him, he couldn't go through the process of coming to terms with his brother's death again.

Aiden was his younger brother. Connor should have been looking out for him. He should have steered him to another profession before he'd gotten tangled up with Sphere. He should never have been proud that his brother had been recruited as a Sphere agent. He should have been the one who'd died, not Aiden. The list of what he should have done was endless. How much of his anger over losing Aiden was directed at Sphere and how much at himself?

"I believe Aiden is alive," Kate said, her voice soft with hurt underlining every syllable. "I want to find him and bring him home. It wouldn't kill you to be nicer and have a good attitude."

Shame assailed him. She was right and her simple

words struck him, made him recheck his words and thoughts. "I'm sorry. I have trust issues."

"I know you do," Kate said.

Connor waited for sleep as his fitful thoughts drifted between Aiden, Kate and Sphere.

Connor awoke to a knock at the door and his hand went to his knife. The sky was dark, the lights from the liquor store below shining through the uncovered window into their room. The whirl of the fan was the only sound.

"Who is it?" Kate asked him in a faint whisper.

Connor pressed a finger over his lips and motioned for her to move across the room. If this got ugly, he wanted her tucked out of reach. Perhaps her rejection of the snake-tattooed man at the bar had invited trouble. Gangs were territorial and perhaps they had underestimated who they were up against. Maybe someone had the wrong room.

Or maybe Sphere had found them. The same information Kate would have learned about Aiden would be available to Sphere. Had they tracked him and Kate to this jungle border town?

"What do you want?" Connor asked through the thin plywood door. The door would pop open with a strong shove, but the confidence and strength in his voice might intimidate a visitor and cause them to think twice about forcing their way inside.

"Let me in and I'll tell you."

A female voice, heavy accented and one he didn't recognize. He glanced at Kate, who was shaking her head. She didn't know the voice either.

A Sphere agent was his first guess. Bush league for them to approach in the middle of the night.

Connor swung open the door and came face-to-face with a stranger. A stranger who, if she wasn't a Sphere agent, was clearly offering sex. Her bright purple dress was similar to one Kate had dismissed in the store as too short, too tight and too low-cut.

When he'd pictured it on Kate, he had visions of her dancing sensuously against him, her body moving to a slow, melodious song.

Seeing the same dress on this woman, he was repulsed. "I don't want whatever you're selling." Drugs. Sex. Booze. He wasn't interested.

The woman leaned against the doorjamb, thrusting out her hip to the right and her breasts toward him. "Give me a chance to show you a good time. Americans love to taste what I have to offer."

The slur of her words indicated she was drunk or high. Pointing out that she slept with whoever paid for it was no lure. Before he could tell her he wasn't interested, Kate's hand slipped around his stomach and she tucked herself under his arm. He hadn't heard her move and he stilled his startled reaction.

"He isn't interested," Kate said.

Annoyance registered on the woman's face. She shrugged and walked to the next room. Connor shut the door. Kate fit easily against his side, her head reaching to his collarbone, his arm around her resting on her shoulder. They fit together well. Too well. Thinking about Kate as if she were his lover made him uncomfortable, especially considering he didn't know much about her relationship with his brother. She had denied they were a couple, and if she was telling the truth, he didn't understand why she had been insistent on coming to Tumara to find him.

Kate dropped her arm, pressing it over her chest and drawing his attention to that spot. "My heart is racing. I thought Sphere had found us." She retreated to her sleeping area on the floor.

Kate's touch had riled his heart rate more than the unexpected and unknown visitor had. He dragged in air and diverted his thoughts to something other than Kate's smell, her soft skin and her bedroom voice. "You didn't need to get involved," Connor said. The feel of Kate's hand on his stomach echoed through his senses.

"I owed you after the incident in the bar with the Snake Man. I figured it would be faster to get rid of her this way instead of arguing. Who knows what else she would have shown you or said to convince you to pay her."

"I might have paid her to go away," Connor said.

Kate let out a small laugh. "Then I saved you some cash."

Connor lay on the floor, staring at the ceiling. He took several more slow, deep breaths to calm his body to return to sleep. Connor thought again of the dress and pictured it on Kate. "Have you ever shown up at a man's door looking for sex?" The question was out of line, but his thoughts had obsessed over it, he'd asked it and it was too late to take it back. Maybe Kate would admit more about her relationship with his brother. That would deep-freeze his body's excited reaction for sure.

"At a stranger's house? No. A man I was dating? Sure."

Her admission heated his body and blood rushed between his legs. She was involved with Aiden in some manner and that alone should put the chill on his libido. It didn't. He wanted her and very little would change that.

Aiden and Connor had never been competitive with each other. The world they'd grown up in was brutal enough without adding brotherly conflicts to it. Knowing it wasn't right to think about her in a sexual way, knowing she was off-limits, made Connor desire Kate more. How juvenile could he be?

Being alone with Kate was a test of his loyalty to his brother. Kate deserved his respect in deference to Aiden. Thinking of her in an inappropriate manner would only make it awkward when Aiden and Kate were reunited.

If they were reunited. Connor hadn't given up on finding his brother, but he wouldn't pin his hopes on it either. Too easy to destroy them. That was a lesson he had learned at a young age from his father.

"What about you? I don't see you as the long-term, monogamous relationship type. Do you like to have a woman in every port?" Kate asked.

Connor had never gotten involved with a local woman while he was overseas on a mission, even if that woman had nothing to do with his tasks. When he had been home, he had attempted to have relationships with women, but they'd ended because he was away for too long. Working for Sphere meant he couldn't talk about his work, which created difficulties. How could he tell a woman he was dating that even though he had been gone for the past three months, he couldn't talk about what he had been doing or tell her anything about his work? When he returned from a mission, he was out of the loop on what was happening in her life. It had become more and more challenging to find conversation to fill the silences. "I rarely returned to the same region after I completed my missions, and I avoid getting involved with a woman while I'm working even if she's only peripherally involved in my missions."

"Did you leave someone waiting for you at home?" she asked.

"Left someone? Yes. Left her waiting? No. It never worked, and after a few failures, I stopped trying. I'm better off alone." It was easier for him to focus when he didn't have anyone's expectations on him. He could live his life how he wanted, come and go when he pleased, and never have to explain himself.

"You're really into the whole solitary thing, aren't you?" Kate asked.

Was that pity in her voice? He did not care for that in the least. "It's not that I'm into it, as you've phrased it, but I prefer it. I've been up front about that and it works for me." Why did it matter? He had agreed she could come along to look for his brother. She should see that as a major win.

"Aiden told me you and he used to spend a lot of time together."

When they were younger and before they had time-consuming, soul-sucking jobs, they had spent a great deal of time together. They had even shared the rent on a two-bedroom town house for a few years. "When we were kids."

"What changed?" Kate asked.

They'd grown up. They'd escaped being under their father's thumb and they'd gotten jobs to support themselves. They'd each wanted their own space. "Life changed us."

"Or you changed," Kate said.

Why was she digging around about this? If she and Aiden were so close, he would have told her all the ugly details of their lives. "Of course I changed. I grew up. I had more responsibilities." Although from a young age, he'd had a number of grown-up tasks. Taking care of Aiden. Finding food when the cupboards were bare because his father hadn't bothered to go shopping. Making sure they had clean clothes and shoes that fit. Getting them to school on time.

"That doesn't mean you needed to cut Aiden out."

Was that her interpretation or Aiden's? "What makes you say I cut him out?"

Kate must have sensed she was walking on sensitive ground. "Nothing. Aiden just mentioned he missed you."

Connor had missed Aiden, too. He'd regretted the distance between them. Toward the end, their conversations had been about their father and how they were footing the bill and the responsibility for his care. They were conversations that had made them both uncomfortable. Aiden believed their father had changed. Connor saw him for the coldhearted, abusive jerk he'd always been.

Connor hadn't wanted their disagreements about Sphere to escalate into the fight that had caused discord between them. It was difficult to live with the idea that they'd never close that distance.

"I've missed him, too," Connor said.

"I hope you'll have the opportunity to see him soon," Kate said.

Hope. There was that word again. It was a fickle word that could end in happiness or devastation. Despite Connor's tortured thoughts, sleep claimed him.

Part III: The Jungle

Chapter 5

The bus would take them to Mangrove. Though Kate had no illusions the intel she'd intercepted was completely accurate, she hoped for Aiden's sake they'd pick up on his trail at the bar where he'd last given a verbal check-in. It had been seven months. Perhaps someone would remember him. In a small town, someone looking like Aiden would make an impression. He didn't look like a local and neither did she or Connor. Maybe someone in Mangrove would know where the Armed Revolutionaries had set up their camps.

Connor was wearing a blue, nondescript ball cap over his hair and Kate had tied a bandanna around hers. It didn't hide her blond hair completely, but it made it less noticeable.

The bus was a remnant of the eighties, rust around the wheel wells and bumper, paint chipped and scratched from the sides, and the cloth seats worn to threads, silver tape around the seams. The air-conditioning didn't work and the small rectangular windows were opened. It was a hot, humid day and the wind wasn't cooperating to cool the inside of the vehicle.

Connor and Kate took their seats in the middle of the bus, keeping their heads bent together and ignoring other passengers. The bus was three-quarters full and ten minutes late when leaving the bus terminal.

"If you want to sleep, now is a good time," Connor said. He shifted in the narrow confines between the bench seats.

During the brief time they had spent together, Connor had shown two sides: cold, detached and mechanical and the side she preferred, warm, protective and considerate. "I am tired." It hadn't been easy to sleep on the floor of the room or ignore the sporadic sounds from the street and liquor store below. The longer into the night, the louder it had become until quiet finally came around 5:00 a.m.

Kate closed her eyes and tilted her head back against the seat. The bus rumbled over potholes, and if she wasn't so tired, it would have prevented her from sleeping. When she awoke, she was immediately aware that in her sleep, she had shifted, letting her head fall to Connor's shoulder, and he had his arm around her. Heat and embarrassment burned through her. He smelled good, an earthy masculine smell, and she felt safe nestled against him. Should she pretend to be asleep and shift away? Or wake up and pretend she hadn't noticed the intimacy?

She decided on the second. When she moved upright, Connor let his arm fall away. She missed the contact the moment it was lost. It was dark and the temperature inside the bus had lowered to a more comfortable level. "How long was I asleep?" she asked.

"A few hours," he said.

That long? "Did you get any sleep?" she asked.

"No, I'm fine. I want to keep an eye on things." His eyes traveled across the aisle to a group of four men, two turned in their seats to face the others, their conversation boisterous. They were passing cards from a playing deck between them.

Were they a threat? Their arms were covered with the same type of snake tattoo the man in the bar had. Were these men members of the Snake Slayers? Were they aware of the altercation in the bar the day before?

"I can keep an eye out if you want to sleep," she said. As she spoke, the men glanced at her, two of them leering in her direction. Goose bumps rose on her arms and an uneasy feeling passed over her.

"Nope. I'll wait," Connor said. For her. He was staying awake to protect her. If she wasn't with him, he could have gone almost unnoticed on the bus.

They were foreigners and it was obvious to anyone who saw them. Some Tumarans lived under the assumption that foreigners, especially Americans, were wealthy and carried cash and jewelry. Would the men approach, thinking they could rob them? The bus driver wouldn't be any help and the people around them were likely to ignore an assault. Getting involved in a fight brought too much trouble, and the farther Kate and Connor were from the city, the more the law of the land changed from the hands of law enforcement to outlaws.

The glances from the four men increased and then

their voices lowered. Kate tensed. They were planning something and she didn't like it.

She gripped Connor's arm. "I'm getting a bad feeling," she said in Italian.

Connor glanced over at the men. "I'm not thrilled about this either, but we'll be okay."

Kate tried to appear confident, lifting her head and squaring her shoulders. She wouldn't let the men intimidate her. She had training. Untested training and no real field experience, but she wasn't helpless.

"Hey, friend, is this your first time in Tumara?" One of the men directed the question at Connor.

"No, it's not," Connor said. He looked at them, but he didn't engage in more conversation.

"What about your lady? She looks like a first timer," the man said, and they snickered.

Connor ignored them, although he shifted in the seat, sitting straighter, turning his shoulders toward them, blocking her between him and the open window. He would defend them in a physical confrontation if he had to, but he wasn't looking for a fight.

"You look like two Americans who brought trouble to town yesterday in our bar," one of the men said.

Then they were aware of the incident. Connor said nothing.

One of the men crossed the aisle and leaned on the back of their seat. He reached to touch Kate. She shrank away as Connor's hand flew up. He caught the man around the wrist and twisted it away. "No touching."

The man winced.

Connor released him and the man rubbed his arm. "Don't be rude, American. You could find yourself and your lady lost and hunted in the jungle. You forget that today, you're outnumbered. When you mess with one of us, you mess with all of us. We have un-finished business."

It wasn't wise to threaten a man like Connor. Not only was his physical appearance a deterrent, but he was also quick and trained. Kate had seen glimpses into what he could do, and she wouldn't test him, even if the odds were stacked against him.

Connor said nothing. The men were irritable and on edge. Watching them closely, Kate recognized the signs of drug use. Bloodshot eyes, twitchy movements and a slight tremor in their voices. Her fear increased. They couldn't walk away. They didn't have any place to go trapped on the bus. People around them were looking away and at the ground, trying not to make eye contact. No one wanted to engage in an altercation with these men.

"We're not looking for trouble. Just passage to our destination," Connor said.

The man gave Kate a long look as if undressing her with his eyes. She shivered with disgust.

"It's a long ride to Mangrove. I was hoping to use the time to settle the score." The man laughed as if he'd made an outrageously funny statement. Connor had no reaction. None. The man pulled out a knife and held it to Connor. "You think you're too good to talk to me? How about you learn the rules here? On our turf, we're in charge. When I speak to you, you say, 'Yes, master Snake Slayer.'"

Connor's expression remained calm. No way would he speak those words.

Kate's heart was racing, and panic caused a cold sweat to break out across her body. "We just want to get to our destination," Kate said, reiterating what Connor had said earlier.

"You'll get there, but there's a higher fee involved for Americans with an attitude. Start by giving me your wallets," the man said.

Kate's muscles seized. What would Connor do? In close spaces with a knife drawn, someone would get hurt. The other three men stood and crowded around, escalating the situation.

How could she defuse it? She'd taken training on dealing with aggressive people and de-escalating problems. What could she say to him that would make him and his gang sit down and keep to themselves for the remainder of the trip?

"Why don't you put that away?" Connor said. "This won't end well for anyone. We're stuck on this bus for another few hours."

The man blinked at Connor, confusion crossing his face. He hadn't thought through his demand. He was looking to prove something to his friends. He wouldn't back down, unless he could somehow save face.

The man lowered the knife to his side. Relief washed over her, but after a few beats, anger flashed across his face. He swung the knife abruptly and a gasp escaped her. Connor caught his swinging arm and squeezed, forcing the man to drop the knife. It fell to the seat of the bus, and Connor grabbed the handle of the blade before one of the man's friends got the idea to jump into the fight.

"Take a seat. I don't want trouble," Connor said.

The man was bleating like a sheep.

The bus slammed to a stop. Kate surged forward, catching herself on the seat in front of her. Brakes squealed and the engine idled loudly. The bus driver walked down the aisle, gun in his hand, waving it at them. He looked at the Tumaran men and then at Connor and Kate. He pointed his gun at Connor and Kate.

"You two, get off my bus. I don't want trouble. Off. Now," the driver said, pointing his gun between them and the back door.

Kate opened her mouth to protest. They hadn't started the fight, although with the knife clasped in Connor's hand, he looked like the aggressor. That, in addition to the Snake Slayers having some control of Rosario, put her and Connor in the losing position.

Connor stood. "We're going," he said to the driver.

Kate waited a moment for someone to speak in their defense and explain what had happened. No one moved. No one lifted their heads. The gangs had made everyone too afraid to speak.

Looking through the window, she felt worry swamp her. The bus was in the middle of the jungle. No other roads led this way, and she couldn't remember the last time they had passed a town or she had seen anyone on the road. They didn't have much with them. Where would they go? How far had the bus gone? How much farther to Mangrove?

"Come on, Kate," Connor said.

He wasn't going to argue and try to stay on the bus? Connor was already stepping down the aisle. Kate hitched her bag higher on her arm and followed Connor. When they were on the ground, the door shut forcefully behind them and the bus pulled away, kicking up dirt and debris. As the bus disappeared down the road, it stole the last of the light, leaving them in the pitch black.

Darkness. No city lights. No streetlights. Nothing.

"Why didn't you argue?" Kate asked. She shivered. It was cold and they were in the middle of nowhere.

"Wouldn't have helped. We're Americans. They were Snake Slayers. The driver wouldn't have believed us, or if he did, he wouldn't stand up to gang members."

"Where are we going now?" Could they hike back the way they'd come? Or were they close to another town?

"We had to get off the bus at some point and hike through the jungle. It's just happening a few miles sooner," Connor said.

He was annoyingly calm. Wasn't he concerned about the change in their plans? Would they run out of supplies? What about finding a safe place to stay? "We don't have shelter."

"We'll make it."

"We don't have enough food or water to last long."

"We'll find more."

Kate blew out her breath. Sphere agents had a reputation for being resourceful. Their extensive training allowed them to survive in the worst circumstances. They were conditioned to remain calm. Kate's training had taught her to do the same while she was behind a computer. What about now? She felt exposed and shaky and worried. She'd participated in training exercises to sharpen her survival skills, but she'd had the comfort of knowing help was a few hundred feet away and the exercise lasted only a few hours.

In the jungles of Tumara, she had no such comfort. She had to rely on her book knowledge and Connor.

"How close are we to Mangrove?" Kate asked.

Connor reached into his pack and withdrew his

flashlight, a GPS locator and the map they'd bought in Rosario. He turned on the flashlight and aimed it at the map. Their partial view of their surroundings was scarier than the pitch black. Lurking in the jungle were jaguars and other predators. Would the light draw them?

Plants and the beaten road were all she could see in the beam of light. No landmarks and no street signs. The road the bus had taken had been paved at some point, but the blacktop was cracked and missing in many places, washed over by mud and leaves.

"Will we follow the road?" Kate asked.

Connor looked at his watch, which had a small compass. "It will be easiest to travel a plowed path, but it's not a direct route and will take more time. We'll stay as close to it as we can."

His words brought to mind the articles she'd read about the area following Aiden's disappearance. Hikers went missing. Tourists were robbed at gunpoint. "Do you have a phone? We should call for help."

Connor walked into the brush along the road. "I have a sat phone for emergencies. Who do you want to call? Your buddies at Sphere? I think that ship has sailed."

It hurt that he believed she would sell them out and run back to Sphere at the first bump in the road. "Don't blame me for this."

"I am not blaming you."

"I have friends at Sphere. I could call them for advice." She could trust her friends to keep her location a secret, couldn't she?

"Not a chance. By this point, every person in that organization is looking for you and will sell you out in a heartbeat. They might even be offering a reward for your capture."

Kate had received those memos offering a reward for the apprehension of or information leading to agents who'd disappeared. Sometimes, the reward was in the millions.

"You have to think like a field agent. We work with the information we have, we trust no one and we stay focused on the mission. In this case, that's finding Aiden."

Kate hated that she wasn't as mentally prepared on this mission as she had thought. She was out of her element. She couldn't admit that to Connor. Not now. She'd have to fake that she was comfortable and competent.

Could they hitchhike if another vehicle drove this way? "We can flag down another car along the road and ask for a ride," Kate said.

Connor gave her a look that was a mixture of surprise and dissension. "What if the people driving the car are with the revolution and unfriendly toward Americans? What if the people in the car are with *el presidente* and they don't believe why we're in the jungle? We'll stay off the road and see who comes by before we reveal our presence."

"It will take days to walk to Mangrove."

"Not if we cut through the jungle."

It was her turn to be surprised. "Cut through the jungle? Won't that take longer?" The terrain could be brutal. Dense vegetation would slow their progress.

"Not if you know what you're doing."

The problem was that she didn't know what she

was doing. Cutting through the jungle meant a rougher landscape and a greater chance of getting lost.

"The longer we're out here away from civilization, the harder it will be on us physically and emotionally. We'll find shelter until the sun rises. Then we'll start moving," Connor said.

"I'll help however I can," Kate said. She'd read how to build a shelter in the jungle, but in the pitch blackness, she had no clue where to start.

"I'll make a fire to keep predators away. Then I'll see what I can throw together."

They walked into the trees. Kate clung to Connor's arm, her body shaking from fear and from the cold. She was with Connor. He was one of the best people to be with in the jungle.

"Relax. We'll be okay," Connor said, his voice soft and comforting. He stopped and turned. "Would it make you feel better to hold the flashlight?" He handed it to her. "Shine it on the ground in front of us so we don't trip, okay?"

She took the flashlight and held it in one hand, gripping him with the other. "I'm scared."

"I know and I'm doing everything I can to make you not afraid."

Though she questioned her reasoning for coming into the jungle and how much her guilt had played into it, she didn't doubt finding Connor had been the best course of action. He was committed, protective and skilled.

They found a location where they could clear an area for a fire. Connor removed the lighter from his pocket. He grabbed some twigs and fine brush and used them as kindling to start a fire. When he had a strong flame burning, he added a few more sticks and then stepped away. In a few minutes' time, he had a good fire going. "I'm going to gather supplies. Wait here."

"Alone?" What lurked in the jungle? Animal predators would avoid the fire, but the members of the Armed Revolution could be patrolling or living in the area. The Tumaran government could have soldiers posted looking for the AR. Distrust and anger between the two ran high and she didn't want to be in the cross fire.

"I'll stay within eyesight. Or at least, within shouting distance," Connor said. He took the flashlight from her.

Kate clung to the straps of her backpack, needing to do something with her hands. "I'll wait here unless there's something you want me to do."

Connor was already gone. If she got crazy about needing to be close to him, she was proving right Connor's doubts about her abilities. Kate had read about the Tumaran jungle. She knew what to expect.

The sound of crackling wood had her jumping. Just the fire settling. She squinted into the dark and couldn't see anything.

The sight of Connor returning from the jungle, his arms filled with leaves and branches, was a relief. Kate uncurled her toes and relaxed her shoulders.

Connor laid broad leaves on the ground, covered them with a plastic tarp and then stacked the branches on top of it. "This will slow down the bugs from crawling over us."

Slow down. Not stop. Kate took a deep breath. She could handle this.

Connor left and returned two more times with items

he'd gathered. Leaves and dried moss created bedding. As she watched him, it dawned on her they'd be sleeping next to each other, side by side, on a bed about the size of a twin mattress. With the amount of effort he'd put in to make one bed, she couldn't ask him for a second bed just for her. This wasn't the time to be modest and ask for sleeping space.

Connor lay on the branches and patted the wood next to him. "Sleep now. We'll get an early start."

Kate set her bag on the ground and sat on the leaf-and-branch bed. It was more comfortable than she'd expected. She set her head on the rolled clothes from her pack. Connor was lying on his side, and Kate shifted, trying to make more room for him. The fronts of his thighs brushed the backs of hers.

Kate shivered.

"Are you cold?" Connor asked, already digging in his pack. He withdrew a flannel shirt and laid it over her.

The temperature had dropped, and with the fire at her front and Connor at her back, the flannel created a warm pocket for her to sleep. "Thank you for the bed and the blanket."

"You're welcome." He slung his arm around her.

It was a place to put his arm, she supposed. It didn't mean anything. His forearm rested below her breasts and his breath blew against the back of her neck. Desire skittered down her body and pooled low in her belly.

"Is my hair in the way?" she asked, reaching to gather it in her hands.

"Nope. Smells like the ocean."

She flipped her hair above them, keeping it from his face. Another compliment? Or was he one of those people who hated the beach? "My next vacation will be to the beach." She was mentally stretched out in the sun, digging her toes in the sand while the water lapped over her legs.

"Which beach?" he asked.

It didn't matter to her. She'd grown up on the East Coast and had spent summers on the Maryland Eastern Shore. As a teenager, she'd taken trips to Florida with her friends and had loved it. She'd been on cruises in the Atlantic and Pacific Oceans. Her favorite place to sit was near the water, where the crowds were thin and the sun was hot. "Anywhere that's quiet and private."

"I could not agree more," Connor said.

Quiet and private was a good way to describe Connor. Kate shifted, trying to get her shoulder in a more comfortable position. Her breasts rubbed against Connor's arm and her backside brushed his hip.

"I could have made the cot larger, but I thought we could share body heat."

Kate made some noncommittal noise. Being this close to Connor affected her on another level. With Connor, she felt safe. Despite his insistence that he was a lone ranger, he was showing significant consideration for her. When she was with him, she felt safe and protected, and falling asleep in his strong arms was easy.

Chapter 6

The air around her was hot and sticky. Her shoulder was sore and her shirt had risen up to her bra. She was facing Connor, her face buried in his T-shirt-covered chest, her hands tucked close to his stomach. Before she could roll away and pretend they hadn't been cuddling, Connor opened his eyes.

"Morning," he said, sitting and running a hand through his hair.

While his had taken on a disheveled appearance, she was certain she looked like a rag doll left out in the rain. She sat and finger-brushed her hair and arranged her clothes. She tied her hair away from her face and secured the handkerchief over it.

"We'll break camp and look for food and water," Connor said.

After she stood, he tossed away the branches that

had made their bed and put damp earth over the fire. Kate's stomach growled, and her tired, foggy brain longed for caffeine.

"You look pretty good in the morning," Connor said.

Was he making fun of her? "I don't have a mirror, but I must look a hot mess." The humidity was playing havoc with her hair.

"I wouldn't use both those words. *Hot*'s a good word. You look like you should, like you've been camping." Connor rolled his shoulders. "My biggest complaint is that you took up more than half the bed. I'll remember that next time. You travel in your sleep."

Kate's cheeks flushed with embarrassment and she dug through her bag to deflect the comment. "Why didn't you slide me away if you needed more room?" Being close to him had made sleep possible, but she felt guilty if she'd made it worse for him.

"I didn't want to wake you by giving you a splinter," he said.

Right. Their bed wasn't a mattress. "Tonight, I'll make my own bed and you won't have to worry about me taking up space."

Connor shrugged and slung his backpack over his shoulders. He looked at his watch and then at the sun. He started walking.

Kate followed. He stopped several times to pull fruit from the trees and hand it to her. Some were bitter and unripe, but they provided liquids and calories. At least he hadn't asked her to eat bugs. They were preserving their limited food sources, uncertain how long they would be hiking.

Determined to keep up with him, Kate didn't complain about the pace he was setting. His strides were long, and by taking the lead, he was doing the most work, moving branches and vines as they traveled. They walked for what felt like hours before Connor broke the silence.

"Tell me how you got suckered into working for Sphere," Connor said.

An interesting way to describe it. She hadn't been forced. She had decided of her own volition. "Why does anyone work for them? They have access to amazing technology, devices I had never seen before, and I thought I was making a difference by working there. Plus, it was flattering to be chosen. You can't apply to Sphere. You're recruited."

"Right. Their recruitment process. I forgot that part of their sales pitch. Like their careful selection casts out the weak, and only the brave and the strong remain to fight the good fight." The edge of bitterness told her he was speaking more of his experience than making a comment on hers.

"I believe the work I did helped someone. Or many people. Stopped wars."

"Or started them," Connor said.

Kate flinched. She wasn't naive. She was aware of the difficult politics and dicey problems Sphere inserted themselves into. "Or kept the casualty list smaller," Kate said.

"I'm guessing there was a man involved."

Kate stumbled over her feet and righted herself before face-planting. "You've already accused me of being involved with your brother. Do you think every decision I make has to do with a man?" He was striking at that part of her that hated when someone assumed her looks, and by extension her romantic relationships, were how she had what she did. Kate thought of her older sister. Elise had parlayed her looks into a spot on Hollywood's A-list, and Kate had seen how vicious that world could be. Kate wanted to be known for her intelligence, not her appearance. She didn't want to be stalked, hounded by adoring fans or made to feel like a commodity.

Connor took her hand, helping her over a large fallen tree. "Before Aiden. When you started training with the organization, you met someone."

How had he known? "A field operative, yes. During one of my first missions, we had worked together, and when we met in person, we clicked." Suspicion and curiosity nipped at her. "How did you know that?"

Connor glanced back at her. "It's a Sphere hoax. They put you on a mission with someone who is similar to you, who you jibe with psychologically and emotionally. You become wrapped up with that person and the mission and do anything to get a mission complete and to protect that person. It's part of the psychological mind trap."

"You really believe that?" Had Michael set her up? Was he a plant for Sphere? Connor was making her think as suspiciously as he did.

"It's just another way Sphere controls its employees. Sphere decides it wants your professional and personal life to be about them, and they make it so. And when you've dumped everything you have into it, when your entire life is consumed with Sphere, they take the person away. At that point, you're more isolated and more invested in the company than ever."

Kate found it hard to believe Sphere would take their tactics to that level. "That seems like an awful amount of effort to isolate me from people outside Sphere."

"When you were in said relationship, did you spend time with him whenever possible?"

She and Michael had spent a lot of time together. That was how new relationships were. When Michael was sent overseas for months without any way to communicate with her, her feelings for him had cooled. Absence hadn't made her heart grow fonder, which was lucky, because when he'd returned, he had told her he had fallen in love with someone else. Had their entire relationship been created, used and destroyed by Sphere? "We spent a lot of time together until he was assigned a series of missions outside the U.S."

"Right. Then you both moved on with your lives, taking your broken heart and filling the void with more Sphere missions and work."

"You're making it sound like I was coerced into falling in love with someone. Like Sphere is a god that plays games with their employees and their emotions."

"I imagine some people within Sphere do believe they are gods."

Kate went over those first months, which in some ways seemed so long ago. She had been young and inexperienced and pliable. "How do you know all this?"

"After I left the organization, I became friends with a woman who had worked on their psychiatric team years before. She was responsible for creating profiles of employees and creating situations to ignite relationships. She called herself a high-paid, highly skilled matchmaker."

"She just gave you this information?" Kate asked.

"Not gave. She had worked up a profile on me before Sphere recruited me. She said I intrigued her and she couldn't figure me out. It took them several tries to find the right woman to lure me."

She couldn't stop herself from asking. "Who was the right woman?"

"Her name is Lauren. She's Italian, a naturalized American citizen, speaks English with a heavy accent that drives me crazy."

That explained why and how he spoke Italian. Jealousy lodged in her emotions. *She* didn't have an accent.

"Petite, curly brown hair, curvy, strong. A field operative like me. Physical, likes to train hard and play hard. I wouldn't get involved with someone I was working a mission with, so it took Sphere longer to get us together." For someone who didn't share much, Connor had a lot to say about Lauren. The woman he described was Kate's opposite. She tried not to let that burn through her.

"You speak of her in the present. Is she in your life?" Unwanted envy for a woman she had never met consumed her.

"We stay in touch. We're no longer romantically involved."

"Even though she manipulated you?"

"She didn't manipulate me. Sphere manipulated us."

Thinking about Sphere having that much control over her life bothered Kate immensely. Had she let Sphere exploit her? Wasn't she smart enough to see through a plan like that?

"Believe what you want. I'm being straight with you because I think you deserve the truth. When this is over, you'll walk away and realize how much of your life was controlled by them. You'll be glad to be free to live your life on your terms."

Kate took the branch he handed her to prevent it from slapping her in the face. When she returned to the United States, her life would be drastically different from how it had been before she'd left. She'd be unemployed and, depending on how much Sphere had smeared her reputation, unemployable. What else could they do to her? They had access to her bank account where they deposited her paycheck. The extensive background checks they'd run on her gave them access to most aspects of her life. If they wanted to, they could torpedo her world into a million pieces. What would her family think?

Kate hadn't taken the path her parents had laid out for her. Neither had her sister. Seeing disappointment in her father's eyes would destroy her.

"You'll find a new job and a new life. With your looks, doors will be flying open," he said.

Again, picking at old wounds. "Can you please stop making insinuations about my looks?" she asked.

"Are you unaware you're gorgeous?" he asked.

Kate's muscles tensed. "I am aware of what I look like. Do you know Elise Burke?" she asked.

Connor glanced at her, confusion on his face. "The actress?"

"Yes. She is my sister. My half sister. She wanted me to follow in her footsteps."

"Life on easy street?" Connor asked. "Why not?"

"First, her life isn't what it seems. Second, I had one acting job in my life and it was a disaster. I hated it. That world is not for me."

"I'm sorry. I didn't realize."

Maybe he'd heard the tension and hurt in her voice. He'd backed down without needing her to explain more.

She was glad about that. She didn't want to talk about her brief and disastrous foray into Hollywood or how much her sister had changed after she'd filmed her first blockbuster movie. Elise became untouchable, uncommunicative and rarely made time for Kate and her family. Kate heard about her sister and her career when the internet alert she'd set up messaged her a news article. It was a sad way to try to be part of her sister's life.

They reverted back to silence. The strenuous traveling through the jungle tired her. Kate put aside thoughts of her life in America and concentrated on taking one step at a time. Forward progress was slow, and as the sun rose higher in the sky, the temperature and humidity increased.

Kate shook her foot free of a vine that had snaked over her shoes. Connor's arm shot out and landed across her chest.

"Stop. Don't move." The words left his mouth in a whisper.

Alarm tore through her. Had Sphere found her? Rationalization kicked in and a host of other dangers flickered through her mind. A jaguar. A poisonous snake. The AR.

Kate didn't know which was worse. She strained to hear whatever Connor was hearing or see whatever Connor was seeing. She couldn't distinguish any human noise from the sounds of the jungle, and with his forearm across her, most of her attention was focused on his strong arm against her breasts.

Connor pointed down to their feet. Razor wire was laid three inches from the ground like trip wire. Nasty trip wire meant to do harm to anyone who crossed it. If they were injured in the jungle, their first-aid kit would help to a point. Open wounds in this climate easily led to infections.

Razor wire meant humans were, or had been, in the area and were protecting something. Kate wasn't sure if that made her feel better. "We could be near a village," she whispered. Most locals wouldn't have access to razor wire, but then again, who knew how the AR and the conflict with the Tumaran government had changed the culture? Communities that had survived thousands of years would adapt to protect themselves and isolate themselves from the problems where possible.

"If this is a welcome to their village, it's an unfriendly one," he said. "But are they unfriendly to us or supporters of the revolution? Or have we found an AR camp?"

No way to know whose side anyone was on or what was being guarded by the trip wire. Kate had read that some communities were sympathetic to the revolutionaries, some to the government, and others wanted to remain out of the conflict. "Let's circle around," Kate said. She'd rather avoid a confrontation, and entering the marked perimeter invited problems.

Connor peered along the ground. "We don't know how far it goes, and we could lose daylight and walk miles off our path." At her wary expression, he set his hand over hers. "If this is the perimeter of a village, that means water. If it's an AR camp, they could have Aiden. Let's cross and see what we can find."

They'd drunk the water from their canteens and eaten some of the food supplies, but they were thirsty and hungry. His touch was as persuasive as his words. Connor was fearless or at least appeared that way. If he was afraid of what they'd find, he didn't show her. He stepped over the wire and extended his hand to help her. "Focus on the positive. The possibility of fresh, cool water."

If her mouth wasn't so dry, it would have watered at the thought. "Water. Yes."

Connor furrowed his brows. "I'll look for more fruit to help us stay hydrated." Connor scanned the area slowly and adjusted the knife at his waist, pulling it to his side. "If my brother is inside, I won't leave him."

Kate wished she had spent more time in Sphere's hand-to-hand combat classes rather than in classes on the latest technology and computer theory. The computer classes had seemed more relevant to her work. In the jungle without her phone, her knowledge of cutting-edge technology was useless.

Connor moved at a slower pace, checking each step. "Put your feet in the tracks I'm making. Land mines could be planted out here."

Land mines? Images from World War II movies flashed into her mind. Explosions and dirt being kicked high into the air and shrapnel being tossed in all directions. Kate grabbed the back of his T-shirt. Closing her eyes for a brief moment, she squelched the thrum of terror that beat in her chest. Dangerous revolutionaries, barbed wire, jungle predators and now land mines. She'd been involved in operations situated in the jungle, communicating with Sphere agents on an hourly basis. She had been safe in her air-conditioned office with access to food, water, coffee and plumbing. How did field agents cope with the pressure and lack of resources?

Then again, the average agent with Sphere lasted less than five years. They were either killed, switched out of the role of field agent or they quit.

Kate took care to keep her steps inside Connor's

larger ones. When he stilled in front of her, she braced herself for an assault. Angry revolutionary? Jungle cat?

"You were right. It's a village," he said. He changed directions, moving to the left.

Through the heavy foliage, mud-brick buildings came into view. After walking for so long with a view of only trees and vines, it was strange to see a clearing with human-made structures. The jungle couldn't be held away from the village completely. Despite the split-rail fence surrounding it, the jungle had pressed inward, giving the village a run-down and disheveled appearance.

Connor moved closer and waited, crouching to the ground. Kate did the same. After long minutes had passed, Connor turned to her. "I haven't seen a single person. It's the middle of the day. Where is everyone?"

She hadn't noticed any movement inside the fence either. "What do you think it means?"

"It could be abandoned." He sounded disappointed.

"I'm sorry Aiden isn't here," she said.

"He's out here somewhere and we'll find him," Connor said.

"Let's see what's left. Supplies. Water."

"Carefully," Connor said, though he seemed as eager as she was to search.

The village was eerily still with no people, no animals and no movement. "It's a ghost town," Kate said.

"Do you want to wait out here while I have a look around?" he asked.

She wasn't waiting alone, unprotected in the dense green. "I'm coming with you," Kate said. Two sets of eyes were better than one.

They searched building after building. Most were stripped bare of supplies. Some furniture remained

inside, some clothing and wood for fires. Kate was
disappointed they had no bottles of water and no ed-
ible food. Either the former inhabitants had taken their
goods with them or she and Connor were not the first
people to find the village and raid it.

"How much did you study religious practices of the
people of this area?" Connor asked.

Kate wiped a trickle of sweat from her temple. She
didn't know how her body was sweating extra fluid. She
was desperately thirsty. "I've read a little. I don't know
anything about summoning water via a rain dance or
using a divining rod to locate a water source." She
meant her words in jest, but Connor either missed the
humor or ignored it.

He pointed to the doors and windows of the nearest
two huts. "Those stick figures. What do they mean?"

A chill trembled up Kate's spine as she looked around.
Why hadn't she noticed them before? Hung with vines
from every door and window were simple stick figures
formed from dried grass. "They're to ward off evil."
She'd seen a picture of them when she'd been researching
the area. A Sphere agent had taken a photo of one while
he was performing some reconnaissance in Tumara and
had found one hanging on his tent in the morning. It
was disturbing for two reasons. First, a Sphere agent
was trained to go undetected and listen for footsteps.
Someone had approached his tent without him hearing.
Second, for the locals to believe Sphere agents were evil
had overarching implications about the successfulness
in obtaining help from them. That was, they wouldn't.

Connor ran his hand over one of the figures. "What's
your best guess as to the evil they are trying to avoid?

Are we talking about the revolutionaries? *El presidente?*"

Kate couldn't be sure. "They could have been experiencing a problem within their community and tried to turn things around with a ceremony to ward away evil. When that failed, maybe they abandoned their village and relocated. The locals are seminomadic. They don't stay in a place for long that doesn't have favorable conditions."

"Like if their water source dried up," Connor said.

"Yes, like losing their water source," Kate agreed, and her heart fell.

They continued to search the village. Kate kept her eyes away from the stick figures. When they moved in the slight breeze, twisting on their grass loops, they were unsettling.

"Kate!"

She had never heard such joy in Connor's voice. She jogged around a hut on the edge of the village. A small stream cut through the dense vegetation and Kate almost wept when she saw it. She rushed and fell to her knees. Scooping it in her hands, she splashed her face, opening her mouth and catching what she could.

Connor pulled her back, shaking his head before she could cup her hands again into the water and drink. "I don't know if that's safe. Let me build a fire and boil some water."

How dirty could the running water be? Her lips were dry. Just a few sips wouldn't hurt. "I'll just drink a little bit."

Connor shook his head. "If there's bacteria in the water, you could have a major dehydration problem."

She had a dehydration problem now. "I won't drink

any. I'll clean up a bit." Her face and body were damp with sweat and caked with dust and debris. Kate rinsed her arms, rolled her pants legs, removed her shoes and let cool water wash over her feet. She restrained herself from drinking and waited for Connor to clean it.

Connor was kneeling on the ground, his cargo pants tight around his hips, his white shirt damp with sweat and clinging to his body. His broad shoulders tapered down to a trim waist. The muscles in his back and arms worked as he removed items from his pack and boiled the water. He must spend time in a gym or doing some form of physical activity. No man looked that ripped sitting around his remote cabin watching television and reading books.

"Do you have any hobbies?" she asked.

Connor glanced over his shoulder at her, the boyishness of his expression charming. "Small talk? I told you I hate small talk."

"It's not small talk. I want to know how you keep in such good shape."

Connor had returned to his task, and for a long moment, Kate wasn't sure he would answer her. "I hike. I climb. I do calisthenics."

He had the body and endurance for it. Throughout the day, exhaustion had dogged her, but Connor had pressed on, not only taking the lead, but never showing signs of needing to rest.

"You're in good shape," she said, wanting to draw him out. He was so different from Aiden. Aiden would have let the question lead to a conversation, not drop it as quickly as possible.

"I have to be."

"You don't have to be. You could sit around your cabin, watch movies and eat chocolate."

He frowned at the idea. "I suppose I could. I don't. Water's almost ready."

He pulled the metal pot from the fire he'd made and poured the water into a cup. Then he gathered more water from the stream. He handed Kate the cup. "It's hot, but drink as much as you need. I pushed you hard this morning."

He had. "I understand you want to get to Mangrove."

Connor looked out into the jungle. "I've been thinking. Why was Aiden out here?"

"That's classified."

"Meaning you don't know or you won't tell me?" he asked.

"Everything about his mission was and is need-to-know," Kate said.

"That's Sphere's favorite line. Makes it easier to hide the truth."

The water was cool enough to sip, and though the liquid was hot, it was a salve to her parched throat. She blew on the water and sipped as fast as she could.

"That's a good look for you," Connor said. "You look like a hiker."

The clothes, backpack and cup. "I call this my out-doorswoman look. All I need is an ax, and I could survive out here for weeks." Joking, of course. Without Connor, Kate didn't think she would survive a night.

Connor removed the pot from the fire and poured himself a cup of water. "Are you sorry you came? Do you wish you were home now, under the spray of a hot shower, then pulling on a pair of soft pajamas?"

The visual Connor created was tempting. It would

be nice to have hot, running water and access to the luxuries she lived with and was accustomed to. But sitting around in her apartment wouldn't save Aiden. "It's mean to give me that glorious mental image when I'm covered with grime, but I'll be home soon enough."

Connor let his gaze move down her body. She felt the look as if he'd touched her. How did he do that to her?

"Had Aiden seen you in the field or did you stay behind a desk?"

"He and I worked together for a few years before we met in person. Most of our interaction was over the phone," Kate said.

"And the sparks flew?" Connor asked.

Kate stared at him. If he didn't want to believe her, that was fine, but his take on events was skewed. "Sparks did not fly, to use your words. I met him and we had a mutual and well-deserved respect for each other. We got along and shared a few beers and conversations. But Aiden isn't interested in dating me."

"I know my brother. You're his type. Tall. Gorgeous. Blonde. Smart. Aiden would be on you like flies on manure."

Her belly fluttered at his compliment. "While that's a darling image, it's fiction. Hear me now, and for once, stop thinking I'm lying to cover an agenda. I am not in love with your brother. I do not have sexual feelings for your brother. I have great respect and admiration for him. I care about him as my friend. That is all." She wouldn't go so far as to tell Connor it was him she had the crush on. It was Connor who caught and held her attention. Connor who possessed that hard-to-define quality that drew her eye. Kate wanted to touch him and kiss him and be wrapped in his arms. Though it defied logic, she was drawn to the more difficult brother.

Given Connor's paranoia that originated in some damaging emotional experience, she shouldn't want to be close to him. She should want to put as much distance between him and her as possible.

"I believe you," Connor said.

Finally. "Good, because it's the truth."

"I can give your water some flavor if you want," Connor said. "Make it more like sipping tea."

Kate blew on the water to cool it. "You travel with tea bags?"

"My mother was English and instilled in me a love of tea, but no, I don't have tea bags. But I've got some sassafras root I picked up this morning."

He set a gnarled-looking stick in his tea. "Have to make the most of the flavors you can find."

"I'll try some," she said.

Connor handed her his cup. "Help yourself. We'll refill our canteens here, too."

Kate took a sip and was surprised how good it was. "It tastes a little like root beer." She handed the mug back to him and their fingers brushed. The heat from the jungle, the mug and their touch could have ignited a fire. "If I have to be lost in the jungle, I'm glad it's with you."

"We're not lost. If you can get past the personality quirks, I'm a handy guy to have around."

His personality quirks were undeniable. The paranoia about security. The bluntness. General distrust of the human population. She could live with those traits.

Half her colleagues had at least one of those qualities. But the resourcefulness, the confidence and the calmness under pressure were strengths she admired. Put to the test, Connor was a man who would rise to the occasion. "What are the chances you can come up with a way to get us some meat?"

"Is that a challenge?" Connor asked.

She had expected him to laugh off her request. "I'm only joking. We have other things to focus on."

Connor shrugged. "We'll stay here tonight and have some shelter. I can set some traps and get us food other than fruit. We have the food we bought. We'll eat some more of it for dinner."

His willingness to go out of his way for her impressed her. "I can make do with what we've found." But now that he had mentioned it, she was looking forward to beef jerky. How her life had changed in the past several days. Prior to coming to Tumara, jerky of any kind would be near the end of her "things I want to eat" list.

"Let's pick a hut here to set up. We've been walking for hours and we need to rehydrate and refuel," Connor said.

Connor walked through the village again, stopping at a midsize hut in the middle of the village. "We'll use this one," Connor said. It was the most sophisticated of the huts, a stone fireplace built into one of the walls and wood sleeping platforms on the ground. Unlike their bed the night before, the wood was sanded smooth. "I'll start a fire and heat some stones to leave around the hut to keep us warm overnight."

"What can I do to help?" Kate asked.

"Can you gather some broadleaves for bedding?" he asked.

Having seen him work the night before, Kate knew what to look for, and she was pleased to be asked to help. She didn't want to be a burden. She left Connor in the hut building a fire in the hearth.

The jungle was never quiet. Birds' songs and bugs' humming filled the air. The strange sense of being watched burned into her back. Kate looked around, expecting to see Connor. He was still inside the hut. Was it Sphere? They had eyes and ears everywhere. Their satellite capabilities were legendary. Could they be spying on her and Connor now remotely?

Kate smothered the laugh that rose to her lips. She was becoming as paranoid as Connor. Sphere could gather intel and they could track her, but how much effort would they put into finding her when they hadn't tried to find Aiden? They'd be more likely to strategically place someone in Mangrove and try to stop her and Connor then.

Trees and brush rustled around her. Kate peered into the green, training her eyes to look for movement. If a predator was watching, she wanted to see it coming. She didn't see any animal appear. She continued collecting leaves.

When she had enough, she returned to the hut, watching over her shoulders. She couldn't shake the sensation someone was out here with them.

Connor had arranged the hut and was laying food on a plank of wood. "Lunch, if you're interested."

She was hungry, although her nerves made her stomach tight with fear. "I felt someone watching me."

Connor's gaze swerved to her. "Did you see anyone?"

His eyes took on the intense look he sometimes got. Intense and focused on her. Being on the receiving end of his attention, she found it was difficult not to reach out and touch him, to complete that connection that burned hot. He aroused a heavy, sensuous sensation in her body. Her breasts felt heavier and her skin ached to be touched.

His hand covered hers. "Did you see anyone?" he asked again.

He'd no doubt meant the gesture to get her attention, but it turned into something primal. She turned her hand over and laced their fingers. "No, I didn't see anyone. I'm tired and jumpy."

Connor looked from their interlocked hands to her face. He didn't drag his hand away as she'd expected. He brought his free hand to the back of her neck and pulled her close, stopping when his lips were inches from hers. "What are you doing?" Darkness danced in his eyes, and though he wouldn't hurt her, she sensed a danger that lay in wait in him.

"What do you mean? I'm holding your hand and waiting for you to kiss me."

Connor drew away a few inches, confusion plain on his face. "Why?"

Why? Didn't he feel the connection? She drew air into her lungs. "From the first time I saw you, I felt something. I want you. I want to know what it's like to kiss a man like you."

"Define what you mean."

Did he have to question and overthink everything?

"Strong. Smart. Handsome." What woman wasn't looking for those qualities?

Connor stared at her for a long moment. "You don't have to pay me for helping you with sex."

She recoiled as if he'd slapped her, pulling her hand away. "I am not trying to pay you with sex. I am not interested in sex." At least, not just sex. No doubt Connor would have some amazing moves in bed. But Kate wasn't looking for that. She just wanted to explore the attraction, get her mind off being stalked by Sphere and do what felt right.

"I don't think this is a good idea. You're bored," he said.

"Bored?" she asked, his rejection stinging her pride and making her feel foolish.

"I'm the only man out here."

She threw up her hands in frustration. "I don't need a man so much that I just throw myself at the closest one. I'm not bored. I'm interested. Or I was before you made this into an overly complicated situation."

"You're looking for ways to pass the time."

Kate glared at him. "Pass the time? No, actually. Making camp here for the night means we have more time to get to know each other." She held up her hand. "And that isn't a euphemism for sleeping together. I thought after what we've been through, we had something. Now I'm mad that you're making me explain myself. Can't you go with the flow and not question everyone's motives and reasoning? Sometimes it's just emotion. Not logic."

Connor jammed a hand through his hair. "Of course I question your motives. I have from the beginning."

Was he dense or was he taking pleasure in seeing

her get mad? She wouldn't give him the satisfaction. "You're a good-looking man." Simple.

Connor's eyebrows lifted. "You're coming on to me?"

She couldn't be the first woman to tell him he was attractive. Why was he surprised? "You must know women find you attractive."

He inclined his head. "I don't know what women think about."

Did this have to do with his trust issues or was he unaware of his sexual pull? It made him more charming that he wasn't aware of it, or at least not arrogant about it. "You've got a lot going for you. Having sex with you has crossed my mind." She'd wanted a reaction, wanted to break through his frosty exterior, and she'd succeeded.

Connor traced his finger over her lower lip. "You are a complicated woman. There's layers here I've only begun to figure out."

Her heart sang. It was the first time a man—aside from her father—had said that about her. Most men she had dated didn't see much past her looks.

"We're alone. You have all night to see what you can figure out," Kate said.

Her words had turned him on. His eyes were wide. "This is an interesting side of you."

"What's interesting about it? I'm just putting it on the table for you to see." She wrapped her arms around his neck.

His breathing escalated. He inched closer. He was into her. He was into this. The evidence was pressing into her stomach. He rotated his hips against hers in a slow, smooth rhythm, giving her the undeniable impression that she had been right: he would be very good in bed.

Her legs weakened and Kate tightened her hold on him. She wanted more, wanted to see how far he would go before one of them stopped this. Her mind swam with warnings, but her body ached for more. She pressed full against him.

His eyes blazed. "You're playing with a fire you can't control."

"You don't know what I can and can't do. Don't underestimate me."

Connor brought his mouth down on hers in a hard, demanding kiss. She melted into him, opening her mouth, sucking lightly on the end of his tongue. His hands went to the back of her head and pulled free the clasp binding her hair. Connor kept his emotions on a tight leash. Too tight. She was getting the raw, intense passion that had been concealed beneath his careful control. Kate lifted her leg, wrapping it around the back of Connor's thigh, anchoring her body to his.

Her feelings for him rocketed from crush to full-on lust. Work hard, play hard. Yes, yes, yes.

A growl sounded in his chest and he tore his lips away. "This has gone far enough." He sounded angry. Angry he had lost control?

"A kiss? That's not far at all," she said. Taunting him.

The brown of his eyes deepened, and she was suddenly very aware of how mercurial Connor could be when his back was against the wall. From kissing her as if passion was absolutely in charge to denying that it could go further in the span of several moments. "Let me walk you through this in ten seconds or less. If this goes further, we'll both be distracted. Instead of tracking Aiden, we'll be worried about getting each other naked as often as possible. That's not good for anyone. If I make a mistake and Aiden suffers for it, I'll blame myself, and resentment will build. You'll get hurt, and it all circles back to my inability to keep it in my pants. I won't let that happen to you. To Aiden. To myself."

She didn't buy that something happening between them would be exclusively about sex. Maybe their relationship ended the moment they located Aiden. Maybe they returned to the United States and never spoke again. The uncertainty of the future was always a challenge with relationships, but it had never stopped her from getting into one. Even with Michael, even if what Connor had said about him was true, she didn't regret what had happened. "You're very good at making reasons to keep people at arm's length." She didn't move away from him. She leaned in closer.

Connor took her arms, holding her in place, and stepped back. "Experience has taught me it's better that way."

It was her turn to be blunt. "You said you weren't afraid of anything but I don't think that's true. I think you're afraid of being hurt. If you keep everyone away, if you refuse to trust people, then you can never be hurt," she said.

"Interesting assessment." A dismissal.

Freezing her out. Unwilling to talk. She wasn't ready to let it go. She could get him to be open with her. "Aiden shared some about what it was like for him growing up. I know the two of you forged a bond from a less-than-perfect childhood. I know you've both overcome obstacles to be where you are today. I know you both have worked to be strong and sharp. But how is Aiden so open and you are so closed?"

"If you and Aiden are close, I assume he would have explained that to you," Connor said, pacing in the hut, putting more distance between them. "We need sleep."

She had pushed too hard and he had emotionally shut down. Kate wouldn't give up, but she wouldn't press him now when it would get her nowhere. She had time. "I'm exhausted. I could fall asleep on a pile of burning coals."

Connor had left the door to the hut open and the grass figure swung as if from a hangman's noose. It caught her attention and Kate wished the creepy figures would disappear.

Connor followed her gaze to the doorway. "I'll remove it if it bothers you." He sounded almost apologetic. She knew it wasn't about the figures.

Superstition prevented her from telling him to get rid of them. "If they have some religious meaning, I don't want to destroy them and risk the wrath of whatever power they were supposed to ward away."

The corner of Connor's mouth lifted. "A religious woman? I never would have pegged you for that."

Her belief system wasn't something she discussed with anyone at work. For the most part, it seemed as if the people she worked with and for didn't believe in a higher power. Perhaps it was because they engaged in life-and-death decisions every day or perhaps it was because they relied on themselves in the field when their prayers weren't answered.

"I'll choose not to take that as an insult. I do believe in a higher power. When I'm in contact with an agent working in the field and something goes wrong, I say a quiet prayer."

Sadness touched the corners of Connor's eyes. "How many of those prayers were said for Aiden?"

Not the response she had been expecting. "Many. But we're going to find him."

The expression on his face was filled with doubt, and Kate wished she could make this right for him. She wished she could guarantee they would find Aiden. She wished Connor would open up to her. And she wished she could tell Connor the role she'd played in Aiden's disappearance without demolishing the little trust that had formed between them.

Connor had almost lost control. When he'd held Kate close, he'd felt it slipping and it had taken him far too long to get it back. He trusted no one and he considered that a good trait. When he was around Kate, she made him too comfortable. She was easy to talk to. She was stunning and her attention led him to feeling energized and powerful.

He'd have to be careful. While he might have mischaracterized her relationship with his brother, knowing she was single couldn't change his boundaries with her. Aiden had to come first. Any distractions could cause a mistake.

When he fell asleep, Kate was breathing evenly. He was tempted to pull his pallet closer to hers. After some internal debate, he decided against it. Being in the same hut was close enough. Though his body ached to hold her as he had the night before, he didn't need to sleep beside her. She was near enough to protect.

Connor was dreaming, a dream he hadn't had in a

number of years, of his mother and her face the last time he had seen her. She was kissing him and Aiden on the cheek, telling them to be good boys. She was crying and getting into her boxy navy blue sedan. When he had turned away from her, unable to watch for another moment, he saw his father standing in the doorway observing them with cold detachment, his hands in his pockets.

How soon after she'd left had Connor become his father's punching bag? His mother had always protected him and his brother from their father's temper. Now that she was gone, Connor had to protect Aiden. Connor had no one to rely on and no one he could trust except his brother. He hadn't wanted Aiden and him to be split up, and he knew if anyone found out about his father, they'd be sent to foster care. Separate foster houses and he'd risk never seeing his brother again. Unacceptable on all levels. He'd had to look out for Aiden no matter what.

Connor awoke to a sound outside the hut. His chest was heavy with sadness and the hurt that echoed across time from a wound that had never healed. An engine revved and then the unmistakable sounds of footsteps and flames. Snapping into the present, Connor was freed of the dream, and the last of his sadness dissipated. His body went on full alert, his mind kicked into gear and he brushed aside remnants of the cutting memory of his mother leaving.

Another human was in the village. Perhaps it wasn't abandoned as he had believed. Were he and Kate trespassing on someone's land? Their fire had gone out, but the heavy smell of burned wood clung to the air. Would their late-night visitors notice and investigate?

Without the benefit of sight, Connor was working at a deficit, and with Kate to protect, the stakes were higher. If he woke her, would she come awake quietly and follow him without question? Could he leave her asleep and carry her away without being seen? A dozen scenarios crowded his head.

This was one of the thousand reasons bringing a newbie into the field was dangerous. A seasoned veteran would know how to respond to being woken abruptly: quietly and defensively. He wouldn't have to worry about protecting a seasoned veteran.

The Sphere agents who had followed them at the airport could be searching for them. Nomadic people from the jungle could have been looking for a safe place to spend the night and found the village. The AR could have a group on patrol. A tourist could have wandered into the village.

Connor was trained to anticipate and prepare for the worst-case scenario. He'd assume an enemy had arrived armed with guns and knives, looking for tourists to either rob or kill.

Would the person or people outside check every hut in the abandoned village? If he and Kate remained quiet, would they leave without an altercation?

Connor reached into his pack for his knife. He grasped the handle and pulled it free. Should he wake Kate? If she woke disoriented, they would waste time they didn't have or risk making noise that brought someone to investigate. She had been quiet and calm when she'd been woken in Rosario by a late-night visitor. Making a decision, he touched Kate's shoulder.

"Kate," he whispered.

"Hmm?" Kate asked.

"Remain calm. Someone is outside. I need you to be quiet and follow me," Connor said.

She sat and squeezed his arm, letting him know she'd heard him. He went to the window and peered out.

Four men exited a vehicle and all four had guns strapped across their bodies. Two carried torches. They wore military fatigues and had black armbands tied around their upper arm. The Armed Revolutionaries.

Three of the men turned toward the tallest. After the large man said something Connor couldn't hear and gestured, two jogged off away from the huts. The remaining pair stood in direct view. One man smoked a cigarette, while the other stood next to him, waiting. When the man Connor guessed to be the leader finished his cigarette, he flicked it to the ground. He and his partner began to open the doors of the huts and peer inside. In his current position, Connor couldn't exit without being seen.

"We have to get out of here," Kate whispered, joining him at the window.

They needed a place to hide. The men were almost to their hut. Without the chance to escape, Connor adjusted his plan from avoidance to offensive. He and Kate couldn't outrun a bullet, but he could hope the men didn't get to their guns faster than he could use his knife. He pressed Kate against the wall of the hut. If bullets started flying, he wanted her out of harm's way. The longer she stayed hidden, the better.

The men opened the door to the hut. Connor's gaze

landed on Kate's backpack in plain view at the same time theirs did.

"There's something in here," the smaller man said, alarm in his voice.

Before the other could respond, Connor disabled the man, striking him on the back of the head. The other man turned and swung at Connor. Connor ducked the attack and landed a well-placed punch to his solar plexus, knocking the wind out of him. He gasped for air, and Connor swept his legs out from under him. The man fell backward, rolled and righted himself.

Keeping himself between Kate and the leader, Connor dodged left and swung right, catching the revolutionary across the face. The man finally fell to the ground unconscious.

Connor pointed to his bag. "Get the rope from my pack. Hurry," he said to Kate. He'd tie up these two before the others realized their associates were missing.

Connor tied them to the large wood pallets where he and Kate had been sleeping. Though it wouldn't prevent them from moving entirely, it would keep them from attacking him and Kate.

"What about the others?" Kate asked.

A radio beeped on one of the men's belts. "Boss, come in."

Connor swore inwardly. If no one answered, they'd return to the vehicle and possibly notice him and Kate. Connor plucked the radio off the man's belt and exited the hut. He hurled the radio into the jungle. If they followed the sound or GPS, it would buy him and Kate another few moments.

"Grab your backpack," Connor said, taking the

weapons from the two men. He threw his pack over his shoulders and Kate did the same.

"What are we going to do?" Kate asked.

"We need their vehicle."

"We're going to steal their car?" Kate asked. "To go where?"

"We're going to Mangrove."

Kate took his hand. "Connor, be reasonable. If these people are with the AR, it won't take long for word to spread that we've stolen a car from them. We don't need every member of the AR looking for us."

"We'll already be in Mangrove before anyone finds out. Come on." Connor needed to find his brother, and he would do anything to accomplish that goal, even if that meant taking risks.

As he left the hut, he froze at the sound of his brother's name. "Aiden? Is that you?" Surprise and unease were heavy in the speaker's voice.

Connor didn't move. It was almost pitch-black and it wasn't the first time he had been mistaken for his brother. The second patrol was returning. How should he respond?

"That's not Aiden. Wait. Stop!"

"To the car," Connor said, taking hold of Kate's upper arm and racing toward the vehicle.

The sound of gunfire exploded in the air. "Stop!" one of the men shouted.

Kate screamed and Connor lost his hold on her. He whirled. One of the men had grabbed her and was wrestling her to the ground. Kate was kicking and flailing, but her strength was no match for the man on top of her. The image brought rage over him. If the man hurt Kate, Connor would kill him.

Connor took the man by the neck and ripped him away from Kate, flinging him to the ground. The second man came at him, and Connor disarmed him and shoved him into the dirt next to his companion. He'd confiscated three of the weapons, and the fourth lay on the ground out of reach.

"Do not touch her. Do not ever touch her," Connor said.

Connor leveled the gun at the men. "Tell me who you think I am." They had spoken his brother's name. Was it too much to hope these men knew Aiden? How many Aidens were in this part of the world?

The men were silent.

"I already killed your buddies," Connor lied. "Tell me what you know or I'll kill both of you, too. A body count of two or four makes no difference to me."

"You killed Bruno Feliz?" one of the men asked.

It was Connor's turn to be silent. They had crossed paths with Bruno Feliz and Connor had attacked him. Starting a personal war with the leader of the Armed Revolution was never his intention. He was outgunned and outnumbered. Except what was done was done. The mission hadn't changed. He still had to find Aiden as fast as possible and get him home. It was just more complicated: he had to avoid the AR and the Sphere agents tracking them. "Tell me about Aiden," he said.

One of the men opted to answer. "You look like a man we knew out here. Aiden West. He disappeared a while ago. No one's heard from him." His voice shook, though he kept his chin lifted proudly. The AR were resilient and persistent. It was one of the few groups that had survived *el presidente*'s counterattacks.

"Where did you last see him?" Connor asked.

"He was at Camp Rome," the man said, "of course."

Camp Rome—an interesting name for the revolutionaries' hideout. Where was it located? "Why 'of course'?" Connor asked.

"Don't tell him anything else. He could be a spy for *el presidente*," the other man hissed. "He killed Feliz. It doesn't matter what he does to us now."

"Your life for the information," Connor threatened. He hated to behave this way in front of Kate. He had no intention of killing these men, but he would get all the information he could from them.

The men exchanged looks. "He was an American. Looked a lot like you," the man said. "He came here and he worked with us against *el presidente*. Then one night, after a raid on our camp, he disappeared."

Whose side was Sphere on and where had they positioned Aiden? He would have done whatever Sphere had asked of him on this mission. Had they asked him to work with the Armed Revolutionaries in order to spy on them for *el presidente?* Were these men lying and holding Aiden captive as punishment for working against the AR?

Connor didn't let his strong emotions for his brother rule him. "Where is Camp Rome?"

"We can't tell you," the man said.

The evasive answers were irritating. "Because you don't know or it no longer exists?" Connor asked.

The men were silent. Connor strode to the two men in the hut. He grabbed the larger one, assuming it was an unconscious Bruno Feliz, and dragged him in front of the other men.

"Last chance. Talk or I'll put a bullet in his head."

"You said he was already dead!"

"I lied. Talk," Connor said.

"We had to relocate it after the raid. The new spot is a few miles north of here," the man said, shaking hard.

Connor dropped Feliz on the ground. He slapped his cheeks, trying to rouse him. The man groaned, proving he was alive. Relief was plain on the other men's faces.

Kate touched Connor's arm. "They weren't bluffing. That's Bruno Feliz," she whispered. "I didn't recognize him before."

Connor looked from Feliz to these men. If he killed Feliz and the Armed Revolution was holding Aiden somewhere, he was signing his brother's death warrant. He'd have to get to Aiden before word spread that he'd attacked Feliz and his men. "I'm leaving you alive. I expect the same for my brother or I will find you again and kill you." Connor had disabled the legendary Bruno Feliz. That should drive home the fear factor Connor was counting on to make someone think twice about hurting or killing his brother.

"Hand her the keys to the car," Connor said. "Slowly."

The man took a lanyard with keys at the end from around his neck and handed it to Kate. She took it and returned to Connor's side. She clutched his arm and her trembling concerned him. He hadn't meant for her to be afraid. A lot of what he had said and done was posturing to work the situation. Surely, she knew that. Her training with Sphere had to have touched on psychological warfare.

"Get in the car," he said to Kate. "Start it and I'll be there in a minute."

With a final squeeze, she ran to the car. When he heard it start, he backed away from the men. He threw the guns in the backseat of the vehicle and climbed in the driver's side.

Together, they sped away from the village, heading north to Camp Rome.

Chapter 7

Trekking a few miles in the jungle was faster with a vehicle, but not by much. Kate's backside was sore from bouncing around the vehicle as it navigated the rough terrain.

"I don't want them to hear our approach. Let's get out here and do some recon," Connor said.

"This could be a trap," Kate said. Connor had gotten the information by force. In her opinion, the more uncooperative the informant, the more questionable the information. A few miles to a camp could mean a hundred miles or they'd been pointed in the wrong direction or the camp was nonexistent.

Kate got out and helped Connor put leaves over the car to partially conceal it. Connor pulled two pairs of fatigues and a set of black armbands from the vehicle. "Let's change into these."

"No one will believe we're AR," Kate said.

They looked all wrong for the part, but it was something. "They'll help us blend."

Kate looked around for a place to change. Connor had already stripped out of his shirt and was tugging the camo-green tank on. It was a sight she would never forget. The man was muscle, tanned skin, sinewy arms and corded abdomen without a stitch of fat anywhere. Kate closed her mouth and took off her shirt. The mental image of Connor was plucking at her desire and she needed it to remain quiet.

She struggled to put on the shirt, feeling as though her hands weren't working properly. Which they didn't when she was jittery. It wasn't that she hadn't seen a man without his shirt before. She had. Plenty of times. The problem was that most men who had a body like Connor's were secured in the pages of a magazine, no risk of her ogling them in their presence.

Connor pulled her shirt down, and his fingers skimmed the soft skin at her midsection. "Looked like you needed some help," he said.

She shivered, wishing he had pulled the shirt the other way. She ached to reach out and touch him skin to skin, if only for a minute, if only to get some comfort. Kate was frightened and it was fraying her at the seams. "I got it. I'm just tired."

Connor waited for her to finish changing, giving her his back. Gentlemanly contact and she wanted for him to be anything but a gentleman.

Hidden by the dark, she took off her jeans and pulled on the camo pants. They were more comfortable than the jeans had been. She liked them.

Connor turned and gave her another head-to-toe look. "You look good in green," he said.

She adjusted the clothes. Not as good as he did. The whole look worked for him.

"Stay close to me, okay?" he asked.

She had no intention of being anywhere else. He was carrying one of the weapons they had taken off Bruno Feliz and the men from the village. Bruno Feliz! They couldn't have tangled with a bigger fish in the jungle unless *el presidente* had decided to start patrolling himself. Kate knew it wasn't the last they would hear of the incident. An assault on the leader of the AR would come back to haunt them.

Connor hadn't offered her a gun and she guessed that was smart. She hadn't trained with a gun that size and that alone was intimidating.

They walked the area for a time before returning to the vehicle. They drove farther north and stopped and searched four more times before Connor took her hand and squeezed it. The sign of affection was so unexpected she almost asked what he was doing. But she kept her mouth closed and followed his pointed finger through the brush.

Another village. This one was obviously populated, and lights were fixed to posts surrounding the area, making it easier to see. Camp Rome? There were no street signs in this part of the jungle. They crept around the perimeter of the camp, stopping and watching for long periods of time. Kate tried to keep track of how many people were inside.

The men at the previous village had indicated Aiden had been here but had disappeared and they believed he'd been working against the government. Her State

Department contact claimed Aiden was being held by the Armed Revolutionaries. Either one or both had bad information.

"If my brother is being held here, we'll find him," Connor said.

"Feliz's group said Aiden was missing," Kate said.

"Just like I lied to them, they could have lied to me," Connor said.

Deception and sorting lies from the truth was part of the game they were playing.

Connor and Kate took their time watching. Connor sat and watched without moving. Kate, on the other hand, had trouble maintaining focus and not swatting at the bugs that buzzed around them. An hour passed. Kate shifted, trying to get more comfortable. Her leg muscles were sore from remaining in the same position for so long. The sun was beginning to rise and Kate hoped it chased away nocturnal predators.

"I need a break," she said.

Connor glanced at her. "Are you okay? Do you need food or water?"

If she said yes, he would go and get them for her. She didn't want him to break from his surveillance. What if he missed seeing his brother? "I'm going to walk a little bit." She pointed behind them, away from the camp.

"I'd rather you stay close," Connor said.

"I'll stay within eyesight of you," Kate said.

Though Connor didn't seem to think it was a good idea, he didn't argue. Kate moved carefully and slowly as Connor had through the jungle. She stretched her legs and her arms. Her body wasn't accustomed to going without sleep and food and coffee, and she needed the movement to wake her up.

A hard object pressed into her side. "Don't move. Don't breathe or I will kill you. Keep your hands where I can see them." The words were spoken quietly, but the accompanying tone was iron.

Kate gasped. A gun. Someone had a gun on her. Kate lifted her hands slowly to her sides and turned toward the female voice. The woman on the other side of the shotgun was startlingly beautiful. Wide, expressive brown eyes, dark hair to her waist, and a mouth that, if it wasn't frowning, would form a lovely smile.

"Are you alone?" the woman asked.

Kate could see Connor in her peripheral vision. Had he realized what was happening to her? "No. I am not." She was too afraid to lie.

"Why are you here?" the woman asked.

"We're looking for a friend."

Connor disappeared from view. Kate held on to the hope that he was coming to help her. Kate kept talking to hold the woman's attention. "My name is Kate. I am looking for my friend's brother. He went missing in this area. We heard he could still be alive. We've come from the United States to find him and bring him home safely."

"You're Americans?" the woman asked and lowered her gun a few inches.

Should she admit to it? Her Portuguese was good, but her accent could use some work. "Yes."

"Did *el presidente* send you?" she asked.

"No," Kate said. "We're not working for anyone. We're just trying to find someone we care about."

Despite the gun and the hardness of the woman's face, Kate saw a warmth in her eyes. "Tell me about the man you're looking for."

Should Kate tell her the truth? If this woman knew Aiden, maybe she could help them. If she knew Aiden and believed him to be a traitor, would she hold that against her and Connor?

Kate kept to basics. She would watch the woman's reaction and then plan how much to say. "His name is Aiden. He's also American."

"Aiden?" From the way the woman spoke his name, a combination of confusion and reverence, Kate discerned this woman knew him.

Excitement trilled through her. Could Connor hear them? This was an exciting lead. "Do you know him? Have you seen him?"

"I know him." The woman lowered her gun to the ground. Sadness was clear on her face.

Sad because Aiden was dead? Missing? "Do you know where he is?" Kate couldn't handle it if the woman said Aiden was dead. It would devastate Connor.

Connor came out of nowhere. Kate hadn't seen his approach. He leaped onto the woman, tackling her to the ground and tearing the gun from her hands. Connor came out on top, swinging the barrel of the shotgun toward the woman, holding it over her head. "Tell me where my brother is."

The woman's eyes were wide and she stopped struggling. "You look just like him."

"Connor, get off her," Kate said. This woman knew Aiden and had personal feelings for him. Connor had been acting in defense of her, but this woman wasn't the threat she had presented. "Please tell us what you know," Kate said.

Connor glanced at Kate before moving his weight off the woman. He kept the gun aimed at her.

The woman was trembling as she sat. "I'm Ariana Feliz. You must be Aiden's brother, Connor. He spoke so highly of you. I am sorry to tell you he's been taken by the Tumaran government and I haven't heard from him in months. I've been trying to find him."

Hope flickered across Connor's face. "My brother has spoken to you? He's alive?"

The woman's eyes filled with tears. "As far as I know, he's alive. I haven't spoken to him." The woman sighed. "He and I spent much time together. He loved me. Loves me. And I love him. He was taken because of me."

Kate's chest ached, hearing the grief in Ariana's words.

Connor's eyes narrowed. "Taken where?"

"I don't know. He didn't want you to come here. He knew you would come if you found out he was in trouble and he didn't want you to be in danger."

"What danger is he in?" Connor asked.

"Things have gotten worse over the past year for us. I tried to tell Aiden to return to the United States before something tragic happened, but he wouldn't leave without me. I can't abandon my post. People are counting on me. Even if I could, I would never get past the border because I'm considered a criminal."

"I'm here now. I can help him. I won't leave if he needs me," Connor said, the pleading in his voice so raw, Kate felt tears welling in her eyes. Connor helped the woman to her feet.

Ariana shook her head in misery. "You don't understand. I brought him into this mess. Aiden came here working for an American company, a military operation. I fell in love with him. It happened so fast, but when something is right, it just is." She sounded close to tears and it took a moment for her to compose herself. "When he left the first time, he told me I would forget my feelings and I would forget him. I didn't. I couldn't. When he returned the second time, nothing had changed. My love for him was true and strong. Though it was dangerous, he decided to stay with me."

Ariana paused and took a deep breath. "I'm sorry. I'm rambling, and I know this must not make sense, but I've felt so guilty. I wanted to tell Aiden's family what had happened to him, but I didn't know how to find you or your parents or if Aiden would want me to."

Connor stiffened at the mention of his parents. "Our parents are not part of our lives."

Ariana inclined her head. "Aiden speaks of his mother and father often."

Connor stared at her. Blinked in disbelief. "Tell me how to find Aiden."

"I've tried to find him. I've worked every contact I have, looking for information. I've hit dead end after dead end. I'm an outcast. I can't return to my family in the city. If I do, the government will punish them for talking to me. I have to hide in the jungle with the other members of the revolution."

"If you don't know where he is, tell me what you do know," Connor said.

Ariana looked away into the dense green, her eyes misting. "There was an ambush in the middle of the night. The government sent out a squad to decimate our camp. We lost twenty-two men that night. If Aiden hadn't been there defending us, it would have been more. I escaped, thanks to him, but he was captured."

"How do you know he's still alive?" Connor asked, his voice tight.

Ariana pushed her hair over her shoulder and sat straighter. "He has to be. I cannot accept any other possibility."

Not the same as knowing.

Connor's gaze swung to Kate. "How will we find him? What intel do you have? Tell me everything."

The last word she had of his trail ended in Mangrove. She hadn't known he'd left Sphere and switched sides to work for the AR against *el presidente* and the Tumaran government. "My contact believes an American is being held by the AR."

Ariana shook her head. "We don't take prisoners or hostages."

Had Kate's contact been mistaken?

Connor swore. "I will search this country from border to border to locate him."

Kate believed him. The look of hope on Ariana's face was both sweet and heartbreaking.

"Aiden said you were tenacious. He didn't want you here, but I prayed you would come," Ariana said. "How did you find our camp?" Her last question was filled with worry.

Kate told her about the men they had encountered at the abandoned village.

Ariana's eyes grew wide. "You assaulted my brother?"

Kate connected the last names, and her stomach churned with worry. "It was an accident."

To her surprise, Ariana laughed. "God has a funny way of working. He sent you to me by way of my brother.

Bruno will be angry, but I will speak to him. He loved Aiden like a brother. He wants him found, as well," Ariana said. "Let me get you something to eat and drink, and we'll make plans."

Kate and Connor followed Ariana into the AR camp, ignoring the curious looks from others. Kate had once believed these men and women to be the enemy. Now she didn't know what to think.

Over cups of tea, they discussed how to find Aiden.

"The Sphere agents who followed us from the States will still be looking for us," Kate said.

"They think we've gone to Mangrove," Connor said.

"Unless they've known all along Aiden wasn't being held by the AR like my contact believed," Kate said.

"Most AR members who are captured by the government are jailed in Carvalo City," Ariana said. "I haven't been able to find out if Aiden is there."

"What if Sphere has been looking for him and hasn't been able to find him either?" Kate asked.

"And they're using us to do it," Connor said, filling in the rest of Kate's thought.

To know Sphere and the government's motivations was impossible. Kate had known Sphere to flip sides as their interests changed. Often, those interests were financially motivated.

Kate looked back and forth between the two of them. She had an idea—a risky idea, but an idea. "Let me float something. I don't want to make this harder for anyone, but my alias Kate Swiss still works for the United States State Department. As Kate Swiss, I can contact friends I have in the Tumaran government and within the embassy and find out what I can about Aiden."

"Won't your cover already be blown? Sphere knows you've turned against them," Connor said.

Kate shrugged. "Could be. They might have contacted the embassy and told them I was fired, but they wouldn't have told them who I really was. That flies in the face of their plans. They could have said I was replaced."

Connor set the rifle on the ground and took a sip of the tea Ariana had made. "You want to go undercover as Kate Swiss."

A more thorough plan was formulating in her mind. "We need to get back to the city. Ariana can drive us and leave us as close as she feels comfortable. She can return the vehicle to her brother with our apology."

Connor looked sheepish. "Yes, with our apology."

Kate's mind was in overdrive. "I'll need a cell phone and I'll need a computer. I'll spoof my email address to look like it's coming from the State Department. I'll send out some feelers to my government contacts and see if anyone was alerted to me being fired. If no one knows anything, I'll tell them I'm making a trip to Tumara. When we meet in person, I'll do all the digging I can."

"And if everyone believes you were fired?" Connor asked.

"Then I'll tell my friends I'm planning to make a trip to Tumara and I'm looking for another job. If anyone asks about the reasons I was fired, I'll pretend it was my ego or that I argued with my boss." She could make herself sound disgruntled without sounding hostile. "If I can get my hands on the right equipment, maybe I can get inside the Tumaran government's databases and look around for information about the AR and about Aiden. If I had known Aiden was being held prisoner by the government, I would have infiltrated their systems from back in the States."

Connor hugged her, throwing his arms around her and clutching her to him. Then he kissed her full on the mouth. It was the most honest and exuberant display she had seen from him. The kiss wasn't just excitement. She caught the passion simmering in Connor.

"I'm glad you made yourself a thorn in my side and insisted on coming along," Connor said.

"Thorn in your side? I like to think I'm tenacious and that's a good thing," Kate said.

Connor ran his finger lightly down the side of her face. "I guess it is a good thing. You're a good thing."

Ariana cleared her throat as if reminding them she was there. Kate took a step back from Connor.

"How can I get to a computer?" Kate asked. Once her hands were on a keyboard, her work could begin.

Part IV: The City

Chapter 8

In her element, Kate had more confidence than she'd had the rest of the trip. Connor arranged financing for the tools she needed from an account unmonitored by Sphere. Trading the clothes she had worn in the jungle for a few suits and a nice pair of heels, Kate checked into a hotel and paid cash for a room for several nights. After she showered and changed into her new clothes, she found a retail technology store and acquired a laptop and the accessories she needed to present herself as Kate Swiss. Connor accompanied her on every errand, keeping watch for Sphere agents and making sure she was safe.

Now that she was working and had more control, she felt better and stronger than she had in days. It took her under five hours to spoof a State Department account and send a few tentative emails to her friends in the State Department and within the Tumaran government. The responses she received were largely business as usual.

"I don't think they know anything about me leaving the State Department," Kate said.

"Not yet. If anyone from Sphere realizes you're actively using the alias Kate Swiss, they'll put a stop to it," Connor said.

"That's why we need to move as fast as possible. I'll arrange to meet with my friend from the government for dinner tonight and find out if he knows anything more about Aiden."

"Wouldn't it be safer to hack into the system first and look for information?" Connor asked.

Humans inadvertently divulged more information than computers did. The best way to go after the information was a socially engineered attack. "The Tumaran government updates their security measures every thirty days. Hacking the system and staying undetected will take time. Plus, there's no telling if information about Aiden is even in the system or if the information is tied to Aiden's real name."

"How much do you trust your friend?" Connor asked.

Marcus was the contact who had initially passed her information about an American being held by the AR and the government wanting to keep it quiet to avoid any alarmist reaction. Marcus had a good heart even if his information had turned out to be wrong. "If he knows anything about Aiden or any other American citizens being held against their will, he may tell me. Meeting with him in person, I'll be able to watch his reactions to my questions and know if he's holding anything back."

"Have I thanked you yet for doing this?" Connor asked. He sat next to Kate on the bed.

Kate was afraid to remove her hands from the keyboard. Close quarters, high stakes and Connor made the temptation to kiss him impossibly high. "You haven't thanked me. This might be the first time I deserve any thanks."

"Thank you. Thank you for finding me when you had information about Aiden. Thank you for not turning around and running when I tried to scare you away from my door. Thank you for putting up with me and my accusations about having an affair with my brother. Thank you for putting yourself at risk and using your computer skills to do this." Connor leaned in, running his nose along the underside of her jaw.

Kate's body heated. "Don't thank me too much. When he's home safe, we'll both have reasons to be grateful."

The truth about her role in Aiden's disappearance was on the tip of her tongue. If she had alerted Aiden about the raid, he could have better protected himself. If Ariana was right and the Tumaran government was holding him as their prisoner, were they using him as a bargaining chip to control Sphere? Making an example of him to members of the AR?

Kate should have told Connor from the beginning the role she had played in Aiden's disappearance.

How would Connor react if she told him the truth now? They had been through so much and a bond had formed between them. How much damage would the truth do?

Keeping it to herself felt like a lie. Connor had deep trust issues and lying to him had to be the worst option she could pick. She opened her mouth to tell him, but the words wouldn't form on her lips.

"Speechless?" he said. He slid his hand around the back of her neck and rested his forehead on hers. "Aiden found a good friend in you. I hope I can return that favor."

Her heart swelled, and thoughts of ruining the moment with an admission fled to the dark recesses of her mind. She slid the computer away. "Aiden was a good friend to me. You don't need to do anything to repay me for helping him. But I am happy to have your friendship." Or perhaps more than friendship.

Connor lifted her and placed her in his lap. He put his arms around her waist. She fit against him, snug as if her body was meant to be folded against his. She threaded her fingers into the back of his hair and let them run down his neck.

Connor smiled and his eyes softened. "You're one of the most courageous women I've ever met. You're loyal and smart and beautiful. I'm lucky to have you in my life."

She had never seen him so relaxed and open. His mouth captured hers in a slow, sensuous kiss that she felt from her lips to the tips of her toes. She kicked off her heels and crossed her legs, tucking herself against Connor.

There was magic in the moment, some undefinable quality that harnessed her to him. His hand slid up her leg, over her knee, to her thigh, moving a few inches under her skirt. Her body sang with relief. She was finally alone in a private space with him. His touch made it obvious he wanted her, and she had wanted him for so long that giving in to those sensations felt long overdue.

Her computer beeped, alerting her to an incoming email. With half a mind to ignore it, she thought about Aiden. What if the email was from one of her contacts?

A groan sounded in Connor's throat.

She and Connor would have more private moments later. Aiden took priority now. Kate pulled the laptop closer. "It's from my friend at the consulate. He wants to meet us tonight."

"Us?" Connor asked.

She hadn't told Connor that part of her plan. "I told my friend that I was bringing my boyfriend. I told him we were talking about relocating and you wanted to check things out." She needed Connor with her tonight. "I didn't feel safe going alone. What if Sphere shows up and we have to run again?" She put her arms around him.

Connor lifted a brow. "Never in all my years as an operative have I played the part of someone's boyfriend. I don't know how good I'll be at it."

Did he have to pretend? They'd acknowledged the heat between them. Couldn't he play off those emotions? "Why don't you make the part an extension of what just happened? Not as much pretending."

"Are you suggesting we make out all through dinner?" His eyes sparkled with amusement.

Teasing her, but her body heard the words and she was turned on by them. Heat pulsed through her in waves. "Something could happen after the dinner. Most men look forward to the ending of a date much more than the date itself." She would be counting the moments until she was again alone with Connor. Prying information from Marcus couldn't take longer than a couple of hours. With any luck, they'd be alone by midnight.

"I assume I'll need to wear something more formal than jeans and a T-shirt?" he asked.

Connor looked good in whatever he wore, but the place where she would suggest to Marcus they meet had a formal dress code. "I'll call the concierge. We'll rent a suit for the night."

She typed a reply to her friend, telling him they'd meet in a couple of hours. "We'd better get ready."

"Maybe you can spare another twenty minutes?" Connor asked.

"What I have in mind will take longer than twenty minutes," Kate said.

Connor groaned and ran his hands over her body. He brought his mouth to her neck and she let her head fall to the side. His teeth nibbled and sucked at the sensitive skin, and lust spiraled through her. She threw her leg across his lap and her skirt slid up her thighs. Connor kissed her mouth—long, slow, deep kisses—and Kate melted against him. Rolling her hips against his, she felt the length of his hardness press against her core.

After a few moments, Kate broke away, panting and straining. If he got much further, she wouldn't be able to leave this hotel room tonight.

"You have more discipline than I do," Connor said.

It was taking everything in her not to rip off their clothes and make frantic, wild love to him. It would be good for both of them, taking the edge off their stress. The completion she knew she'd find in Connor's arms would be, oh, so satisfying and needed. "We can't be late."

Connor released her, and Kate hurried to the bathroom to get ready before she canceled plans with Marcus and, instead, spent the night finding new and exciting ways to make love with Connor.

An hour and a half later, Kate was sticking a few more bobby pins in her hair to hold it into a chignon. The navy dress she'd purchased off the rack fit well enough without needing alterations. She tapped on the door to the bathroom. Connor was inside getting ready.

"Everything okay with the suit? Does it fit?" she asked. Last-minute arrangements left them with a limited selection.

"It fits. I feel ridiculous. Like I'm wearing another man's fatigues."

"In a way you are." She hoped the suit wasn't too small across the shoulders or too short in the arms and legs or...

She lost her train of thought when he stepped out of the bathroom. He had showered and shaved, his hair combed away from his face. The suit fit him well. Too well. It accented his wide shoulders and trim hips. He turned, looking over his shoulder with a strange expression on his face. The pants fit around the waist and the legs of the pants were perfectly tailored, not too baggy or too tight.

"Does this look right? I feel odd and you've got a funny look on your face," Connor said.

A funny look? Was desire being written plain on her face funny? She schooled her expression. "You do not look strange. You look amazing."

"These don't have enough pockets," he said, patting the pants legs.

"Why do you need pockets?" she asked.

"Where will I put my gear?" he asked.

He didn't need gear in a five-star restaurant, the only one in the city. "You can leave the rope and knife here."

He frowned. "You want me to venture out without my equipment?"

"You'll have your good looks and your charm." Both of which could disarm her. When he wanted to, Connor could talk someone into doing whatever he wanted.

"Those are hardly my best tools and we both know it."

He underestimated himself in that regard. "You'll have me and I'll have this," she said, holding up her clutch bag. "I've got my new smartphone inside, but I have more room. If there's anything you cannot live without, I'll carry it."

He looked at the small bag. "Not much will fit. But we'll do this your way." His eyes drank her in. "You look pretty great, by the way."

Kate was glad he'd noticed. "I want my friend to be impressed. This is the first time we're meeting in person."

"Won't it be awkward for me to be sitting across the table from a man who wants to sleep with you?" Connor asked.

Kate set her hand on her hip. "What makes you think he'll want to sleep with me? We've spoken on the phone and over email a hundred times. He's never once said anything inappropriate to me."

Connor gave her a skeptical look. "Do you joke with each other?"

Some of their conversations had a light overture to them. "Sometimes."

Connor deliberately raised his eyebrows. "And he's never seen you?"

"No. He could have looked up my State Department information, which has my employment picture."

Connor adjusted his suit jacket. "He wants to sleep with you. He gets that you're funny, he knows you're pretty, and when he gets a look at you in that dress, it will be the first and most persistent thing on his mind."

Kate shook her head. "You'll be there. You're my boyfriend."

"He'll be thinking of ways to get rid of me and have you to himself."

Kate rolled her eyes. "Not everyone is out to get you. You're such a conspiracy theorist."

"Not a conspiracy. One man. Him. Trying to get in the pants of one woman. You. Which is going to royally annoy one person. Me."

"When you meet him, you will see how wrong you are," Kate said.

"Shall we make it a wager?" Connor asked.

"Name the stakes," Kate said. Marcus might want to sleep with her, but he would never say anything or do anything unprofessional. As a high-ranking Tumaran government official, he had a lot to lose if he behaved inappropriately.

"When I'm right and he makes a pass at you, then you owe me breakfast in bed."

"We're in a five-star hotel. You can order breakfast in bed."

"No, the deal is that you order it, bring it to me and

serve it to me." He waggled his eyebrows and Kate laughed.

"And when I'm right and nothing untoward happens, what do I get?"

"Name it."

A list of lewd suggestions came to mind. She dismissed them for something that would be harder to entice Connor to do. "I want to ask you ten questions and get honest, straight answers to each and every one."

Connor smirked. "Done. When you order my breakfast in the morning, tell them I prefer my eggs over easy with a little bit of salt on the side."

They were dining at the most exclusive restaurant in the city. It was quiet, dimly lit, and the chances of running into Sphere agents were low. Connor liked those odds.

The moment Connor laid eyes on Marcus, Kate's Tumaran government contact, he knew Kate would be serving him breakfast in bed. He wouldn't go so far as to demand she wear anything in particular, although requesting she wear just his T-shirt or something to show off her shapely legs did cross his mind. He'd just enjoy his eggs, gloat and then share them with her, of course.

Marcus approached her. A slow smile built across his face as his gaze took her in from head to toe. "Kate?"

Connor wanted to punch that look off his face. Marcus moved closer to her, extending his arms to hug her.

"Marcus?" Kate asked, joy erupting across her face.

She was good. Connor didn't know if she was genuinely happy to meet him or pretending. He guessed the former. Although Marcus was their mark and they were using him to get information about Aiden, Kate had spoken highly of him. He had been the person who had clued Kate in to the possibility that Aiden was alive. Though his information had been inaccurate and it was the Tumaran government that was holding Aiden prisoner, that didn't mean Marcus had intentionally misled her. Connor wouldn't decide either way until he had a chance to talk to Marcus.

"Kate Swiss, it is wonderful to finally meet you. You are even more dazzling in person." Marcus released her and took Kate's hands in his, kissed both her cheeks and let his eyes and hands linger on Kate for several long moments before he turned to Connor, smiling thinly and looking annoyed that Connor was there.

Marcus's fake smile reaffirmed that he'd been right. Marcus had jumped at the chance to see "Kate Swiss" and take her out to dinner.

"Thank you for your warm welcome," Kate said. She introduced Connor to Marcus, and he shook the man's hand. Marcus's palms were damp and his blinking rapid. Nerves over meeting Kate or was he hiding something?

Marcus moved to Kate's other side. "I've made reservations for the three of us. Luckily, we refer a number of international visitors here and I've gotten friendly with the maître d'. Otherwise, we would have been eating at 10:00 p.m. or at the pizzeria down the street."

Kate laughed. "I've had my fill of pizza in America. I want to try the local cuisine."

Connor loosened his jaw, realizing he'd been clenching it watching Marcus and Kate. He didn't like Marcus, although he owed him a debt for alerting them that Aiden was alive. Was it that the man was practically drooling over Kate or were his instincts picking up on a deception?

The high ceilings of the room allowed the string quartet to play without overwhelming the space with noise. Polite conversation floated among the diners at the small linen-covered tables. Nearly everyone was wearing suits and dresses. Connor wasn't familiar with the locals, but he guessed the tables were filled with the wealthy upper class who could afford to spend a few hundred dollars on a dinner. The income gap in Tumara was huge. The rich were very rich and the poor were very poor and the middle class didn't exist.

Connor didn't care for the way Marcus slid his hand to Kate's lower back, walking her to their table. Connor followed behind. If Marcus's hand slid lower to Kate's rear end, Connor would grab it and break it off, information or no information. The streak of possessiveness was intense and unexpected.

Kate had gotten through to him, and when he stopped putting effort into rebuffing her, he found he wanted her in his bed. He didn't want to share her.

They were shown to a table situated close to the dance floor, and Marcus took the seat closest to Kate. At Connor's pointed look, Kate subtly shook her head as if to say, "No, you didn't win the bet." She'd wait for Marcus to do something more overt before admitting he had been right.

Connor shrugged and sat. At the rate they were going, he'd win their bet by the time their drinks arrived.

Marcus leaned close to Kate, angling Connor out of the conversation. "Kate, tell me what brought you to Tumara so unexpectedly. I didn't hear from anyone at the consulate that you were planning a trip here."

Kate took her dinner napkin and folded it on her lap. "Just between you and me, I've had some problems at work. My boss has gotten more and more demanding. I'm working nights and weekends, and he still isn't happy. I'm stressed-out to the max."

Marcus nodded in understanding.

Connor watched Kate work this guy, a mix of pulling on his sympathies and playing the damsel in distress.

Marcus took a sip of his water. "I'm surprised to hear you say that. You seem so put together and confident on the phone."

"That's part of the job. But, Marcus..." Kate paused and set her hand on Marcus's. Marcus looked at their hands, and the smug smile on his face irritated Connor to no end. Connor had to suppress his jealousy—yes, pure, unadulterated jealousy. He wanted to reach across the table and wipe the dopey look off Marcus's face with his fist. "I know with everything going on in the country, it's getting harder and harder to keep the peace and do our jobs. I believe in this country. I believe *el presidente* is doing his best to address the people's concerns and the problems facing the lower class.

"I've worked for the State Department for years. I love the work I do. I want to be part of the solution," Kate said.

Marcus was clinging to her every word. If the guy weren't attractive and muscular, it wouldn't have bothered Connor as much. It wasn't a crush from some pathetic, sniveling loser grasping at the attention of an attractive female. Marcus, in his tie-less suit and with his stiff, gelled hair, could pick a number of women in the room to take home. But he wanted Kate.

Connor didn't blame Marcus. But he was territorial when he desired someone or something. It wasn't a trait he enjoyed about himself, but he didn't like watching another man flirting with the woman he wanted.

"Are you asking me for a job?" Marcus asked.

"Not asking you," Kate said. "But exploring the possibility."

"You want to move to Tumara?" Marcus asked.

The interest in the guy's eyes bordered on yearning. This guy needed to calm down. He was sitting at the table ogling another man's girlfriend, and that other man was in the same room, at the same table, staring at them. This guy was either led around by his hormones or was ballsy.

"I'd like to, yes," Kate said. "Connor and I are here to look around. He's not as hot on the idea as I am. I'm hoping to convince him."

Good idea to imply some underlying tension and give this weasel the impression he might stand a chance with Kate.

Marcus turned slowly to Connor. "You don't like our country?"

Connor shrugged noncommittally. "I haven't decided. It's my first time here. Kate says good things about the politics and the people. She lives and breathes it. Am I wrong to think moving here will mean I'll see even less of her?"

Marcus returned his attention to Kate. "We work long hours. Especially lately. You've seen the news. The world loves to cheer for the underdog, and the

AR is doing its share of barking. No one realizes how much trouble and violence they bring to the people."

The conversation was naturally leading around to the AR and the government's problems.

The waiter arrived with drinks and took their order. Marcus ordered appetizers for the three to share, promising they would delight.

"It is a privilege to work for the Tumaran government. I will see if I can find anything available that might suit your skill set," Marcus said.

Connor guessed any job that Marcus found for Kate would be working in close proximity to him.

"That's so nice of you. Kate is a woman of many talents. I'm sure you can find something for her," Connor said.

"I hate to ask a favor on top of a favor, but if it's possible, I'd like to work on projects that will keep my hands near the fire. I can't see myself being happy filing paperwork," Kate said. "I do enough of that now and I'd like a change."

Marcus turned his chair to face Kate. "I wouldn't recommend something boring. Not for the woman who single-handedly resolved several problems with the AR."

Kate lowered her head and blushed. "I had the right intel at the right time to make sure the government was ahead of their plans."

Sphere was firmly on the side of *el presidente* and the government. It didn't surprise him. Then again, Sphere wasn't on anybody's side but their own. They would switch allegiances if it was beneficial to them.

"You never told me how you knew what you did about the AR," Marcus said.

Kate laughed and winked at him. "I can't reveal my sources. At least, not yet."

Connor was starting to feel as if he was on someone else's date. A bad date. A sleazy date. The longer Connor was with Marcus and watching him talk to Kate, the more irritated he became.

Marcus took a sip of his wine. "Kate, are you sure you want to stay mixed up in the problems *el presidente* has with the AR? They're dangerous. Pockets of rebellion are springing up every week. We stamp out one group and two more pop up."

Kate patted her hair. "The government has it under control." She sounded naive, as if she had every confidence in *el presidente* and the Tumaran government. Connor guessed it was her intention.

"Do they?" Connor asked, hearing the challenge in his voice. Kate had been handling the conversation well, but Marcus's characterization of the AR grated on him. His brother had chosen to fight on the side of the AR and that meant something to Connor. Ariana was a motivating factor, no doubt, but what else had stirred his brother to change sides?

"We do," Marcus said, a chill in his voice. "We're routinely looking for members of the group and we have investigators question them. We find out what we can about their plans, their movements and their locations. Those who are willing to work with us get much more leniency. Those who insist on maintaining silence are punished to the maximum extent allowed by law."

Connor's ears tingled. Marcus needed just a little push and he would give up more information, information they needed to locate Aiden. "No loyalty among thieves? I imagine most are quick to spill what they know to get out of trouble."

"You'd think. Most like to play the big, strong hero. We break them eventually."

The idea of his brother "breaking" gnawed at Connor's control. That word could mean anything: prison, torture or death. Heat flushed through his body and it took him a moment to gather his control. He stood. "Please excuse me. I need to use the men's room." If he didn't get away from the table and from Marcus, he didn't trust his next words.

"He seems uptight," Marcus said, signaling to the waiter for a refill on his drink.

Kate rolled her glass between her hands. "Connor? I guess you could say that. He's not comfortable being here. He wants me to stay in America and find a new job there."

"If you want to be one place and he wants to be in another, what can you do to change it?" Marcus asked.

Pretend relationship aside, Kate found it difficult to get on the same page as Connor. He was closed off, distrusting and harsh. Breaking into his thoughts, earning his trust and seeing his softer side had been a wonderful experience. Marcus didn't know how much his comment resonated on an emotional level with her. "I don't know that it will work. If I find the right opportunity and Connor doesn't want to live here, I can't change his mind. Connor does what he wants to do," Kate said.

Marcus had come close to detailing the work she'd done in support of *el presidente,* which might have divulged the role she'd played in Aiden's disappearance. She hadn't told Aiden about the government raid on the

AR before it had happened even though she knew he was undercover with the AR. Her boss had asked her to hold the information. She should have questioned why instead of blindly accepting that Sphere was acting in the best interest of their agents. If Sphere had learned that Aiden had changed his loyalty to the AR, they would have wanted him dead, and a government raid could have met that purpose. Kate didn't want Connor to learn from someone else that she could have warned Aiden and saved his life. She'd have to tell him the truth. Kate refocused on Marcus, not wanting to miss anything important.

"Can I speak frankly for a moment?" At Kate's nod, he continued. "You're a strong woman and you've learned the art of negotiation. We know the only way to get things done is to play nice in the sandbox. How can you make a relationship work with someone who is strong-willed and who doesn't understand life is a series of compromises?"

Kate had a feeling she was about to lose the bet with Connor. She leaned away, hoping to dissuade Marcus from using Connor's absence to make a pass at her.

Marcus covered her hand with his. "I don't mean to upset you. But if you decide your relationship with Connor is unworkable, my heart is open to you. Both as a friend and a colleague. I've felt a connection with you since we first spoke, and now that we're together, I feel it more strongly."

Marcus was willing to blow apart their friendship for the possibility of sleeping with her. Typical. She couldn't cut him off at the knees. Not when she needed him on her side and to remain an ally. Kate fished for more information. "We've always had a good rapport.

I've trusted you with information my superiors thought I should keep to myself."

"I've done the same with you."

Kate nodded, seeing her opening to ask about Aiden. "You sent me a picture of an American a short time ago. Have you located him?"

Marcus shifted. "Initially, I believed he was being held by the AR. But I've heard some disturbing rumors lately that he was found to be a traitor and arrested. I don't know what information is true or who I can trust."

Kate waited for him to continue.

He took a sip of his drink. "We have some Americans in La Sabaneta."

La Sabaneta was the worst prison in the country. Violent offenders were housed there, and controlling the prison population sometimes meant taking extreme measures. Was Aiden one of the Americans held inside the prison? "If the American consulate finds out, it will create an international incident."

Marcus rubbed his forehead. "I am aware. It's why I sent you that picture the first time. *El presidente* doesn't want any further interference from the international community, and Americans in danger in this region will bring that interference. But what can we do now? If the Americans are released, they'll sell their story to the press. If we don't release them, someone could still find out about them. We're in a difficult position."

Kate nodded in sympathy. Inside, she was boiling. Misinformation was part of the game, but she and Connor had wasted time tracking Aiden to the AR only to learn he had been a prisoner of the Tumaran government. Was he still alive?

"I wish I could offer something to help," Kate said.

"My position is precarious. My boss doesn't listen to me." By getting the information and then distancing herself from it, she hoped to avoid suspicion. She turned the conversation back to something personal. "If I were to find a job here, I'd stay. Connor is returning to the U.S. at the end of the week. I don't know what that will mean for our relationship."

Marcus seemed happy about her response, and she hoped it had distracted him from reading more into her questions about the Americans in La Sabaneta and Aiden.

The waiter arrived with their appetizers and Connor returned a few minutes later. He focused his attention on Kate and heat spread up her back. As he watched her, she felt something akin to desire and excitement. Connor was rougher around the edges than Marcus. He wasn't as outwardly warm. He lacked the polish of careful breeding. For her, there was still no competition. Connor was it. Connor was the man she could see herself with. Connor made life an adventure. He was strong and confident and made her feel safe and secure, and not just in a physical sense.

She was dying to tell Connor what Marcus had told her about Aiden and La Sabaneta. It was unverified and it could be another false lead, but it was the most promising information she'd gathered.

"Kate, we have to dance," Connor said.

Connor knew how to dance? It would have been as shocking if he had said he enjoyed painting pottery on the weekends. She wiped the surprise off her face. As his girlfriend, she would know he could. Unless they got on the dance floor and made a spectacle of themselves.

"I'd love to," Kate said.

Connor circled the table, and the moment his hand touched her waist, she knew he had the moves. Those moves. A man who danced as if it were part of a seduction. His feet glided across the floor and his arms led her, making her feel as if she could dance, as well. Of course, she'd had lessons on the waltz, the fox-trot and other ballroom dances, but Connor took those elementary lessons to another level. His hands guided her; his hips swayed to the music in a sultry, yet completely appropriate way.

"What did he tell you while I was gone?" Connor asked, bringing his mouth close to her ear in an intimate gesture.

His intention wasn't to seduce her. His intention was to trade information. He could have waited until the end of the night to speak with her, but she knew he was anxious about finding his brother.

"They have Americans inside a prison called La Sabaneta. Aiden may be one of them."

Connor tensed in her arms. "Can you get us inside?"

"Not yet. Not with my current clearance and not without raising a thousand red flags," she said. To complicate matters, knowing where Aiden was and getting in touch with him were simple compared to freeing him.

"Then I'm going to work a jailbreak," Connor said.

"What?" The question popped from her mouth too loudly. She lowered her voice. "What do you mean *a jailbreak?*"

"I mean a jailbreak. I'm trained for it. I need to run surveillance and gather the intel. I'll get Aiden out."

"Impossible." How were he and Aiden going to

avoid guards and guns, and get around locked metal doors?

She recognized the determination in his eyes. "Possible. Aiden's trained on escape-and-evasion techniques. If he's inside, he's already planning how to get out. I need to figure out what's keeping him in and work from the outside to free him," Connor said.

Sphere agents had training to overcome the most difficult circumstances. Among the skills they had were lock picking, lying without detection and maneuvering to get what they wanted. If the prison had a security flaw, Aiden would exploit it. With Connor working with him, the two could free him.

"That's a tall task," Kate said.

"No task is too tall to find my brother." Connor's hands slipped to her back and his fingers dangled low over her rear end.

"Your hands," Kate said. She didn't mind the touch, but they were in a public, formal place. Despite the seriousness of the conversation, being close to Connor stirred her desires. He was holding her close, her body was molded to his, and she could feel every movement as they circled the dance floor.

"I want Marcus to know we're together. Nothing inspires a man to impress a woman as much as competition with another man," Connor said.

"Are you saying your hand on my rear is solely for Marcus's benefit?"

"Not solely," Connor said. "But I am taking delight in watching him over your shoulder scowling at us."

"I implied to him we were having relationship problems," she said.

"Giving the guy false hope?" Connor asked.

"I need to find out everything he knows about Aiden," Kate said. Her chest skimmed his and electricity zipped through her. She wanted to return to their hotel room, where she could slip off her dress and back into Connor's arms.

Chapter 9

When they returned to their table, Marcus stood and held out Kate's chair for her. Connor said nothing, but Kate noticed his eye twitch. He didn't like Marcus, which was okay, because she didn't like Marcus much either. She didn't know where his loyalty lay and that made him undependable and under suspicion.

"I didn't realize you were such a skilled dancer," Marcus said.

Kate heard the possessiveness in his voice. "Skilled dancer? I know enough to fake it. It's easy to appear competent when I have a talented dance partner."

"Could you both excuse me?" Connor asked.

Marcus nodded and Kate smiled at him. He was leaving her alone with Marcus. With the current mood, Connor would win the bet. Connor was away from the table for less than three minutes when Marcus tucked his chair close to the table. "Why don't you extend your trip? Plan to stay a few extra days with me?"

Kate took a sip of her water. "That's a tempting offer." She would be staying longer than she had initially told Marcus. Planning a jailbreak would take time, and Connor wouldn't leave the country without his brother. Similarly, Kate wouldn't leave Tumara without Connor.

"Think about it. We could be very good together." He set his hand over hers and squeezed.

Kate would be bringing Connor breakfast in the morning. Kate pulled her hand away and reached for her wine.

A distinguished-looking man approached their table and Marcus stood. Kate did the same, though she didn't recognize him. Marcus and the man shook hands.

"General Alva, please allow me to introduce you to Kate Swiss. She works at the American consulate."

Kate recognized the name. He held a prime position in the Tumaran Army and an aggressive stance on Tumara's handling of the AR. He believed the only way to stop a revolution was to wipe out every member of the AR. He served on the board of advisers to *el presidente.*

General Alva didn't smile, though he extended his hand to her. "Kate Swiss. The name sounds familiar. I've seen your signature on some paperwork pertaining to our arrangement with Americans in Tumara who are sympathetic to the traitor's cause."

The traitor's cause—a hostile way of referring to the Armed Revolutionaries. She'd have to tread carefully. She didn't want to show sympathy toward the AR or Bruno Feliz in front of Marcus or General Alva. However, working at the embassy, she wouldn't take either side in a political standoff. "Our goal at the embassy is to promote peace and see as little bloodshed as possible."

General Alva sat in Connor's seat. He seemed ready to engage Kate in a debate and she didn't want to argue. The less time she spent with this man, the better. If he mentioned her to any of his colleagues or looked into her position at the consulate, her cover was blown. "We have to root out the source of the problem and take swift and severe action. We can't allow ignorant, quick-tempered nonconformists to dictate how to run this country. They make unreasonable demands. Bruno Feliz is a child having a temper tantrum. The only way to deal with him is to show him who's in charge."

Bruno Feliz was hardly a child. He was at least fifty years old and had captured the hearts and spirits of many in Tumara. The Armed Revolutionaries adored him and were willing to give up their lives for him and the cause. "I understand your perspective," she said. It was as neutral a comment as she could muster. She didn't want to agree with him. Even knowing it was lip service felt traitorous to Aiden.

"They are unreasonable, ridiculous and foolhardy," General Alva said.

Connor arrived at the table and Kate was struck again by how dashing he was in his suit. Seeing him dressed up was a shock to her libido. He owned the polished look. "Connor, hello." She reached up to kiss his cheek, grateful he had returned, partly worried the general's comments would inflame him into saying something that would give away their real identities.

General Alva stood and introduced himself to Connor. "You look familiar. Have we met before?" he asked.

Panic rose in Kate. If General Alva knew Aiden, he could see the likeness to Connor, just as the Armed Revolutionaries in the jungle had.

"I don't believe so," Connor said smoothly. "This is my first time in Tumara. Unless we've met elsewhere. I served in the United States Army ten years ago. Any chance you spent time in America?"

A mental path to lead him away from thinking about Tumara. "Not on military business," Alva said. He took another sip of his drink and looked around the table. "I'll leave you to your meal. Marcus, we'll have drinks later this week. I have a few open issues I'd like to discuss with you."

"Looking forward to it, sir," Marcus said.

As they took their seats at the table, Kate braced herself for a tension-filled dinner.

"Am I getting breakfast in bed or won't you concede that Marcus can't wait to get rid of me and get you alone?" Connor asked, pulling off his tie and tossing it on the back of the wooden chair across from the bed. He removed his knife and set it on the bedside table. She hadn't realized he was carrying it, though she supposed she had never seen him without a weapon close at hand.

Kate laughed. "I'll concede the point. When you left us alone, Marcus asked me to stay in Tumara for a few extra days to spend time with him."

Connor came behind her and wrapped his arms around her waist. "Just you? How interesting." He lowered his mouth to her neck and nibbled. Hot pleasure danced across her skin.

Kate let her head fall to the side to give him better ac-

cess to the sensitive skin at her nape. "Not interesting—
not at all. Expected and you know it. I assumed you'd
gloat about being right."

Connor's hands slid down her dress. "I am not gloat-
ing. I like to bet on a sure thing. Wagering on a beautiful blonde in a sexy dress picking up a man? Easiest
bet I've won in years."

Kate turned in his arms and began pulling the bobby
pins from her hair and tossing them to the ground.
"You're saying all the right things."

He watched as every strand of hair came free. He
brushed his hand along her cheek and into her hair.
Flicking her long tresses over her shoulders, he watched
as they fell. His complete attention was focused on her
and she loved it.

Connor kissed her and Kate melted against him. Her
body pressed to his, chest to chest, her heartbeat hammering with anticipation. This was the moment she had
been waiting for all night. Connor's hand tugged at the
zipper along the back of the dress and slid it down. His
hand followed the zipper, touching her bare skin. He
peeled away the top of her dress, letting it fall to her
waist. She was bared to him, and she arched forward,
encouraging him.

Dropping to his knees, Connor took her breasts in
his palms, rubbing his thumbs lightly over her sensitive peaks. White-hot excitement slipped around her
body, centered on where Connor was touching her and
spiraling out over her.

Fiercely aroused, Kate slid her hands into his silky
hair. He pulled her dress to the floor. He swore under
his breath when he realized she wasn't wearing panties.

"Surprise," she whispered and stepped out of the dress.

"If I had known about this before we left the hotel room, we never would have made it to the restaurant."

The memory of the heated kiss they'd shared sprang to mind and Kate was eager to pick up where they'd left off.

Connor kissed her stomach and her belly, going lower and then switching directions away from where she most wanted his touch, kissing the fronts of her thighs.

She reached down to take off her shoes and he shook his head. "Please leave them on. Just your heels."

This was never where she'd expected to be. In this room with a man who was dangerous, exciting and sure to break her heart. She dropped to her knees and her lips found his in a slow exploration. She could have spent the entire night just kissing him.

Kate wanted to feel his naked skin pressed against hers. She took the lapels of his suit jacket and shoved it over his shoulders. It hit the floor and crumpled into a pile. Off came his shirt, falling on top of the suit jacket. She reached for his belt buckle and paused, the significance of what they were doing not lost on her. It struck her hard that this was Connor. Strong, independent, closed-off Connor and he was letting her touch him. She knew the difference between sex and intimacy. This felt wonderfully private and had the makings of a torrid, intense affair.

He looked at her as if he were drinking her in. She unfastened his pants, and he stood, pulling her with him and scooping her into his arms. He carried her to the plush chair in the corner of the room. Kate was a tall woman, but Connor moved with her in his arms as if she were weightless.

Holding her with one arm, he shucked off his pants and sat with her on his lap, pulling her thighs open over his. He ran his hands along the outsides of her legs as she knelt over him. His mouth captured hers in a fiery kiss. Her knees were braced on the cushion under him and against the arms of the chair. It was an unconventional place for two people to make love the first time, and it made her love it that much more.

From the beginning, her relationship with Connor had been different. He hadn't hit on her or assumed she was a dumb blonde with an empty head. He had protected her and treated her with respect. She loved how she felt when she was with him. Beautiful and smart, strong and powerful.

She loved everything he was doing and she loved him. The realization came so naturally, she didn't break stride. She looked at him, wanting to remember the moment she'd lost her heart to Connor. The roughened angles of his face didn't detract from how handsome he was, his shoulders roped with muscle, his broad chest hard and his ripped abdominals sexy and alluring.

She had fallen in love with Connor West. Her instant crush on him had deepened and grown into something more, something built on a pressurized situation she knew made the future rocky.

On the heels of her realization, she knew it wasn't the time to tell him how she felt. If she spoke the words, he wouldn't return them. Brushing that aside, knowing it was part of loving a man like Connor, she focused on this moment and how she felt. Warm, cherished and undeniably desirable.

He conjured a condom as if from nowhere and slid it on. Lifting her hips over his body, she impaled herself on him, grasping his shoulders to steady herself. The burn of that first thrust scorched her. His hands clutched her hips and she set the pace. In his arms, she felt light, breathless and carefree.

She rose and dropped, rocking her hips against his and riding him. She took him deep and pivoted her hips, watching his face and his reaction. Pleasure. Happiness. His excitement spurred her to move harder and faster. She gauged what he liked best as their gazes locked and everything that needed to be said was in their eyes. Even if he never spoke words of love, she had this moment, this expression of her love and how he was making her feel.

Being with him was as pleasurable as it was a release of the pent-up stress she'd been living with for months. Connor lifted her hips and his hand went where their bodies met. He rubbed a small circle around the tight bundle of nerves at her core. He found the right spot, pressure and rhythm almost immediately.

She came quick and hard, and he held her tight. When her climax eased, with one smooth motion, he rolled her under him, laying her flat on the chair, her hips and legs over the edge of the seat cushion and her heels flat on the ground.

"More?" he asked.

"Yes, more," she said. He moved slower as he held his body over hers, and her sensitized nerves were grateful for the care he was showing.

He increased the pace of his movements, and she felt her body responding again, tension building until another tremor ripped through her—this time, taking him with her.

They lay sprawled in the chair, a tangle of arms and legs. With a quick kiss, Connor got up and disposed of the condom. He returned and coaxed her to the bed. She took his hand and they climbed onto the fresh, crisp sheets. She kicked off her shoes and Connor made a face.

"Can you wear them all the time?" he asked.

"All the time?" she asked.

"They look great on you," he said.

"I'll see what I can do. If we go back to the jungle, I will not be hiking in heels," she said.

Connor laughed. "Fair enough."

Facing her with their legs intertwined, Connor kissed her forehead.

"This is the second time I have been extraordinarily happy you came here with me," Connor said.

"An unexpected bonus?" Her heart was still racing and her breathing was returning to normal.

Connor appeared more relaxed than she'd ever seen him. Gone was the tense readiness, and his eyes weren't wandering the room looking for a threat. "I thought you were in love with my brother. Based on that, I wouldn't have thought sex was an option."

"I care about Aiden a great deal, but I've always wanted you," Kate said.

Connor gave her a curious look. "Always?"

"From the first time I saw you, I felt a connection. Like you were meant to be in my life."

"Even though we had never spoken?" he asked.

That finger-snap connection was unlike anything she'd experienced. "Even then." Though his brother's memorial service had likely been one of the darkest times in his life, she had been drawn to Connor. Maybe it was the stories Aiden had told her. Maybe it was the legends that were whispered around the watercooler at Sphere headquarters about Connor West. Maybe it was just that Connor was everything she had been looking for in a man and had never found in one person. "Can I tell you something and you promise you won't say anything back?" she asked.

Connor ran his hand down her arm. "If it's a criticism of what we just did, I'll give you advanced warning. I won't stay quiet. I'm going to plead for another chance to impress you because I thought it was awesome."

She laughed. "Nothing wrong with what we did in that chair. This is a different but somewhat related matter." Her nerves shimmered. If she told him the full extent of what she was feeling, would he withdraw? Shut her out? She didn't want him to feel obligated to say anything to her in response. Her love for him was without conditions.

His face turned serious. "I'll listen. I won't say anything."

Kate took a deep breath, unsure until this moment what she would say, if anything, about her feelings for Connor. An excited utterance during the throes of passion didn't mean much. She wanted to give her feelings the reverence they deserved. "I love you, Connor." A simple statement and a complex message at once. She had no expectations of a reaction and she was glad she didn't.

His face didn't move. His eyes were still and his mouth was drawn into a straight line. Was he hiding his reaction because she had told him he couldn't respond? Or did he truly have no reaction? With a man like Connor, trust came slowly. She regretted prefacing her statement with a request for silence.

Connor shifted on the bed. "You've put me in a tough place. You don't want me to respond, but I've never had a woman say those words and not have them create an overarching issue that needs to be addressed."

An *issue?* That was a softer word for *problem.* He thought her loving him was a problem. She wasn't sure what she'd wanted his reaction to be. Happiness? Contentment? Or maybe deep, deep down, she had wanted the words to burst from his lips in return. She fumbled for an explanation as insecurity consumed her. "I know you aren't ready to say those words. I know it takes time. But I wanted to say them because they are true for me and I wanted you to know how I felt."

Connor blinked at her. "You don't want my thoughts on the matter?"

Based on him calling her words "an issue that needed to be addressed," she didn't think him elaborating would make her feel any better. "Can my words just be what they are? No discussion is needed."

He hesitated a moment and then kissed her again. "Okay, no discussion tonight."

At some point, they would talk about it. But for now, she welcomed quiet and fell asleep in his arms.

"Go over it again. We missed something," Connor said, his hands fisting and unrolling in frustration.

"We haven't missed anything," Kate said. They'd reviewed the spreadsheets, diagrams and charts they'd created to organize and analyze the data they had gathered about La Sabaneta. The prison was locked down. No one had ever escaped except in a body bag. Thirteen men had tried. One had made it to the final checkpoint hiding inside a food-delivery truck, but he had been discovered and shot on sight.

Supply trucks came and went on a seemingly random schedule. The back, undercarriage and inside of every truck was checked by two separate guard stations both entering and leaving the jail. As old and decrepit as the prison was, their security system and use of technology were cutting-edge.

"What about bribery?" Connor asked. "Let's go over the employee list again. Someone must be in desperate straits and need money. A gambling problem. Loan debt. High alimony payments."

Kate had performed analyses of information for Sphere for years. She understood the underhanded methods of buying someone off or manipulating someone's fears and finding a weak link that would help achieve the end goal. Even with a hundred policies and rules in place, by finding a weak link, they could exploit it and they could free Aiden. As yet, Kate didn't see it. "Connor, we've gone over this. We would have to bribe an entire block of guards, every single person who patrols Aiden's cellblock or interacts with him." As extreme as that would be, it had other challenges. They hadn't confirmed the cellblock where Aiden was being held or if the prisoners were rotated. They hadn't even confirmed if Aiden was in La Sabaneta.

Connor paced the room. "How can I get myself thrown into prison at La Sabaneta?"

Shock knocked Kate's thoughts on their side. "You cannot be serious. Never mind the thousand problems with getting arrested, once you are inside, how will you talk to Aiden? How can you be sure you'd be jailed there? Would you leave me out here to figure out how to get both of you out?"

Connor threw his hands in the air. "What can I do? I can't leave him there, and we have nothing. We've gone over this a dozen times."

Frustration was getting the best of him. "Then we'll go over it a dozen and one times. I know you are used to being in the field and taking action. What do you think went on at headquarters during every mission while you were in the field? Analysts were sorting and filtering information until we found how to do what was needed. It doesn't happen easily and it sometimes takes more information or a certain amount of creativity to find a way. We don't need to do anything rash and drastic. Not yet." Kate moved her computer from her lap and crossed the room to Connor. She put her arms around his waist and rested her head on his chest. He needed to calm down so they could think clearly. "We are not leaving Aiden there. But we also are not putting you into a prison when we have no method in place to free you. Even if you could commit a crime and be sent to La Sabaneta and placed near Aiden, what can you do once you are inside? If there was an easy way out from the inside, Aiden would have already found it."

Connor held her against him. "Aiden and I can put our heads together. My brother and I are good at what we do, but when we're together, we're even better. We've never worked a mission together, but growing up, whenever I went to Aiden with a problem or he came to me, we'd work it out."

Kate stroked Connor's arm, hoping she was offering comfort. She and her sister, Elise, had never liked each other. Generally, when they were together, they brought out the worst in each other. "You are lucky you had each other. My sister and I never got along."

"Would you risk your life to find her if she were jailed in some remote hellhole?" Connor asked.

Kate didn't have to think too much about it. Of course she would. She wasn't sure if Elise would do the same for her, but differences aside, she loved her sister. "Yes. I would get her out."

Kate broke away from Connor. Being wrapped in his arms made her ache for him. While sex was relaxing, it wouldn't help, and they were on a deadline.

She thought about the methods they had used at Sphere to gather intel or provide resources. Calling in favors, networking and bribery were typical techniques used. "What about pulling strings?" Kate asked.

"Whose strings do I need to pull?"

"Is there anyone who owes you a favor? Political allies who you worked for in the U.S. who might be able to get us inside the prison or in touch with someone in power in the prison?" Kate asked.

"I can make some calls. I've worked with Senator Allen a few times in dicey situations. I don't think he would publicly acknowledge that he knows me, and I don't have any hold over him to compel him to help me."

"Senator Allen?" Kate asked, surprised Connor was in touch with the well-respected and highly feared member of Congress. He was the senior member of the secret committee that oversaw projects at Sphere. Senator Allen moved mountains and found miracle solutions when others had long given up. "Why did you meet with him?"

"Classified exchanges of information, briefings on missions and once for a personal favor," Connor said.

"A personal favor?" Kate asked.

"He needed my expertise on a family matter. I can't discuss the details."

"Perhaps, then, he does owe you a favor," Kate said. She considered his position. "Would he help us even though he's working with Sphere?" Kate asked. So many people who worked with Sphere were corrupt. With Sphere looking for them, could they take a chance and bring someone else into their mission? "Perhaps he would go out on a limb and help you."

"It's worth a call," Connor said. "It's worth doing anything I can to help Aiden."

Connor called the number he'd been given for Senator Allen's private line. The number was disconnected. He tried the senator's office number next, and as he'd expected, he wasn't put through to the senator. A perky, but firm-sounding woman promised she would deliver his message to the senator. Connor had his doubts about that. He'd had to leave a vague message in case the senator was working closely with Sphere and wanted him and Kate found and brought back to the United States for prosecution.

If his message was passed along at all, it would be given to the senator along with the hundreds of other calls he received during the week, half of them from crazies with unreasonable demands. Connor supposed his request wasn't far outside the realm of crazy.

The senator wouldn't risk communicating directly

with Connor. Connor was a former secret agent and his hands were dirty. Now that the senator's daughter had been returned to him safely, he had no use for Connor. Though the senator played a role at Sphere, he kept that part of his work hidden from the public.

Connor picked up the sketch Kate had drawn of La Sabaneta. Wild ideas sprang to mind, blooming from desperation and fear for his brother. Catapulting himself inside the perimeter. Climbing the fifty-foot wall and braving the razor wire and snipers posted around the gate. Dropping in via a parachute and trying not to be shot as he drifted to the ground wearing a colorful chute.

Even if one of his off-the-wall ideas got him inside, finding Aiden and then navigating a way out was uncertain. Connor didn't know his brother's physical or mental state. He could be near starvation or have suffered from beatings.

Connor had known secret agents who had been left lame or limbless after being imprisoned in a foreign country. He'd known some that had gone absolutely bat-crap crazy and had been unable to function in society after their ordeal.

Connor promised himself that if Aiden needed lifelong support, he would provide it. If his brother needed a caretaker, he would be it. He wouldn't let his brother down and he would see that the people who harmed him paid dearly.

Kate was on the phone with some contacts she had from the State Department. She was still in her role of Kate Swiss and she was good. Diplomatic and kind, she was sweet-talking information out of people with practiced ease. She also pulled some scams, pretending to be tech support, obtaining log-ins and passwords to get inside systems she didn't have authorized access to. Cup of coffee in one hand and keyboard in the other, she was amazing.

And she loved him.

It was hard to believe and even harder to hear. Connor wasn't an easy man to love. He didn't need a shrink to tell him he was closed off from the world—both emotionally and physically. Connor didn't like people being close to him or in his space. He didn't like turning his back to anyone, sure a knife would be stuck in it the moment he did. He had a firm grip on the reasons for that. His mother had left when he was a boy and he might have been better off if his father had, too. It was textbook abandonment issues. He had no close family except Aiden. Aiden was the one man he trusted.

Ariana had mentioned that Aiden had spoken to his parents. Connor spoke to his father when he had no other choice, but what about their mother? Was it possible that Aiden had reestablished a connection with her? Aiden was bent on seeing the best in people. He gave more chances than he should. He forgave and forgot. Hardships in life didn't hold him back or keep him down. That trait in Aiden was something Connor had fought to protect and deeply envied.

In the past, Aiden had tried speaking to him about their parents. Over the years, Aiden had brought them up in conversation, but Connor had shut down those discussions quickly. He didn't want to talk about the painful past. He wanted to get on with his life, and going over those long-past events seemed pointless.

Yet, Connor hadn't moved on fully with his life. He seemed stuck in the same patterns of keeping people at bay, expecting them to leave him just as his mother had. Even when he attended college, changed jobs, changed hobbies and changed diets, those changes were superficial and didn't open him to others in the same way that came easily to Aiden. Deep down, Connor had never changed. He stayed in protective mode and waited for someone to screw him over. It was something he hated about himself and yet he was unsure how to change.

Except Kate had gotten in and she'd gotten in more than a little. He'd had girlfriends before, but he'd never shared anything with anyone about his life. He had shared much with Kate in the short period of time that he'd known her. She'd affected him. She'd gotten past his reservations and proved to be loyal and steadfast.

If those qualities weren't enough for him to question his reluctance to trust her, she brought so much more to the table. Like her intelligence, her keen mind, her humor and her beauty.

His phone rang and Connor hesitated answering. A withheld number could be Sphere trying to trace him. He had his signal rigged to bounce around cell towers across the world, but Sphere could have technology to counter his attempts to hide his location. He braced himself. "Yes."

"Connor West?"

Connor recognized the voice he'd last heard years ago. Senator Joshua Allen. That was fast. Almost too fast. Perhaps the senator had been alerted by Sphere that he and Kate were people of interest and the senator was establishing contact for them. "Senator."

"You needed my help?"

"How did you get my message so quickly?" Connor asked.

"My incoming calls get logged to my phone-message system. I set an alert for your messages to be sent to my phone directly."

"Why?" Connor asked.

The senator chuckled. "You can take the man out of the paranoid agency, but you can't take the paranoia out of the man." He cleared his throat. "You saved my daughter's life. That's reason enough. I owe you and I pay my debts. I won't pretend I'm unaware what's going on between you and your former employer. I know you and an analyst have gotten involved in complicated matters and you've landed in some trouble."

Connor appreciated Senator Allen being up front with him. "Someone from my family is in trouble. I'm trying to help him."

"I wasn't asking for an explanation. You rescued Chelsea. You did things I couldn't have expected or asked for to have her returned safely. That's enough for me."

The no-explanation-needed return of favor was unexpected. "I need help. I need access to someone in a prison in Tumara."

A long beat passed. Connor expected a "Sorry, I can't help you."

"I have someone who might be able to get you what you need. He's a specialist in that region and he does work for me when I need it."

That simple? "Tell me where to find him."

"If he's worth anything and still has his edge, he'll find you," the senator said. "I'll send him. Eyes and ears open. You know Sphere wants you brought in on treason charges. You'll need to evade them. They don't give up."

"I'm aware I'm being hunted." *Hunted* was the best word he could think of to describe what Sphere was doing to him and Kate. It was one of the reasons Kate's State Department alias, Kate Swiss, had a limited life. It wouldn't take long for word to get back to Sphere that she had shown up in the city. Perhaps the only reason they hadn't yet was that Sphere didn't openly operate within the embassy and would want matters with Kate to remain under the radar.

"This makes us even," the senator said. "I will deny that I helped you if asked. If something worse happens as a result of this incident, I will not assist you."

The senator was taking a big risk talking to Connor directly and then sending assistance. "If your contact can help me, the debt is paid," Connor said.

"I have to go. Good luck to you," the senator said and disconnected the call.

Connor would be especially on guard over the next twenty-four hours. His call with the senator had been brief, and with his bouncing cell signal, he didn't think enough time had passed for anyone to trace the call or pinpoint his location. Even so, he would watch his and Kate's backs in case Sphere was faster or more savvy than he believed.

When he returned to the room where Kate was working, she was setting the phone on the bed. She smiled, her eyes bright and excited. "I have good news."

Finally. "Me, too."

Her eyes widened. "You go first."

"I have help coming," Connor said.

"Who?"

"A friend of a friend," Connor said.

Kate lifted her brow. "I will never understand how you all operate. And by 'you all' I mean secret agents. You don't name names or speak aloud about information. How do you know a secret agent from a stranger on the street?"

"If the agent is good, you don't know he's a spy. Divulging information is a slow and careful process," Connor said. "Tell me your news."

Kate clasped her hands together. "I have a way for us to get inside the prison. I haven't figured out how to get near Aiden, but if we can get inside and have a look around, it might help us look for security flaws we can exploit."

Getting access to the prison was a major score for them. "How are we getting in?"

Kate almost danced with happiness. "I found my own friend of a friend through one of my social networks who works as a volunteer chaplain in La Sabaneta once a month. He holds a small religious service for those prisoners who are permitted to attend. He asked on his social-media page for volunteers to take confession. Apparently, the warden is the son of a minister, and he's convinced *el presidente* that religion inside the prisons will help control the prisoners."

Connor stared at her. "Beyond that being almost unbelievable, why would your friend want *us* to do this?" They had no experience as ministers. Connor hadn't been to church since his mother had taken him when he was a boy.

Kate grinned at him. "You're an ordained priest and I'm an experienced missionary, at least according to my freshly edited online profile. You can listen to confession."

"I have to pretend to be a priest?" Connor asked. He had never been to a mass held by a priest. How would he fake it?

"You've been undercover as plenty of people—why not a priest? The service is nondenominational and we can make stuff up," Kate said.

"If one of the prisoners asks a religious question and I have no idea what I'm talking about and can't answer him, won't that be suspicious for a priest?" he asked.

"You can take a Bible in with you. Just look in the Bible, read a few verses and answer cryptically. From what I remember from private school, it's all very mysterious anyway," Kate said.

Her confidence in him bolstered his willingness. "What's involved with confession?" Connor asked.

"I don't know. We'll get a book on it," Kate said.

As if it were that simple.

"What role will you play to explain why we're together?" Connor asked, dragging her into his arms. "It is my understanding that priests don't have lovers."

Kate twisted her lips in thought. "We can keep our relationship secret for a few hours."

Wouldn't someone notice a casual touch or a longer-than-usual glance? Ignoring her could raise suspicions just as easily about the nature of their association. Connor had never been in the position to pretend he didn't care for someone when he was in the field. And pretending he didn't care for Kate was almost impossible.

"I don't like the idea of you being inside a prison, missionary cover or not. It's a dangerous place for a woman to be. Any woman." La Sabaneta did not allow conjugal visits for inmates, and not a single female employee came into contact with the prisoners day-to-day.

"You'll be with me," Kate said, running a finger along his jawline and then tapping his lips. "When you're with me, I know I'm safe."

She pressed her lips to his and Connor kissed her back. "Safe in some ways—in deep, deep trouble in others."

Kate laughed as Connor pulled her shirt over her head. Piece by piece, he stripped away her clothes. Then she turned serious as Connor walked her back toward the couch and covered her with his body. They momentarily forgot about priests and missionaries as they tumbled into each other's arms.

Chapter 10

Connor watched Kate adjust her loose-fitting pantsuit and high-necked blouse. As a missionary and a woman inside a jail that housed violent offenders, she didn't want to draw any more attention to herself if she could avoid it. She had secured her long hair at the nape of her neck. She was going for a no-nonsense look.

Even her attempts to dim her appearance hadn't dimmed his attraction to her. Knowing what was underneath those conservative clothes tormented him. He had to remind himself he couldn't—shouldn't—touch her. He'd made love to her four times over the past twenty-four hours. It wasn't enough. Being close to her turned him on. Her scent, her soft hair, her long, lean body called to him. They couldn't get through this fast enough. Once they had more intel on the inner workings of the jail, they could find a way to get Aiden out. Connor was banking on it.

They waited in the visitors' area of the prison. Their identification had been checked and hadn't raised questions, they had been patted down and they were waiting for clearance and an escort to enter the chapel. Clasping her Bible in her hands, Kate's expression was serious, but her eyes danced with excitement. Connor had sunk deep into his role, holding a gospel in his hands and having procured a black priest outfit complete with stiff white collar. In the past twelve hours, they had studied and crammed as much about Christianity as they could. They had found a children's Bible online and had read the stories. Connor had so many stories and quotes whirling in his brain, he had dreamed of sheep and plagues and poisoned fruit. He'd awoken several times through the night, each with Kate sleeping peacefully beside him. The sight of her had eased some of his worry.

If getting into La Sabaneta was complicated, getting out would be even harder. Locked doors, high gates, metal detectors, patrolling guards and sniper towers were expected. The complex electronics and thumbprint readers to open doors were more complicated than they had anticipated. The Tumarans took guarding their inmates seriously, and it was evident that a conventional escape, like causing a commotion and rushing out, was unlikely to work. How much could Kate's computer expertise help? Could she crack the codes on their security system?

The regular chaplain, Father Luca Elias, had given them additional information on the layout of the prison and the schedule as he waited with them. When their escorts arrived, they were taken directly to the chapel

accessible by a long hallway barred from the visitors'
area by a metal gate.

The chapel was furnished with long wooden benches,
a confessional, several folding chairs and an altar constructed one step up from the concrete. A table and
cross were the only other floor fixtures in the room.

"Father Luca, thank you for allowing us to serve
here," Connor said. "I worked in a prison in the United
States and I found it to be very rewarding."

Father Luca smiled. "Father George," he said, using
the name Connor and his fake identification had sup-
plied, "we're glad to receive help from wherever it is
sent. The warden's asked the inmates to learn more
about the Lord. It's hard to convince ministers to serve
here. This prison operates differently than those in the
United States. The day-to-day realities are harsher.
We have more murders per hundred inmates than any
prison in the United States. The men here have little
hope of being released and their behavior reflects a
devil-may-care attitude."

He paused and clasped his hands in front of him.
"But, that said, I see hope here. The men who attend
service are trying to find the Lord. They want forgive-
ness for their sins, both from the Almighty Father and
from within themselves for what they have done. Expect hard facades but warm hearts. Only inmates who
have not violated the prison's rules are permitted to
come to service. One infraction and they are confined
to their cells for six months."

Connor's thoughts turned to his brother. Had Aiden
committed any infractions or was he playing along,
giving the warden and the guards perfect, acquiescent
behavior? From what he and Kate had read, good be-

havior was rewarded by giving the inmates one hour in an outdoor, wire-fenced area once a week. It killed Connor to think about Aiden getting so little sun and exercise. How was he surviving the isolation and captivity?

Connor wouldn't trust a single man who walked into this room. Sociopaths and psychopaths were always working an angle. If they thought they could use the weekly religious service to get something they wanted, they wouldn't hesitate to lie. With Kate in the room with him, the stakes were high.

"We did have an incident a few months ago." Father Luca pressed his lips together. "One of the inmates, who I believe was mentally disturbed, stabbed one of the missionaries because he thought he was inhabited by the devil. Since that incident, more guards have been assigned to this post and we have panic buttons throughout the room to summon additional help. If you feel threatened, do not hesitate to use it."

But a panic button wouldn't stop an attack in progress. It would take time for additional guards to arrive. Connor wouldn't rely on a button to protect Kate. He would protect her.

Kate straightened in her chair. "God puts challenges in front of us to test our commitment and love for Him. For Tumarans, raised with polytheistic beliefs, to embrace the one true Lord is an undertaking, but we're ready," Kate said.

She was laying it on a little thick, but at least she appeared calm and was remaining in character.

"Is there a place where Sister Kate will be safest during the Bible study?" Connor asked, earning him a glare from Kate.

"Yes, Sister Kate. Please stay close to me or one of the guards at all times. You may speak openly to the inmates about our Lord, but do not let them distract you or lure you from this room. This room is our sanctuary and the inmates are told to respect the people in this space."

As if hardened criminals would care about a room and some rules pressed upon them in said room. The inmates had already proved they would break the law.

"This is not my first prison visit," Kate said. "I know how to conduct myself."

"You and I will conduct the Bible study in the main portion of the room while Father George takes confession. We will start the service at five, and you are welcome to join me at the altar or take a seat on the benches. We keep the service as unthreatening as possible. No spouting threats of fire and brimstone from these lips," Father Luca said.

With a warning look at Kate to do as Father Luca had said, Connor took his post in the confessional and pulled the gray flannel sheet across the opening. Between him and the area where the inmates would give confession was a metal screen. On the wall next to him was a panic button.

Connor wasn't certain what he was supposed to do while he waited. He heard Kate and Father Luca greeting people. So far, it was a quiet, solemn occasion. Connor hoped it would stay that way. Connor bowed his head and folded his hands. Not quick to call on a higher power or use prayer to achieve his ends, he took the time to ask for help. After such a long period of silence between the two of them, Connor couldn't imagine that God was listening, but it was worth a shot.

Besides, prayer seemed like the appropriate way for a priest to spend his time.

An inmate stepped into the confessional and sat heavily. He was sweating and his jumpsuit hung limply on him.

"Welcome," Connor said.

The man closed his eyes and rested his head against the wall. For a moment, Connor wondered if he was using the tiny enclosure as a safe place to rest or maybe to see something different from the gray, dirty walls and iron bars of the prison. What would a priest say? Or would a priest wait in silence for the other person to collect themselves?

It struck Connor as an odd custom, to tell a virtual stranger deep, dark secrets. What would Connor tell someone? That he'd fought with his brother and almost lost the most important person in his life? That he was sleeping with a woman who was in love with him and he hadn't told her how he felt in return? If he went back far enough, Connor figured he'd be in a confessional for most of the week unburdening his soul. Some of his sins would give a priest nightmares.

The man finally spoke. "Bless me, Father, for I have sinned. My last confession was two months ago."

Connor opened his gospel for his cheat sheet of what to say. "The Lord gives you His blessing and welcomes you, as He does all His children, to His home."

"I have a lot to confess today," the man said heavily.

Connor did not interrupt.

The man listed his sins, ranging from dark thoughts to openly cursing others to carrying rage in his heart for the people who had sent him to prison.

The prisoner scrubbed his hand hard across his face.

"Something bad is going to happen in cellblock D. I know it. Every inmate knows it. I can't tell the guards or they'll think I'm involved or I'll be beaten to death. But it's going to be bad. I needed to tell someone, Father, and I thought if I told you, you could do something about it. The warden respects priests and the sacrament. He won't make you tell him how you know."

Connor wasn't sure if he could or should pry. Wasn't there some kind of sacred silence between priest and confessor? Then again, Connor wasn't a priest. He hadn't taken vows to maintain silence about anything said in this booth and the inmate had requested his help. "What do you mean by something bad?"

The inmate shifted and cleared his throat. Dropping his voice low, he leaned toward the screen between them. "They keep us apart. They don't want us to rebel. But we get news from the outside. We know out there our countrymen are fighting for change. We want to join them."

Connor's instincts tingled with an ominous, heavy feeling. "How can you join them when you are here?"

The man sighed. "Father, you're not from around here. I can hear it in your voice. This is a dangerous country. Something has to change and it's got to start from the inside."

"You mean from inside the jail?" Connor asked.

"From inside Tumara," the man said. He wiped his sweating face on his sleeve. "I haven't seen my family in ten years. My wife left me. My children are embarrassed to tell their friends who I am. All because I didn't agree to swallow the trash I've been fed all my life. I tried to make a difference and the government was afraid of me."

Prisons were full of inmates who claimed they were innocent or that they'd been misunderstood or unfairly punished. "Tell me what you think you can do to help."

The man looked at Connor quizzically. "Are you telling me that instead of being in here with you, Father Luca and the chick, I should join the rebellion?"

Right this minute? The man was speaking as if the danger of a rebellion was imminent. "I am telling you to do what is right for you, your family and your country," Connor said, remembering he was a priest. Encouraging a rebellion wasn't something a priest would do, was it?

"We outnumber the guards two dozen to one. They might stop some of us, but they can't stop all of us."

The hair rose on the back of Connor's neck. "Is the riot planned for today?"

The man was silent.

Panic sharpened Connor's senses. Aiden was inside one of those cellblocks and Kate was in this room. In a mass riot, the guards would keep control with tear gas, shootings, beatings and whatever means were necessary to put it down. Many people would be hurt and some would die. "In times of trouble, I do not recommend making it worse by adding to the violence."

"Then this room is the safest place I can be. Talking to a priest when it starts is the best alibi I can get."

The inmate's angle for being in confession was to stay out of the inevitable fallout and punishment for a rebellion. Connor had to warn Father Luca and Kate, and the three of them needed to clear out of the prison.

Alarms went off at that moment. The high-pitched blare was deafening. Connor fled the confines of the confessional and looked around for Kate. The twenty or so prisoners who had come to service were beating at the locked doors, and the guards were swinging their billy clubs, yelling at them to get on the ground and not to move. Several listened. Most did not.

"They're staging a riot," Connor shouted to Kate and Father Luca.

Father Luca clasped his Bible to his chest and called to the prisoners to do the right thing and sit down. He was ignored. Connor grabbed Kate, not caring that it might be inappropriate for a priest to touch a woman. The prisoners could turn on the three of them, and Connor needed Kate close.

The guards weren't having success in gaining control over the inmates. One of the guards lost his club and fell to the ground. The other was flailing his stick in a mad act of violence he couldn't sustain for long.

"When that alarm blares it means the warden has called for a lockdown. Doors lock automatically and no one gets in or out until it stops," Father Luca said, trembling.

"There's no other way out of this room besides the main door?" Connor asked, pointing to the door being beaten down. It was bowing under the hammering it was taking.

The prisoners picked up the folding metal chairs and hurled them at the door. One guard dragged the other from the melee. One of the inmates turned. With dark, angry eyes, he stared at Connor and then Father Luca and then Kate.

A wicked smile spread across his face. Connor's reaction was swift. No one would harm Kate. She was no one's hostage and she was no one's victim. Not while he took breath. Connor put Kate behind him. The man approached, moving with an almost drunken swagger, every step heavy and exaggerated.

"I haven't seen a woman in over three years," the man said. "Get out of the way, Father. This is between her and me."

The situation was spiraling out of control and Connor had to make a stand before they were overwhelmed by angry prisoners. Hitting the panic button would likely do nothing as every available guard was probably attempting to control the rioting prison population.

"You will not hurt her," Connor said.

The man laughed. "Who's gonna stop me? You and what army?"

The man advanced on Connor, and though he was bigger, Connor reacted swiftly, bringing his knee into the man's chest, knocking the wind out of him. When he doubled over, Connor hit him on the back of the neck, knocking him unconscious.

"Anyone else?" Connor asked. He hoped showing himself to be aggressive would put off more advances. It wouldn't be easy to protect Kate against the other people in the room.

Someone hurled a chair at the glass window high above the altar. It bounced off, slamming back into the crowd. A second chair flew through the air, piercing the window. Glass rained down. Others pounded at the door until it finally bent open under the assault.

A far-off chant grew louder. "Power to the people. Power to the people." Once the men in the room caught the words, they joined in. Groupthink was taking over and the air vibrated with fear and violence. The inmates shoved the table on the altar to the wall beneath the window and climbed on each other in a bloody, frantic scramble to get out of the room through the window.

It wouldn't lead outside the gates, but it was one step closer.

Connor was alone in the room with the guards, Father Luca, Kate and the man who had come to confession. The lone remaining inmate was sitting quietly on the floor by the confessional.

"I didn't know you could fight," Father Luca said to Connor. "Thank God you were here."

"I told you I'd worked in a prison before," Connor said. He didn't want to raise suspicions about who he really was.

He knelt on the ground where one guard was unconscious. He was breathing and his heartbeat was strong. "I think he'll be okay. We need to get him help," Connor said.

"Where?" Kate asked. "You heard Father Luca. The prison is on lockdown."

"We'll put him in the confessional to hide him. We'll drape him in our priest robes so if any inmates come through here, they'll think he's a minister and not a guard. Our black shirts and white collars will have to be enough for us." It wasn't a foolproof plan, but it might buy them some time and safety, and it was the best chance they had. Connor couldn't quickly search for an exit while carrying two hundred pounds of deadweight. Connor and Father Luca removed their robes. Working together, Connor, Father Luca and Kate dressed the unconscious guard in one of the ceremonial robes and carried him to the confessional. The other guard pulled the second robe over his uniform.

"Aren't you planning to run?" the remaining guard

asked the inmate sitting on the floor as he wiped at his bloody, bruised face.

"Nope," the man said. "Won't get over the fence. Snipers'll get anyone who tries. What's the point?"

Aiden. Connor's body tightened. If their intel was correct, his brother was somewhere inside this prison. He could be hurt, bleeding, broken or shot and Connor wouldn't know.

"Tell me who started this riot," Connor said to the prisoner.

"I told you already. Cellblock D. They've got leaders from the AR in there, spouting about freedom and ruling by the people. Got everybody stirred up."

The AR. If Aiden was with them, how was he involved? Connor's chest tightened thinking of his brother needing him.

The inmate crossed his legs and waited. "I have no plans to run. Put that on my record. No plans to run."

A commotion in the hallway drew Connor's attention. Connor flipped the table on its side and shoved Kate and the guard behind it. He took the one remaining billy club and slid it through his belt.

"Father Luca, pray with me."

The two men knelt in front of the table. An angry mob of prisoners waited at the door. They scanned the room.

Connor turned. "Welcome. Father Luca and I are praying for you all."

The men seemed confused. The leader of the group looked at the holy men and growled. "Get out of here. You're not part of this. I don't want to kill no man of God."

"We are compassionate allies," Connor said.

The men lost interest. A chapel with two priests and an inmate didn't add fuel to their fire and they moved on down the hallway. Connor had gotten lucky with the ploy. With the rage and adrenaline surging through this prison, their luck wouldn't hold. He needed to get his Kate somewhere safe and hunker down.

His beautiful Kate. His. The possessive thought caught him unaware. It wasn't the first time he'd had those feelings for her, but they were stronger than before. She was his and he would protect her.

When the hall was clear, Connor spoke to Kate. "We need to get you out of here."

"How's that possible? It's more locked down in here than usual. Where will we go?" Kate asked.

Connor jammed a hand through his hair. He turned to the guard. "You must know a way out."

The guard was badly shaken, beaten and scared. "They took our radios. We can't call for help. There are a few entry points throughout the prison. If we don't get to them before someone finds us, we'll be killed."

Connor knew the stakes. He didn't add to the man's fear by admitting they had slim hopes of getting out unharmed. Connor's behavior had cemented his role as their leader and everyone was looking to him to get them to safety.

The overhead intercom crackled. "This is your warden speaking. Hands on your heads and return to your cells. If you do, you will not be held responsible for what has happened today. If you do not, we will use violence to maintain control. I have given the order to the guards to fire at will."

"What are the chances anyone will listen to that?" Father Luca asked.

The man who had been sitting by the confessional stood. "I'll listen. Those who value their lives will listen." He put his hands on his head and exited the chapel.

The sound of automatic gunfire blared over the alarm. Connor hoped Aiden had returned to his cell. Would Aiden have seen an opportunity and made a run for it in the chaos? His brother had to know he would come for him. Connor never should have accepted Sphere's lie that his brother was dead. He could have saved Aiden seven months of suffering.

An opportunity had dawned. Connor could use the chaos to look for his brother. It would be hours, if not days, before what had happened inside the prison was sorted out. That confusion worked to his advantage. Connor could stalk the halls of the prison and look for Aiden.

"What are you thinking?" Kate asked, taking his arm.

"I want to find my brother," he said to her in English.

"No, a hasty attempt now will get both of you killed."

"This could be the opportunity we've been waiting for." Connor was inside the prison. Aiden was likely somewhere inside, too. To be this close to his brother and not try to find him seemed wrong. But he couldn't leave Kate. If more wandering gangs of prisoners passed by, Connor needed to protect her.

"Be reasonable," Kate said. "We can find a way out. But this is a dangerous place to be. You know what happens during prison riots. Thousands of men are incarcerated here. They could be armed and they are most definitely dangerous. You heard the warden. The guards will shoot anyone they want."

"I need for you to be in a safe place," Connor said. "Then I can look for him."

Kate shook her head. "I'm not leaving you. We're staying together and we'll get out of this together."

Father Luca and the guard were looking at them strangely, perhaps unsure why they were speaking in English.

"Let's find a way out," Connor said in Portuguese, and he led them out of the ransacked chapel.

Kate could see in Connor's eyes the desperate desire to look for Aiden. With the chaos around him, one more man running, especially one dressed as a priest, could have access to more places. If a guard stopped to question him, he could claim he was looking for a safe path out and had gotten lost. Who wouldn't believe a priest?

She understood the desire, but she didn't agree with him acting on it. Field operatives often made decisions as the situation unfolded and exploited opportunities to the fullest, but this decision was fueled by too much emotion and not enough logic. Connor could be shot or teargassed or beaten. The longer the riot went on, the more guards would arrive to control the prison population and the more people would be hurt or killed.

The sound of gunfire persisted. How many men had been shot? How many were dead? Kate wouldn't add to the body count by allowing Connor to search for Aiden. She loved Connor and she had to make sure he saw reason. They would find out everything they could, and if given the chance, they would rescue Aiden. But even finding Aiden was a long shot. They would focus on gathering intel. That had been their mission objective.

Not only that, as darkness fell, the guards would use

floodlights to illuminate the yard. Floodlights would create shadows and darkened areas. Connor could be mistaken for an inmate and killed.

"Let's follow the guard to the nearest exit," Kate said. Learning about undocumented escape routes could help them when they returned to free Aiden.

They ventured into the hallway. It was still and quiet. The alarm had stopped screaming, though bright white lights flashed from devices posted along the hallway. The warden's voice came over the speaker system. "This is your warden. Return to your cells. This is not a request. This is a command. Those who do not return to their cells are considered escapees and will be shot on sight." The statement was punctuated by the sound of more gunfire.

The bloodshed would be high. Connor allowed the prison guard to take the lead. Screaming echoed around the building. Kate clutched Connor and his arm went around her. She'd been on the phone with operatives in bad situations and had been terrified for them. This experience was a thousand times more intense. How did field operatives do this every day and keep their cool?

"We'll be okay. I won't let anything happen to you," he whispered in her ear. His voice was soothing and she focused on that and on him. Connor West was a legend around Sphere for a reason. He had completed missions against all odds. He had performed tasks others could not. He would keep her safe. They would get through this together.

The men clustered around her as they jogged along the deserted hallway. They turned the corner and Kate covered her mouth and whirled away at the sight of a dead prisoner.

Father Luca stopped and knelt, closing the man's eyes, blessing him and whispering a prayer. Staying in character, Connor mimicked his actions. When they finished, they continued. Kate braced herself for more devastating sights.

"There's a stairwell ahead," the guard said. When they reached the unmarked door, the fingerprint reader that controlled it had been smashed to pieces.

"Can we force the door open?" Father Luca asked.

"Unlikely. These doors are pure steel with four-inch bolts along the door. They are meant to remain locked," the guard replied.

"Where's the next closest exit?" Connor asked. They heard yelling nearby. Through a metal post railing, they could see a floor below. A group of inmates ran past, perhaps searching for an exit.

"Cellblock D. There's roof access on the far side," the guard said.

"Cellblock D, where the riot started?" Connor asked.

Kate didn't like the idea of running into the thick of the riot.

"It's the closest cellblock to the exit," the guard said.

"Any other options?" Connor asked.

"We can try to get to the main entrance and signal for the guards to let us out," the guard said.

"Will they be able to open the doors?" Kate asked.

If the prison was still in lockdown mode, could the guards override the system and open the doors? If no one was allowed in or out, that included them. The guards would be nervous and twitchy. Kate didn't want any mistakes to cause a friendly-fire shooting or for their cover to be blown.

"We'll have to see. The alarm stopped. I don't know

if that means they have it under control or if that blasted noise was adding to the confusion," the guard said.

"Only one way to find out," Connor said. "Let's go." Hearing footsteps approach, he added, "Quickly."

Guard stations were abandoned and cells were open and vacant, locks broken and bedding strewn about in disarray. When they arrived at the main gate, it was closed and locked.

The guard shouted through the gates. "Is anyone there? It's Cesar with the chaplain and his missionaries."

No one appeared.

Cesar ran his thumb over the fingerprint reader and typed in his passcode. Nothing. No sound of locks opening and no one came to investigate. Cesar rattled the gate. "Please, someone. Open the gate." Panic gripped his voice, giving away how frightened he was.

Connor touched his shoulder. The shouting would bring inmates, and identifying himself as a guard was dangerous. They had to remain as inconspicuous as possible. Without a place to hide, that was difficult enough.

Cesar banged at the door. "Let us out." Fear trembled in his voice.

"Easy," Connor said. "We'll find a way out."

They had to keep level heads and Kate sensed Cesar was on the verge of losing it.

"If we can't get out, can we find a safe place inside the prison?" Kate asked. "Are there offices for staff? Maintenance rooms? A control center? Can we barricade ourselves inside a cell and wait for a guard to find us?"

"The west control center is near here," Cesar said.

His cheeks were flushed. "The cells don't have enough inside to build a barricade."

"Come on, Cesar. Show us. Lead the way," Connor said. If Cesar lost his cool, they were without their guide.

They changed directions and stopped when the sound of shouting drew closer. A group of seven inmates rounded the corner armed with wooden sticks and clutching shivs. They took an offensive stance, spreading out around Connor, Kate, Father Luca and Cesar. They were outnumbered and weaponless, and Kate didn't know how capable of a fighter Luca and Cesar were. She had training, but it was untested in the field.

"Where are you going?" one of the inmates asked. "This is our territory now."

Roving gangs inside the prison looking to stake out a claim? Why? Didn't it make more sense to get out of the prison? Kate didn't question their logic. Questions could get them killed.

"To the chapel," Connor said. He appeared calm, but Kate knew otherwise. He would react with swift and deadly force if pressed.

Connor stepped between the men and Kate. "We aren't looking for trouble. Your quarrel is not with us."

Kate took his arm. Connor couldn't take on seven men alone.

One of the men advanced on them, and Connor leaped at him, slamming his hand against the cinder-block wall and forcing him to drop his bat. Kate grabbed it. Now she was armed and it made her feel slightly better.

The inmates lunged at them. One grabbed Kate around the waist and hot rage coursed through her.

She brought her knee up to the man's midsection and he doubled over. She slammed him again and used the stick to hit the man again and again. Though her fighting technique was frantic, it got the job done. The man fell to the ground. She stared at him for a long minute, horror at what she had done careening into her.

Father Luca was standing over another inmate, rubbing his knuckles, his eyes wide.

Kate didn't have long to contemplate the situation. On the ground were six of the men who had attacked them and Connor was fighting with the seventh. Cesar was on the ground, as well, doubled over, clutching his abdomen. Kate knelt next to him. He was bleeding from his stomach, pressing his hands over a wound.

With a final punch to the face, Connor dropped the final inmate.

"How is he?" Connor asked Kate.

"He's bleeding from the stomach, maybe cut by a shiv, but he's conscious."

Cesar moaned as if to emphasize he was aware and in pain. Father Luca knelt next to Cesar and prayed.

"We can't leave him here, but he can't walk," Kate said.

Connor knelt down. He removed his button-down shirt, taking off the white cotton undershirt beneath it. He pressed it over Cesar's stomach. The man groaned in pain.

"I know that hurts, but I won't let you bleed out. You stay with us and we'll have you out of here in a few minutes," Connor said.

Kate helped Connor shrug into his black shirt, and Connor lifted Cesar while Kate held the white shirt over Cesar's wound.

Carrying him would slow them down, but they had no choice. They couldn't leave him in the open to be assaulted again.

"The command center?" Connor asked Cesar.

Cesar pointed down the corridor. They took two flights of stairs up and trekked down another hall. The prison was filled with bursts of shouting and gunfire breaking up the silence. When they arrived at the west-command-center door, the fingerprint scanner was broken just like the one at the other exit point.

"How will we get inside?" Father Luca asked.

"Can you hold this?" Kate asked Father Luca, gesturing to the white shirt.

Father Luca held it, freeing Kate's hands, and she stepped forward. Kate examined the device. She had seen this model of scanner before, and while she was working at a disadvantage with the mangled parts, it wasn't as badly smashed as the other one had been.

"Watch my back," she said to Connor.

Connor and Father Luca set Cesar against the wall.

"Hang in there. We're getting help," Connor said.

Cesar watched her through slit eyes. "Please hurry."

Kate knelt to look at the device. Some of the parts were intact but torn apart; others appeared damaged.

"Do you think you can fix it?" Father Luca asked.

Kate wasn't sure. If they could get inside the command center, they would have safe haven from the inmates and the violent response from the prison guards. "I'll try. I took a few electronics classes in college." It was a reasonable explanation for how she had acquired the skills to fix the lock device.

The loudspeaker crackled. "This is your warden. The riot is falling apart. Some of your comrades have returned to their cells. Others are dead. This is your last chance to surrender. Air reinforcements have arrived. Anyone who attempts to get past the gate will be shot down."

Kate ignored the sounds over the loudspeaker, the gunfire and the whirling from a helicopter. She had to fix this. The warden's message confirmed one thing to her: things were getting worse as the riot collapsed and the inmates grew more desperate.

Wishing she had her tool kit, she did what she could. She reassembled the device, took out her phone, ripped off the back and attached it to the fingerprint reader's wiring. Though her phone didn't have a wireless signal inside the prison, she could use the operating system to control the lock. Sweat dripped down her back. She wished she could see the device's electronic configuration.

Several minutes and failed attempts later, and she'd hacked inside the lock's master configuration and control. She entered a dummy password, forced the lock to accept it, and the locks flipped open with a satisfying click.

"We're in," she said. "Good thing I had those classes."

"Hallelujah," Father Luca said. He was too grateful to question her further.

Connor and Father Luca lifted Cesar and climbed the short stairwell to the command center. Kate removed her phone from the lock. She didn't have a way to relock the doors from the inside and her phone might come in handy again. It was the one computer device that she had on her person. Just having it made her feel better.

Connor liked his knives. She liked her electronics.

The command room had two chairs in front of the numerous computer monitors and servers.

"Brace those chairs against the door," Connor said.

Though the chairs wouldn't stop someone from getting in, it might slow them down. Kate did as Connor asked and Connor set Cesar down.

"Is there a first-aid kit in here? Something we can use to stop the bleeding?" Connor asked.

Cesar shook his head. "Just call for help."

Kate sat at one of the keyboards and began typing. She needed a way out, a way to lock the command-center door or a way to call for assistance. Connecting her phone to the server, she started a download of the prison's databases for review. She also uploaded a small Trojan horse that would give her external access, just in case. First priority was keeping them safe, but Aiden's rescue was on her mind. Plugging in directly to a terminal computer gave her access without firewalls and the prison's intrusion-prevention system blocking her.

"What are you doing?" Father Luca asked from next to Cesar. He held the man's hand with one of his and was pressing the T-shirt over his injury. Based on the color of the once white shirt and the robe he was wearing, it didn't look as if it was slowing the blood flow.

"Looking for a way out," she lied. While her phone downloaded information and compressed it, she went to another computer and pulled up the displays for the closed-circuit security system. Picture after picture of destruction and devastation hit the screens. She gasped at the sight of men lying on the ground bleeding, fires burning and active combat among the guards carrying large shields and the rioting prisoners.

She sent a message from the control room to the

main entrance. No response. The system was likely thinly manned, all able-bodied guards working to control the prison population. She sent another message. Nothing. "I can't get through to anyone," she said.

"We're on the top level of the prison," Connor said. "If we can get out on the roof, we can signal for help."

Kate crossed the room and looked out the window. Response helicopters flew overhead. Explosions sounded through the air.

She felt dizzy looking down. "We can't climb out the window. We don't have ropes or a way to climb up."

"Look at that ledge," Connor said, pointing along the wall. It led across to a tiered roof. "We can shimmy across, get on that lower roof and climb to the top. From there, we can signal for help."

Kate stared at him. He knew about her fear of heights. "That's a terrible idea. We're safer here. I can get someone to send help." Eventually, someone would respond.

"Cesar needs medical assistance immediately. We can't wait for someone to find us. Prisoners are roaming freely through this building and we don't know how long it will be before they come in here. You've seen the inmates' reaction to a woman. We need to get you out of here to somewhere safer. You're safer on the ledge than you are in here.

"Father Luca, will you stay with Cesar?" Connor asked.

"Yes, I will pray with him," Father Luca said.

Cesar was unresponsive, his eyes closed.

"Keep talking to him. Try to keep him with us," Connor said.

Kate looked out the window again. "I can't go out on that ledge." She returned to her phone and the computer. Computers were comfortable. Playing with data and code made her feel safe. Leaping out of a window terrified her.

"Yes, you can," Connor said. "I will hold your hand the entire time. You'll be safe."

"Sister Kate, this is a trial from God. A test. He will protect us. Have faith that this will work," Father Luca said.

"Kate, look. Father Luca needs to make sure Cesar doesn't bleed to death. I need to signal for help. You are safer with me. If someone comes into this room and I'm not here, what do you think will happen?" he asked.

Kate didn't need to use her imagination much to understand. She would be violently assaulted. The roof was her best and only option.

Kate took her phone from the console, hoping she had copied enough information to help them find Aiden. She slipped her phone into her back pocket.

"I'll go out on the ledge first, then you," Connor said. "We'll flag down help."

Kate mustered every ounce of courage and followed Connor onto the ledge.

The wind felt as if it was blowing hard enough to knock her down. Helicopters were circling and guards were shooting from their sniper posts. Below them on the prison grounds, bodies were scattered and smoke rose from the prison. Nausea and dizziness hit her. She closed her eyes and tried to restore balance to her shaking legs.

"We're okay. This is almost over," Connor said.

Kate pressed her back to the wall and scooted a few inches along the ledge. Wooziness swamped her. She would not look down again. No good could come from that. Inch by inch, she and Connor shimmied along the wall.

"You're okay, Kate. You got this. You can do it," Connor said.

Any other man, and she wouldn't have made it. But she had faith in Connor. With him next to her, she could do this. Somehow, she would do this.

When they reached the lower roof, she knelt onto it. Connor maneuvered to get behind her. The roof shingles were hot under her hands, but it felt safer to crawl rather than to walk. Carefully, every motion slow and easy, Kate kept her eyes pinned to the next tier of the roof. It was flatter, and from there, they would signal to the helicopters.

Her foot slipped, adrenaline and fear shot in her veins, and Connor's hand went to her body, bracing against her hip. Her heart slammed hard and fear shook her body. She had almost fallen.

"I will not let you fall," Connor said. "Trust me."

"It's easier when you distract me," Kate said.

"From this position, I have an amazing view of your legs and butt. That's all the distraction I need. Too bad you aren't behind me. I could wiggle in just the right way to keep your attention."

Kate smiled. Despite the situation, she couldn't help herself. "Is that all men ever think about?"

"Not all—only a good portion of the time. I also spend time thinking about food."

"You're the only man in this world who could have talked me into coming out here," Kate said.

"Are you telling me I have the power to talk you into doing stuff I want?" he asked, not disguising the lewd overtone of the question.

"In matters of the bedroom, only when it's something I want to do, too," Kate said.

"Put your hand up to that ledge and I'm going to push you up," Connor said.

They were at the other roof. Kate reached her hand and clasped the edge. With a shove from Connor, she gripped it with both hands and pulled herself onto the roof. Kate sat, closing her eyes and clutching her knees to her chest. She hadn't fallen. With Connor's help she had crawled out of a window at least six stories above the ground.

When Connor slid next to her, he stood and waved his arms, trying to flag down a helicopter.

Two helicopters were patrolling the sky. One slowed down and hovered over them. The site of a priest and woman had them sending down a harness. Connor strapped her in first, and Kate kept her eyes shut until she was safely on the ground.

Chapter 11

When the prison riot was over, forty-seven inmates were dead, including the leader of one of the most violent prison gangs, and over a hundred were injured. Three men had escaped and a city-wide search was under way to find them. Thirty-four guards had been injured, five in serious condition at a local hospital.

The helicopter Connor had flagged down had rescued Father Luca and Cesar. The other prison guard they had left in the chapel was rescued and was in stable condition at the hospital.

Connor had no news of Aiden. He was working every contact he had, making calls and pretending to be a reporter looking for a list of casualties, pretending to be a hospital administrator calling for prison medical records to be sent, and the list went on and on. No one could confirm if Aiden was among the dead or wounded. No one could confirm where Aiden was.

Connor had been close to his brother. In the confusion, with more time and with less at stake, he might have figured a way to get Aiden out of La Sabaneta. But Kate had needed his protection, he'd needed to be certain she was safe, and recklessly running through the prison to find Aiden could have gotten him killed. Kate had been the voice of reason when chaos had reigned and the temptation to throw care to the wind had been strong. Connor didn't like admitting she'd been right; he liked to think of himself as unstoppable. But her caution had been the better choice.

"I know the information is here somewhere," Kate said. She had downloaded the data she had taken from the prison into her computer from her phone and she was mining through it. She had been working with it for over thirteen hours. She hadn't stopped for a break. "Aiden is in that prison. I need to figure out what name they have him under."

They had tried every combination of Aiden's name, as well as looking for strangely named inmates that could be aliases for Aiden.

Connor watched the television news report, hoping to catch a glimpse of his brother. The prison riot was receiving national news coverage. During the riot, major portions of the prison had been damaged. Fires had been started. Entire areas were flooded during the efforts to put out the fires.

No sign of his brother.

The riots had a terrible impact on Connor's plans to free his brother. The prison was now under watch by the Tumaran National Emergency Reserves, who would provide additional monitoring of the prison while the mess was cleaned up, the prison repaired and every prisoner accounted for.

The prisoners had lost good-behavior privileges such as being outside and attending church services. All meals would be eaten in their individual, tiny cells.

Aiden's morale would be at an all-time low. As a man who liked to run wild, being locked in and locked down would be trying for him.

"We have to find him," Connor said to Kate, disconnecting his phone in frustration. He couldn't find out any more information than what was publicly available.

Kate crossed the room and put her arms around him. "Connor, we will. I will find him. I won't give up."

"He could be dead."

Kate hugged him tighter. "He is not dead. We'll find him."

She was keeping him from losing it. She was his anchor. Her support and having her beside him was keeping him from falling over the edge of sanity. "What if all that's left to find is his body?" Connor asked. Kate had never lost faith that they would find Aiden alive. Connor wished he shared her sense of optimism.

"Don't think that way. Don't think all is lost because then it really is," Kate said.

"I need to know he's okay," Connor said.

When he looked at Kate, tears shone in her eyes. "It kills me to see you hurting."

He felt vulnerable and exposed in a way he never had before. When he'd thought Aiden was dead, the sense of loss was absolute, but he'd had to accept it because he couldn't do anything to help him. This situation was different. He could do something to help Aiden. He could if only he could find him.

A knock on their hotel-room door. Connor's brain, lacking food and sleep, shot into overdrive. Sphere had found them. More disasters were calling.

"Did you order food?" Connor asked quietly.

Kate shook her head. "No."

Connor motioned for Kate to go into the bedroom of their suite. "Wait there."

Kate shook her head and pointed to his side. She was bent on staying with him. Connor approached the door and looked through the peephole.

Confusion and worry shot through him and he pulled open the door. "Ariana, what are you doing here?"

Ariana entered the room, rushing past Connor and Kate. She removed the hat that she'd been wearing low over her face. Her eyes were puffy and her face red from crying.

"Ariana, what's happened?" Kate asked. She steered her to the couch and sat beside her, slipping her arm around Ariana's shoulders. Connor brought her a box of tissues.

"Ariana, I know this is a difficult time, but I need to know if you were followed," Connor said.

Ariana shot him a look as she dabbed her eyes. "Of course I wasn't. I've been running and hiding for years. I know how to get somewhere unseen."

"How did you find Kate and me?" Connor asked. It worried him that he and Kate had been traced to this hotel.

"I heard from some spies the AR has in the city that two Americans were staying in this hotel."

Connor swore. "We need to change hotels. Immediately. If the AR's found us, then Sphere can find us."

Kate nodded. "Let's go. Let's go now."

Ariana held up her hand. "Please. I have information about Aiden."

They went stock-still. "I've been in touch with one of the men who escaped from La Sabaneta. He said Aiden is still inside and he had last seen him just before the riot."

"Was Aiden part of the riot?" Connor asked.

"Yes, but my contact said it didn't go according to plan," Ariana said.

"Meaning?" Connor asked.

"Meaning he didn't know if Aiden was dead or alive."

Their new accommodations were smaller and farther away from the prison, but they'd needed to relocate to prevent anyone from following them.

After taking a sleeping pill, Ariana had fallen asleep on a cot in their hotel room. Kate started her computer program and set her laptop on the end table. She needed something to shake off the tiredness that dogged her. Drinking more coffee would make her jittery, so she went to the minifridge for some water. Connor had gone to pick up dinner and would return soon and they could eat together. Perhaps he would settle enough to rest with her.

As anxious as she was, Connor was worse. He was restless and edgy, needing information about his brother, worried about what had happened at the prison and how it affected their chances of getting Aiden out. Kate wanted to find information that would put Connor's mind at rest, to exploit a security hole left open after the prison riot.

Kate opened the door to the small fridge and an arm clamped around her waist, a hand clamped over her mouth and she was jerked upright. It wasn't Connor. It didn't smell like him and it didn't feel like him. Kate reared back, trying to slam her attacker or knock him off balance.

He avoided her attack and shook her hard, lifting her off her feet. "Be still and be quiet." A quiet, threatening male voice.

Kate screamed despite the hand over her mouth and jammed her elbow behind her. She wasn't going down without a fight. Though she made contact, the man didn't move. Kate lifted her legs and kicked the wall, pushing off it and sending the attacker back several long steps.

Ariana remained asleep. The sleeping pill had her out cold.

"I will release you, but if you attack me or scream, I will stop you."

Kate stopped struggling and the man let her go. She whirled to face him and came eye to eye with a dark-skinned man with black hair wearing sunglasses, a gray T-shirt and jeans.

"Did Sphere send you?" she asked.

The man snorted. "No one sent me. I took a job and I came here. I'm only late because you moved hotels this morning. Threw me a little. But not enough."

An assassination job? Was the man playing with her, releasing her to have the thrill of catching her again before he killed her? Kate looked around for a weapon. "My boyfriend will be back soon." How many minutes had passed since Connor left?

The man folded his arms across his chest. "Connor West? Good. I want to talk to him."

He knew Connor's real name. They had checked into

the hotel under pseudonyms. Sphere had sent this man and he was planning to kill them both.

"Your problem is with me," Kate said. Connor didn't work for Sphere anymore. She was the one who had ignored her boss's demand that she not get involved in looking for Aiden. Connor was just a concerned family member.

Her phone was across the room, connected to her laptop. She couldn't call Connor and tell him not to return to the hotel. When she heard someone at the door, she shouted a warning.

"Run, Connor! Get out of here."

Foolish, hardheaded man didn't run. Connor came through the door, body poised to attack, scanning the room for the threat. The men both pulled knives at the same instant and Kate watched in horror. Someone would get hurt. The two men circled each other, knives clutched in their hands.

"I'll give you a chance to realize the mistake you made in coming here and run," Connor said.

"Run? You asked me to come here," the man said.

Connor regarded the man through a wary expression. "Who sent you?"

"Our common friend." The man relaxed and straightened, but didn't lower his knife.

"Common friend?" Connor asked. "Did you see the sun set yesterday?"

Kate rolled her eyes at the question. It was a test question Connor and the senator had set up when he had helped him rescue his daughter to confirm who was working on their side and alert the other if they had been compromised in some way.

"I did as I have every day," the man said. The man put his knife away.

Connor grinned and slid his knife into the sheath at his waist. "I hoped the senator would come through. Took you a few days."

Connor and the man clasped hands.

"Took me a few days because you were involved in a prison riot and then relocated," the man said.

Kate wondered how the man knew they'd been involved in the incident at the prison.

"I'm Finn," the man said.

"Connor West. This is Kate."

"The senator was vague, but I've heard of you. I was intrigued," Finn said.

"What have you heard?" Connor asked.

"You've operated in every corner of the world. You've never been caught. You don't work for anyone but yourself anymore," Finn said. "It's a position I can respect given my preference for being an independent contractor."

"We're looking to get someone out of La Sabaneta," Connor said, getting to the reason they'd asked for help.

To his credit, Finn didn't laugh at the near-impossible mission. He also didn't flinch or roll his eyes.

"Is that why you went into the prison? Hoping to break him out?" Finn asked.

"Not exactly," Connor said. "We were doing recon and were inside when the riot started."

"Riots are happening every day in this country, and *el presidente* is increasing his police and security teams. Uprisings have been sporadic and unorganized and put down quickly, but the more momentum the movement gains, the stronger the Armed Revolutionaries grow. I've had to be more careful about who I work for. I have no intention of being caught and jailed in a sting," Finn said.

"How long have you been in this area?" Connor asked.

"Too long. There's enough work. I could stay for another decade and not be bored a single day," Finn said.

"Are you willing to help us?" Connor asked.

"I could help with your problem. The senator's offered diamond-level support," Finn said.

Meaning the senator was paying Finn handsomely for his time. Given the state of affairs in Tumara, operatives could command a high price.

"Kate's working to get confirmation that my brother's inside the prison," Connor said. He strode to the door and picked up the bags of food he'd left in the hallway, then closed the door.

"Was he part of the riot?" Finn asked.

"Unknown," Connor said.

"Too bad you didn't exploit the riot as a chance to get him out," Finn said.

Connor shook his head. "I considered it but extenuating circumstances prevented it. I couldn't get to him without too much risk."

She was the risk. Connor had been worried about her while they were inside the prison and she had insisted they stay together. Did Connor blame her for not being able to look for Aiden? He hadn't said anything to her after they escaped. The guilt that had urged her to first find Connor renewed. She had a hand in Aiden being in Tumara. Connor set the food on the small coffee table.

Finn rolled his shoulders. "Three inmates escaped

yesterday. The government will close those security holes. We'll have to be creative and aggressive."

"I'm willing to die to get my brother out," Connor said.

Though Kate had long known of Connor's commitment to the cause, she was shaken by hearing him speak so plainly. "I'd prefer if no one died," Kate said. "Is there a way to get Aiden out without anyone being hurt?"

Connor and Finn looked at her as if she were crazy.

Connor scanned the newspaper again. A list of the men who had lost their lives during the prison riot was printed in the morning newspaper alongside the pictures of the destruction caused. Aiden's name wasn't among those listed. A brief flash of relief was followed by dread. The government-run newspaper wouldn't print the name of an American they had been holding. They wouldn't allow his name to be leaked to the press and risk creating an international incident.

Ariana and Finn were away working their street contacts, trying to get confirmation of Aiden's location.

"Oh. Oh, look. Connor!" Kate called.

He couldn't tell from her voice if she was panicked or scared. He raced to her. Kate was pointing at an article showing more damage at the jail. Reporters were speculating how the government would continue to keep the jail open considering how much had been destroyed.

"Is that Aiden?" she asked. Her voice was tight to the point of breaking.

Connor leaned over her shoulder to look at the picture. In the background of one of the photos, several inmates were lined up along a wall, being patted down by guards. After the riot, every cell had been emptied and anything that could be used as a weapon or for entertainment was removed. Books, pencils and extra clothes were taken and destroyed. Inmates would be eating their food with their bare hands. The government intended to break the will of the inmates in the prison to ensure they stampeded every last intention of another riot.

"I can't tell. Can you make it bigger?" Connor said. It could have been his brother. He wanted it to be his brother. He clasped her shoulders, needing to lean on her.

Kate had gone above and beyond to help him look for Aiden. His emotions surged in his chest as he looked at her. Never in his life had he had someone who was so much a partner to him, both in his life and in his work. She had remained steadfastly at his side, devoted and true.

Kate opened the picture in another application and zoomed in on the image. Though it was grainy, it looked like his brother.

"If I can get a copy of the original picture…" She was already dialing her cell phone. She pretended to be a reporter from an American newspaper covering the story, and she promised to give the small Tumaran news company credit for the photo and content they provided. She amazed him with her fast thinking.

"They're sending them," Kate said, taking his hands. "We're close to finding him. I can feel it."

Connor pressed a kiss to her mouth. He couldn't get over how close to her he felt. He had never before felt this way for a woman. She worked beside him during the day and she slept beside him at night. Kate was integrally part of his world and their lives had intertwined during this rescue effort. Would that change after he found his brother? He couldn't think about them going their separate ways, not after all they had been through.

"Are you okay?" Kate asked, smoothing his hair away from his face.

"I'm fine. I was thinking about how much I appreciate what you're doing."

She smiled from under her lashes. "I'm happy to help however I can."

"Even though you know there are consequences for what we've done." Her job and reputation would be in tatters. Sphere could make living a normal life impossible for her.

"I know there are consequences. I'll face them," Kate said.

"You won't face them alone," Connor said.

Kate leaned her head on his chest and he held her. A few minutes later, her computer beeped, and Connor reluctantly let her go so she could check her email. The newspaper had sent the original photos.

On her computer, they could see the image of Aiden more clearly. His face was angled down and partially blocked by a guard, but Connor felt sure it was his brother.

"It's him," Connor said. Relief and happiness ballooned through him. To know Aiden had survived the riot brought him immeasurable happiness.

Kate stared for a few more seconds at her screen. "I think you're right." She flipped through the other pictures the newspaper had sent her. She paused and opened the folder where she'd saved the snapshots.

"These are called '3B' and then a sequential number. Does that mean he's being held in cellblock 3B?" Kate asked. She pulled up the map she had on the prison layout. Destroyed, uninhabitable parts of the jail were blacked out. 3B was in part of the jail still in use.

"It's the best we have to go on," Connor said.

Kate tapped her nail against her computer. "We won't have much time to look for him. Once I doctor the prison's security system, it won't take them long to figure out what's going on. If we make a mistake and target 3B and he's somewhere else…"

"We'll have to move fast and roll with the punches," Connor said.

They wouldn't get another shot to save his brother's life. They would give this operation everything they had and hope it was enough.

Chapter 12

"Are you nervous?" Kate asked. Fresh from a hot shower, which she had hoped would calm her nerves, she was eager to get a solid seven hours of sleep before the jailbreak attempt in the morning. She, Connor, Ariana and Finn had gone over their plan, and the details whirled in Kate's head. Disable the security system in Aiden's cellblock, put in a prison helicopter-flyover request and have it approved and get out of the area before anyone figured out what was going on. The timing needed to be perfect. They were counting on the confusion and miscommunications that came with new staff and the Tumaran National Emergency Reserves working inside the prison to pave their way for the jailbreak.

Kate sat on the bed as she brushed her hair, watching Connor. He was lying in bed, wide-awake.

"I'm not worried about the jailbreak. I'm worried

Aiden will have been moved or that, with the new security measures, I won't get to him in time," Connor said. "I don't know if the Tumaran government has figured out who he is or if he's assumed another name. I don't know if Sphere is aware he's in prison. I don't know all the pieces and that means there's a high probability of not accounting for a serious problem."

Kate set her brush down and crawled across the bed to Connor. She rested her head on his chest. "We'll find him. I'll be there to help. So will Ariana and Finn. We all want him rescued." She kissed the bare skin of his chest. He played with her hair, running his fingers through it.

"Why don't you come with us? I don't like the idea of you being on the ground. What if you miss the rendezvous point? What if you're delayed? The timing is tight," Connor said.

"I won't be able to think if I'm in a helicopter whirling around and I need to be clearheaded. The prison might have updated their passcodes or their system and I'm relying on the information I gathered in the control center to give me access. If I can't get in or I get shut out, I'll need to think on my feet. I can't do that high in the air. You know how I feel about heights."

"It's sexy when you talk nerdy to me," Connor said.

"Are you making fun of me?" Kate asked and tickled his stomach.

Connor caught her hand and grinned at her. For a brief instant, he seemed happy and carefree without the weight of Aiden's rescue plaguing him. "I would never make fun of my personal geek service. Without you, we wouldn't be able to get to Aiden."

"Are you using me for my brain?" she asked.

"Would it be bad if I wanted both your brain and your body?" Connor asked, rolling on top of her.

She had never had a man interested in both. She stretched her hands over her head. "You can have whatever part of me you'd like." One day, she wanted all of him and she would have it.

Connor kissed her and didn't take the intimacy further than that. Though the kisses ignited something white-hot in her, Kate needed to be sensitive to how he was feeling. The next twenty-four hours would be stressful and key to saving Aiden.

"We should sleep," Kate said, stroking the side of his face. "You need to be in top form tomorrow."

"I can't. I feel restless," Connor said.

"Do you want to talk about it?"

Connor lifted a brow. "You already know what's on my mind."

She touched his back, running her fingertips along his side. "How about a distraction, then?" She rolled her hips back and forth, teasing him. "A little physical activity to help put you to sleep."

His eyes widened and Connor pretended to think about it. He rocked his hips into hers, and she was aware he was turned on and tuned in to her. "I can't imagine what you have in mind."

Kate parted her legs and wrapped them around his waist. "Does this give you a clue?"

Connor arranged the pillows behind her head and a teasing smile crossed his face. "No. Make it more clear."

Kate grabbed the sides of her T-shirt and pulled it up over her head. She tossed it on the ground. "How about this?"

"I'm still not sure what you're getting at," Connor said.

Kate pushed at the waistband of her panties, and Connor slid them down her legs, leaning back on his haunches. "How about now? If you're still confused, maybe you're all brawn and no brain."

He laughed. "You're the whole package. How can I hold on to you?"

She brought her finger to her mouth in mock thought. "That could be a problem. Maybe all I'm after is arm candy."

He grinned at her. "You're too much and I can't get enough." He buried his face in her neck and kissed her.

He smelled of soap and spice, a combination she found exhilarating. His hard muscles flexed under her hands as he moved lower over her body. Everywhere his mouth lingered, heat flared along her skin. She closed her eyes and enjoyed the sensations tumbling over her.

He lowered his head between her legs and she gasped when he kissed her at the apex of her thighs. His mouth and fingers stroked her intimately, and she lifted her hips, wanting more, wanting to make him feel as good as he was making her feel.

She forked her fingers into his hair, and his name escaped her lips in a gasp. He didn't respond. His tongue stroked her, and the feeling was accompanied by such a strong rush of emotion, tears came to her eyes. He held her thighs open as the heat of his mouth coaxed her to the brink. "Connor, wait. Too fast."

If he heard her, he didn't heed. He slid one finger into her and then two. Shivers coursed through her body and she shouted his name one last time and melted against the bed. He flopped on his back beside her, one hand behind his head, looking extraordinarily pleased with himself. "Feeling better?" he asked.

She put a hand on his chest. "Yes and no. I wanted to relax you. I feel great, but you still feel tense."

"I'm okay. Try to get some rest."

"No way." She pushed herself up and over him, straddling his hips. "Let me see if I can get you to chant my name."

"I'm not much of a chanter."

She smiled. "Is that a challenge?"

"Not at all. I'm more the strong, silent type," he said.

Kate loved this man. She knew being in love with him wasn't easy, especially when it was unreciprocated. He was closed off at times and utterly stoic when she desperately wanted emotion from him. But she would win him over. She would make him see that she was good for him, that they were good together. She was helpful in this mission and more than a lover. She wanted to be his partner in the most complete sense of the word.

She found a condom and rolled it on him. Connor watched her, his dark eyes soulful. She didn't wait for him to say anything. Her body was primed from the careful attention his mouth had given her. She took him deeply and swiveled her hips, letting him move all the way inside her. He moaned. She withdrew and plunged down again. She lifted and lowered her body, slow and steady. He reached for her hips to hasten the movements, and she took his hands and placed them on her breasts instead.

Another groan. But not her name. "Connor?"

"Hmm?" he asked through half-lidded eyes.

"Tell me what you want."

"Faster," he said.

Up and down. He closed his eyes and she let her head fall back against the sensations scorching through her.

"Tell me again," she said.

"More. Faster," he said. A sheen of sweat covered his forehead.

Ever so slightly, she ramped up the speed. "Kate, honey, please, you're killing me."

There it was. Her name, as she had wanted. She planted a kiss on his mouth and rode him hard, fast, driving him over the brink. When he found completion, to her supreme delight, he spoke her name again.

She collapsed next to him on the bed and closed her eyes.

Connor pulled her against him. "You're really something else."

"Meaning?" she asked, sleep tempting her. She cuddled closer to Connor in bed.

"Meaning, I have never trusted anyone how I trust you. You've been there for me. You've put yourself at risk for me and for Aiden. I owe you more than I will ever be able to repay."

"You don't need to repay me," Kate said.

"Can you look at me?" he asked.

Kate opened her eyes and tilted her head up. "What's wrong?"

"Nothing's wrong. Nothing. But I've wanted to say something to you for a while now."

Her heart pounded harder.

"I love you, Kate."

Warmth spread over her. She had spoken those same

words to him and had wanted and waited for them to be returned. That they came freely meant everything to her.

Guilt, like a bucket of ice water, dumped over the tenderness of the moment. If Connor learned the role she had played in Aiden's disappearance, she would irrevocably break his trust. If she told him now, would he change his mind about her? Take back the word *love* and replace it with hateful, angry words?

Aiden meant everything to Connor. Kate had known that from the beginning. At first, she had resisted disclosing anything to him because she couldn't risk him refusing to help. Then she had wanted to earn his trust. Now that she knew she hadn't been responsible for Aiden's disappearance, had been just another pawn in Sphere's game, could she tell Connor what had unfolded and the role she'd played and keep his love?

She couldn't leave the heavy secret between them. At some point, he would find out. She'd blurt it out when she couldn't hold it inside a moment longer. Sad as it was to admit, she had become skilled at lying while she worked, pretending to be other people and playing a role. But she couldn't lie to Connor. Being his lover wasn't a character she was pretending to be. She loved him. She wanted honesty and truth between them.

She had to tell him now. He would see that she had made the only choices she could at the time with the information she had. They could move forward and put this behind them.

She struggled to find the words. "I have something I need to tell you and it might be hard for you to hear."

Connor tensed. Was he waiting for the bomb to explode? Had he expected her to deliver bad news on the heels of something wonderful between them? For a moment, she reconsidered. She was pushing them to shaky ground. She had already started speaking and the words found their way out of her mouth.

"I thought I was responsible for Aiden's disappearance."

Connor sat up and inclined his head. His eyes slightly narrowed. "What do you mean you thought you were responsible for his disappearance?"

The whole horrible story came tumbling out. Not delivering the message to Aiden and then finding out he had gone missing. Believing he was dead and how guilty she had felt knowing she was his ground command and she had made an error. If she had delivered the warning about a government raid, she believed he could have protected himself.

"Why didn't you tell me this sooner?" Connor asked. His voice had taken on an edge.

She shifted, knowing he was upset and unsure how to defuse it. "I didn't want to lose your trust."

"You know Aiden is important to me." His voice had gone soft and quiet.

"That's why I felt I had to tell you now. I didn't want secrets between us."

"You didn't want secrets, or because if we rescue him tomorrow, the role you had in this operation could come out?" Connor asked. "Is this a 'cover your rear end' move or are you trying to absolve yourself of the guilt you feel?"

"I don't want lies between us."

Connor's eyes narrowed. "Did you come to find my brother out of concern for him or guilt?"

"A little of both," she said. The admission hurt.

Connor said nothing for a long time. Kate read anger on his face. Hurt. Betrayal. Giving trust was difficult for him. He had told her he trusted her and loved her and she had bludgeoned him with this information. She should have waited. Or told him sooner. Her timing was all wrong.

"I should have told you sooner," she said.

"Yes." He wouldn't meet her gaze. He had drawn his knees up, the sheet draping over him, and his arms were folded on top of the sheet. He was staring at some blank spot on the wall.

She set her hand on his forearm. "Connor, please don't be angry about this. Please don't shut me out."

A muscle flexed in his jaw and he pulled away from her touch.

"I won't keep things from you like this again," she said. She didn't know what train of thought his mind had taken, but she guessed it wasn't positive about her or trust and love in general.

Connor looked at the ceiling and then at her. "I anticipated this."

He had? He had suspected the role she had played in Aiden's disappearance? She didn't know whether to be relieved or insulted.

"I knew you worked for Sphere. How could those backstabbing, two-faced liars not rub off on you?" Connor asked.

Kate winced. That wasn't the response she had been expecting.

"I knew I couldn't trust you to be honest with me. Why did I let myself believe you were any different from everyone else?" he asked. He stood from the bed and grabbed his pants off the floor. He pulled them on quickly, every motion punctuated with anger.

"Connor, please don't go. Let's talk about this."

"What is it that you want to say to me? That despite lying, you can be trusted? That it's fine now because we know where Aiden is?"

"I just want to tell you that I'm sorry and I never meant to hurt you or Aiden."

"If we hadn't located my brother, would you have told me this information?" Connor asked. "If we had come here only to learn he was dead, would you have said anything?"

Kate wasn't sure. She hadn't considered not finding Aiden. Her focus had been on their mission. "I knew we would find him and I didn't think you and I would get this close."

Connor stared at her. Gone from his face was his anger. Now she read cold indifference. Maybe it was his training to hide his emotions and he couldn't help it, but the indifference was worse than the anger. Indifference meant he didn't care. Indifference meant he had written her off. The thoughts pierced her and she struggled not to cry. How could she explain this and not lose his trust? Not lose him? She felt herself dangling on the edge, holding on with her fingertips.

"I'll sleep on the couch," Connor said under his breath.

"Connor, please."

"Connor, please what?" he said, his voice raised. At least it was a hint of the emotions roiling inside him.

"Please forgive me. Please don't let one small mistake ruin what we have."

Connor's eyes met hers. "You think lying to me is a

small mistake? Clearly, we are not on the same page. I don't even think we're reading from the same book."

Connor had left the hotel early in the morning to meet Finn. He'd said nothing to her.

Her and Connor's final conversation the night before weighed heavy on her heart. But now wasn't the right time to talk. Not only were she, Finn and Connor linked via their headsets and in constant communication about the jailbreak, but Kate also couldn't afford to lose focus.

She and Connor would talk later today. Once Connor had rescued Aiden, he would see that her not telling him that information was minor. Wouldn't he? She couldn't think anything else or she would have a breakdown, and today she needed to concentrate and remain alert.

Ariana had spent the night in the home of an AR sympathizer and had returned to the hotel room. She wanted to be close during the jailbreak and be on hand if Kate needed anything. Finn was meeting Connor before the jailbreak to prepare.

Kate had been a bundle of nerves since Connor had left. She couldn't eat. She was fidgety, checking her computer and waiting for the headline Botched Jailbreak to splash across the local news site. She was careful to keep track of the time, needing to be sure she completed her tasks according to the schedule they had created. Finn, Aiden and Connor were counting on her.

Kate adjusted her headset and focused. She got into the zone, listening to some music from an earbud in one ear and holding a cup of coffee. Four minutes until go time.

She needed to hack into the prison's security system, make her changes and exit before the intrusion-detection system alerted anyone she was in. The prison security system was modern and complex. If she hadn't gotten inside the control room during the prison riot and left behind a Trojan horse, she didn't know if she could have gotten inside on her own in a short time frame with her limited resources.

"K, it's F. I'm in the chopper. I'll be in the fly zone in three and a half minutes. Copy."

Finn checking in with her. "Copy that. I'm on it." The prison had brought in the National Emergency Reserves, independent contractors and a slew of support staff to clean up after the riot and to prevent another. Security around the jail was tighter.

After several tense minutes of coding, Kate broke into the prison's computer system. She submitted her request for a helicopter flyover. Helicopters were regularly flying over the jail, monitoring the grounds, and though her request was off schedule, she had spoofed the credentials to make the request appear from the warden. Unless the warden was in the room to deny he had sent the request, it should be approved in a timely manner.

Should be. No guarantees.

She waited anxiously and checked the status of her request. No change. She checked again. Nothing. Her body heated and she felt slightly dizzy. She took a deep breath. Checked the status again. Finally, the request's status flipped to approved.

"F, you have approval," she said, hearing the pride in her voice. So far, two hurdles down.

If everything went according to plan, Connor and

Finn would be in and out with Aiden in less than five minutes.

"Thanks, K. You work miracles, girl," Finn said. The sound of the chopper clicked through their shared headsets.

Kate monitored the air-traffic radar system surrounding the jail. She waited for Finn and Connor's chopper to appear. When it did, she experienced both simultaneous relief and terror.

"The prison system can see you," Kate said.

"Roger that," Connor said.

Hearing his voice sent a shiver of sadness through her. She wished it had gone better between them the night before and that they hadn't left the rift between them. He was the man she loved and he had said he loved her, too. They would work through these problems. They had to.

"We're close, K. Disable the locks," Connor said.

"Copy that. I'm on it." Kate entered the prison locking system. It would cause havoc, but she needed to unlock the doors from the prison to the yard in cellblock 3B and temporarily shut down the air-traffic radar system.

It would allow Connor to jump from the copter on a rope, find Aiden and grab him. Finn would airlift them out. Simple plan, fraught with complications like guards with automatic weapons and violent, desperate prisoners.

This was the most time-critical portion of the mission. It would take the guards a few seconds to process that someone was dropping *out* of the copter, and if they called for assistance, Kate planned to delay their radio signal and electronic messages. Without confirmation from the radar system, the appearance and disappearance of the helicopter would cause confusion. They were hoping to use that confusion to get Aiden out before the guards started shooting at will.

Kate typed the command to unlock the doors in cellblock 3B. Her request was denied. She swore under her breath.

"What happened?" Connor asked.

"Doors aren't open. I repeat, doors aren't open."

"Delay or denial?" Connor asked.

"Denial. Trying again," Kate said.

Her fingers were already flying across the keyboard and her brain had snapped to that place of complete and total in-the-zone focus. She tried again using a different technique. Denied.

"K, give us a status," Connor said.

"I need a few more seconds," Kate said.

"We don't have extra seconds to spare," Finn said.

Kate tried again, her brain screaming for her to hurry. This time she was rewarded with a task-complete message. Relief rushed through her. "Doors are open. Make it fast."

Flipping to another program she was using to monitor electronic transmissions, she saw a text message from the guards to the warden requesting confirmation of the appearance of the copter. Kate intercepted and delayed it. When they tried to use their radios, she jammed the signal.

"Guards are suspicious. How's it going?" she asked, knowing her stall tactics wouldn't buy them much time.

"Connor's almost touching down," Finn said.

After a couple of seconds, shouting overwhelmed

their shared communication and Kate couldn't pick Connor's voice from others.

"What's going on?" she asked.

No response from Connor or Finn. They might not have heard her over the noise.

Her screen flickered and changed. She moved between programs and a cold chill of fear shot down her spine. She had been booted out of the prison's network. A connection problem? Or had someone discovered she was inside the system? She tried to get access again so she could run interference for Finn and Connor. Nothing. She was locked out.

"F, C, they know," she shouted. "They caught my trail. I can't help you. Do you hear me? Please acknowledge." She was screaming and Ariana came running.

She watched Kate with quaking eyes.

"K, get out of there now. If they know you were in here, they'll trace you," Finn said.

Kate was already one step ahead. She powered off her computer and grabbed it. She would have left it, but she might need it. The mission was going off the skids fast.

"We're going to the rendezvous point now," she said to Ariana.

Ariana leaped up, keys in hand. Their things, all except the computer and phone, were loaded in the car. Priority one was getting to the rendezvous point to meet up with Connor, Finn and Aiden.

The sound of gunfire sounded through her earpiece. "F, are you hurt? Is C hurt?" Terror clutched at her chest, but she kept moving.

"The prisoners realized the locks were disabled and are streaming into the yard. I lost sight of C. I don't know how much longer I can hold this position without getting shot out of the sky," Finn said.

"Don't leave without C and A. We need them." In that moment, she and Ariana were "we." How would she get Connor out if he were trapped in the prison?

Kate pulled open the front door of their hotel room. Marcus stood in front of her, his hand poised to knock and three armed guards behind him.

"Marcus?" Kate asked, confused about why and how he was at her hotel room. She wasn't staying at the hotel under her State Department alias. Why the armed guards? She gestured behind the door for Ariana to run and hide.

Marcus shoved the door open wider. "Where is he?"

The other men entered the room and fanned out, searching. One grabbed Ariana as she tried to climb out the window. Ariana was on the government's most-wanted list as a high-ranking member of the AR. Would Marcus recognize her? Ariana was traveling under an alias, but she hadn't changed her appearance much.

Kate stared at him, hot anger coursing through her. "What are you doing? What's going on?"

"Stop with the act, Kate. We know what you're planning. Where's Connor?"

How had they tied the jailbreak to her so quickly? Or had they uncovered the intention, but didn't know when the jailbreak was taking place? If Marcus knew Connor was at the jail, he wouldn't have questioned his whereabouts.

"I don't know," Kate said. "He went out for breakfast."

Ariana was dragged next to Kate. Marcus rolled his head, his neck cracking. "You've made this much more difficult than it needed to be. I know who you really are. You lied to me and pretended to be my friend."

Was Marcus working for *el presidente?* Or Sphere? Terror took hold of her. She had believed him to be an ally. "Let us go, Marcus, please. We are friends."

Marcus shook his head. "I've been paid to do a job and I'm going to do it. I need to bring you in. If you tell us where Connor is, perhaps *el presidente* will spare your life."

"He went to get breakfast," she said. She would stick with her original lie.

Marcus shook his head. "You're not helping yourself."

She might not be helping herself, but she was buying Connor time.

Had Connor gotten to Aiden? She hoped Finn and Connor were hearing this conversation with Marcus and were warned that the Tumaran government and *el presidente* knew who Connor and Kate were and had made the connection to Aiden.

"What are you planning to do to him?" Kate asked.

Marcus reached to the side of her head. She flinched, thinking he was going to hit her. Instead, he ripped her comm device from her ear. He smiled, perhaps hearing Connor's voice. "Hello, Connor. So nice to talk to you again. I have Kate here. I don't know what you're planning in your current position, but I'd like to make you an offer. Come to *el presidente*'s palace and turn yourself in. We can work something out so that your ladies keep their lives." He threw the comm device to the ground and stomped on it.

Marcus clamped his hand over her arm. "Don't

think about running. Your pretty little head has a price on it and it's a price I plan to collect."

Finn was a good chopper pilot, but leaping out of a moving aircraft and climbing down a rope into a yard filled with angry, abused prisoners was chilling. The guards were on high alert for any signs of rioting and Connor knew they would use excessive force if the situation required it. They wouldn't let a disturbance in the prison swell into another prison riot.

Connor and Finn had agreed that Finn would pull out and flee if his life was in danger. Finn's time and skills could be bought, but his life was worth too much and he had no real devotion to the cause.

Connor landed in the yard, his feet hitting the ground hard. Confusion ensued. "Aiden West!"

Prisoners mobbed the helicopter and Finn pulled up out of their reach. When the guards caught on to what was happening, Finn might have to flee, leaving Connor in the prison.

He called his brother's name and searched the sea of faces. The prisoners were taking full advantage of the open cells. The guards hadn't descended yet to the yard. Having been inside the prison during the riot, Connor knew what to expect. He guessed the warnings would be briefer and responses faster.

Connor charged into the prison as inmates streamed out of it. The short hallway opened to rows of cells. "Aiden!"

Connor listened for his brother's voice, his ears straining, hoping to hear the low, slow drawl that belonged to his brother. He ran past rows of cells, every step plunging him deeper into the prison and away from freedom.

"Aiden!"

When he heard his brother's voice, Connor wasn't sure if he had imagined it. He called his name again.

Then he saw him. His brother limped out of a cell and squinted in his direction. Aiden was dirty, his hair too long and his beard scruffy. He had never looked better. Connor ran to him. No time to talk or explain. He looped his arms under his brother's shoulder. They needed to run and get out of the prison. Connor had already spent more time than he'd planned.

"My leg," Aiden said, wincing.

What was wrong with his leg? "Don't be a pansy. Ignore it. Let's go."

If he could charge his brother with adrenaline and fear, they could overcome anything. On the other side of the helicopter ride was medical care, food and water. Even better, on the other side was freedom and the woman who loved him.

When Kate's face flashed to mind, Connor stamped it out. No time for distractions.

They pushed past inmates who had stepped out of their cells. Then the alarm blared. The alarm would clear up the confusion some of the guards might have had about the helicopter. The helicopter was now a target.

"Faster," Connor said, urging his body to pick up the pace. He was half dragging Aiden, but he didn't care. He would get his brother out even if he had to carry him.

The sound of gunfire peppered the air. If the guards were shooting at Finn, he would fly away. He wouldn't hang around and wait to be shot down. It did them no good to all be trapped inside the prison. Over the gunfire, Connor could still hear the rhythmic tick of the chopper blades. As long as Connor could get to the chopper, hope, however slim, existed of an escape.

Outside in the yard, Connor waved to Finn. He lowered the chopper once, and Connor seized the dangling harness, fighting off prisoners who grabbed at it. He didn't trust that Aiden had enough strength to hold on to a rope. Strapping his brother in, Connor wrapped himself around Aiden. Other inmates reached for the chopper like a lifeline. They couldn't airlift anyone else. They didn't have enough fuel to support more weight.

"Let go," Connor shouted. Some of the inmates were staring in shock as if they couldn't process what was happening. A few stepped back. Only one clung to the metal frame. His small body didn't release at Connor's command.

"You're going to be killed," Connor said. "We don't have enough fuel."

The man wouldn't be reasoned with. He had latched on and wasn't letting go. It was his life, and Connor didn't have the heart to rip the man off the chopper and throw him to the ground. Taking his chances on a risky jailbreak was his decision. Falling from hundreds of feet in the air and hitting the ground was an ugly way to die.

Finn was pulling the chopper off the ground. Connor held on to the rope and his brother with every ounce of strength he had. Amid the gunfire, a flash of hot searing pain speared through his leg. He needed his hands to support his weight and he ignored the burn and focused on staying conscious. The most important part of the mission was complete. Aiden was out.

Connor looked at his leg. Bright red colored his pant leg. He'd been hit by a guard's bullet. Dangling from the end of a rope swinging from a chopper while under fire, he'd be lucky not to be struck again. Aiden was in bad shape and Connor didn't know if he would survive more injuries. He hadn't had time to assess his brother's condition.

The rope began to retract into the chopper. Finn was a miracle worker. The farther they got from the prison, the safer they were.

"Are you okay?" Connor asked his brother.

Aiden nodded and closed his eyes. The thin man from the yard continued to cling to the chopper. Tenacious little man. Hopefully, his small stature wouldn't affect their fuel and fly time too drastically.

Despite the burning pain in his leg, Connor had never been happier to see his little brother. They were close to the chopper's cabin when he realized he hadn't heard Kate's voice. The shared line was silent.

"K, are you there?" Connor asked.

Finn's voice came on the line. "Two immediate threats. Someone named Marcus was with K, demanding you go to *el presidente*'s palace and turn yourself in to rescue K and A. And I've got someone on my tail."

Connor looked around and saw a helicopter racing toward them. They didn't have enough fuel to engage in a chase. Considering the extra hundred-plus pounds they were carrying, they were in bad enough shape. "Pull us in."

"I'm trying," Finn said, veering the chopper in another direction. Connor had never been afraid of heights, but after this experience, he might change that and join Kate in her terror of it.

As the rope got shorter, Connor pulled himself into the cabin and then dragged Aiden inside. He tossed the rope down and, against his better judgment, helped pull the small man into the cabin with them. The man was surprisingly strong and nimble.

"Thank you," the man said, his entire body trembling with fatigue and fear.

Connor's leg was covered in blood, and dizziness overwhelmed him. "I've been shot."

Finn looked over his shoulder. "Wrap that before you bleed out. I can't help at the moment. I haven't shaken the tail."

Aiden reached for the first-aid kit, and he and the small man helped with Connor's bleeding.

"Hold on back there," Finn said. "This maneuver might make you green."

Connor controlled the contents of his stomach as Finn lowered the chopper. He had lost too much blood. He was thirsty, and shock and adrenaline were wearing off, giving way to pain and dizziness.

"Where's K? Did she shake Marcus?" Connor asked. She was his priority now.

"She'd better be at the meeting point, but it sounds like she ran into trouble. I'll get us down and we need to bolt. These jokers are persistent," Finn said.

Aiden pressed hard over Connor's injury and spoke to the smaller man. "I saw you around the prison. You never spoke to anyone. Who are you?"

"Hyde," the man said and nothing else. He sat quietly with his legs folded as if staying quiet and tiny enough would make him disappear. Though La Saba-

neta contained some of the most dangerous men in the
country, it was difficult to picture this man being capable of such a title.

Finn brought the chopper down in an open field in a
landing that surprised Connor with how gentle it was.
Given the situation, he was bracing to be slammed to
the ground. They climbed out of the cabin and grabbed
the camouflage sheet. With some struggle and with
Hyde's help, they pulled it over the aircraft. Detection
from the air would be more difficult, but not impossible. None of their precautions was foolproof. The Tumaran government wouldn't give up looking for them
that easily.

Connor's chest tightened at the empty off-road vehicle waiting for them. Kate and Ariana hadn't made it.

"Where are they?" Connor asked, pressing down
on the injury on his leg. Had Kate fought off Marcus?

"They?" Aiden asked.

"Ariana and Kate Squire."

Joy erupted across Aiden's face. "Ariana is alive?"

"Yes, and she's supposed to meet us here," Connor said.

"We need to go. We won't have long before someone finds us," Finn said.

"Give them a few minutes," Connor said. His argument with Kate the night before flashed into his mind,
and he tamped down the guilt and frustration that came
with it. He had told Kate he loved her and he still did.

He was disappointed that she had lied to him. Was
it necessary for every person he loved to betray him?
Couldn't he have just one relationship where the other
person treated him with honesty and respect? He hadn't
spoken the right words to her and he hadn't known

what to say that morning. Did she understand how important the truth was to him in matters of his heart? Connor shook off those thoughts. Of course Kate understood what was important to him. No one else in the world had ever understood him as deeply as she seemed to. Fight or not, why hadn't he told her that this morning?

The state of their personal relationship wasn't important at the moment. All that mattered was that she was part of this mission; therefore, he had to help her. He left no man—or woman—behind. That meant he had to find Ariana and Kate.

"You coming?" Connor asked Hyde.

The man nodded and climbed into the vehicle. It was either his lucky day or the last one of his life.

Chapter 13

Connor stared at Aiden. Just stared at him. It was like seeing someone who'd come back from the dead. In some ways, Aiden had.

"Want to talk about it?" Aiden asked, catching his brother looking at him. He put down his fork and took a long drink from the cup next to his plate. It seemed as if Aiden had been eating and drinking since the moment they had crossed the border from Tumara into Theos. Theos wasn't an ally or enemy to Tumara, and they maintained their neutrality. Theos was the Switzerland of South America.

Connor winced. He wasn't great at talking about problems, and while he wanted to improve, starting the conversation was hard. To make it worse, his leg burned like fire. Though the doctor who'd performed the surgery on his calf had advised against it, Connor was putting weight on his leg, testing it and forcing it to bear weight. Though the bullet that hit him had been a through and through, Connor still needed time for it to fully recover. Time he didn't have with Kate and Ariana being held at *el presidente*'s palace. "When you disappeared all those months ago, I thought I would never get over it. There was so much unsaid between us."

Aiden took a seat next to his brother. His limp was less noticeable. He would need an orthopedic surgeon to repair the damage that had been done when a broken leg hadn't been set properly and had healed incorrectly. "Then say it now. Tell me what you wanted to say and couldn't. I'm listening now."

With his brother in front of him, Connor's throat grew tight with emotion, and the words lodged in his chest, unable to form on his tongue. Why was this so hard for him?

Aiden rolled his eyes. "We'll start with an easy one. How is it that you fell in love with Kate?"

Connor looked away. That wasn't an easy question. His feelings for Kate were a mix of love, betrayal and camaraderie. "She asked me for help to find you."

"No kidding," Aiden said, leaning back in his chair. "I knew there was something special about that woman. Have you seen her on the computer? I have never seen fingers move so fast. A real thinker. I'd heard of her before I met her, and when I found out we'd be working together, I did a jig. I had the best computer and analytical support looking out for me."

"She made a mistake that caused you to be captured."

"What mistake?" Aiden asked.

"The night you disappeared, she had intel about a planned raid against the AR. She didn't pass it on to you."

Aiden arched a brow. "The government is always planning raids against the AR. I knew Sphere suspected I had flipped sides, and I knew they were coming for me. They wanted the Tumaran government to kill me and make it look like I had been a casualty of the war with the AR or one of their victims."

"Why didn't they kill you?" Connor asked.

"I made for better leverage alive than dead," Aiden said.

"Maybe Sphere didn't know where you were after the raid and they were using me to find you," Connor said, the theory gaining some traction. When Kate had brought evidence from Marcus to Sphere that Aiden was alive, Sphere could have decided to use her to find Aiden, a task they hadn't been able to accomplish themselves. They had her psychological profile. They had to know she wouldn't have walked away and left Aiden in danger.

"Was her contact in on it the whole time? Did he feed her the bait?" Aiden asked.

Hard to say, but it didn't jibe with Connor, not after what he had seen of Marcus. "I don't think so. Marcus works for the Tumaran government. I think he was helping Kate and then he flipped on her for cash. The Tumaran government knew where you were. If they had shared that with Sphere, you would be dead and Sphere wouldn't have needed to use me and Kate to find you."

Aiden dropped his head, and when he lifted it, he looked exhausted. "Best-case scenario, I'm facing treason charges for helping the AR. Worst-case scenario, I return home in a wooden box."

"I won't let them kill you," Connor said.

"I've made a lot of enemies. I'll find Ariana and we'll be together. In Tumara, somewhere else—it doesn't matter to me as long as I'm with her," Aiden said. "Probably what you're thinking about Kate."

Aiden was wrong on that count. Connor hadn't made any future plans with Kate. "She lied to me." The burn of her lie coursed through him all over again. What made her lie worse was that she had earned his trust. He had stopped believing that she was outright conning him and started thinking about her as a partner and a friend.

Aiden inclined his head. "That doesn't sound like Kate. You mean she lied about something regarding Sphere? Because you know we've all lied about that place and the work we've done for them."

"No, not about Sphere. About you. She knew more about your disappearance than she initially told me."

Aiden lifted his brows. "So you said. What's your point?"

His brother wasn't upset that she had withheld information that could have helped them? "She should have told me everything. Your life was at stake."

"Come on, Connor. I'm calling you out on that. Do you really believe she should have confided in a stranger classified information about my disappearance?" Aiden asked. "You know that's not how it works. Sphere agents are conditioned to be tight-lipped. We've each signed the agreement to stay quiet on matters related to and affecting our missions."

Connor propped his leg on the coffee table. It was throbbing hard and aching. "She should have trusted me."

Aiden threw back his head and laughed. "She should

have trusted you? This coming from the man who trusts no one? Who suspects everyone is out to get him? Who lives in the freaking woods in the middle of nowhere so he doesn't risk interacting with a neighbor because God forbid you make a new friend?"

Connor stiffened. "That's not true." Not all of it.

"Connor, I love you. You're my brother and you're the only one I'll ever have. But sometimes you are too hard on other people and too hard on yourself. You're even hard on the people who love you. Put yourself in Kate's shoes for a minute. How much courage did it take for her to find you?"

A lot. Massive brass. "I never said she was cowardly," Connor mumbled.

"Cut her a break. Cut yourself a break. When you talk about her, you actually smile. Will you let her get away because she didn't give you classified information on day one?"

"She had plenty of opportunities to tell me after day one." His argument was sounding lame even to him.

Aiden shook his head. "You can't write people off the first time they make a mistake. If you do that, you'll never get close to anyone. You'll never get to that point where the relationship has substance and really matters." Aiden brought his finger to his lips. "Oh, wait. That describes you exactly. Everyone is allowed in to a very shallow point, and then, at the smallest infraction, they're done and you throw them out."

Connor held back the denial. He had known he had overreacted to Kate's admission, but Aiden was helping him see it from Kate's point of view. Perhaps she had done the best she could. Perhaps she had told him everything she could at the time. In this instance, Connor had made a mistake, too. He had been quick to dismiss her. She had said she loved him and cared about him. She deserved better from him. An honest conversation, or at a minimum, he could have listened to her and not stalked away, running from the situation. He was ashamed of his behavior, and deep regret sluiced over him. He needed to talk to her and couldn't. She was somewhere at the hands of *el presidente,* a man known for his ice-cold detachment, severe punishments and general ruthlessness.

Aiden sat forward. "No sharp reply? Let me put it to you another way. I talk to Mom. I even talk to Dad about more than the obligatory 'how is that place treating you' topics. You know why I've never talked to you about it?"

Connor replayed Aiden's words. Aiden spoke to their mother? The woman who had walked out on them and had abandoned them years before when they'd needed her? "I have many questions about that trinket of information, but I'm guessing you never told me because you didn't think I cared." If that was Aiden's assumption, he would have been right. Connor wouldn't have wanted to hear about it.

Aiden shook his head. "Nope. I never told you because every time I've tried, you cut me off. You make it impossible to tell you or talk to you about it. You don't want Mom and Dad in your life and you've made that clear. What was I going to do about it? Hammer you with it until I beat you into submission and made you listen?"

"You could have told me," Connor said, questioning how he felt about this. His curiosity about Aiden's relationship with their parents was a surprise. He shouldn't care what his brother chose to do or say to them.

"You don't listen, so I don't talk about it."

Connor hadn't realized his brother felt this way. "What is there to say about them? Mom left us and Dad hated us. Why would I want people like that in my life?" For the first time since he was a child, he wanted Aiden to give him a reason why it was worth having them in his life. Almost losing Aiden had opened Connor's eyes to how precious time with family was. If something happened to their parents, would Connor have to live with the same regret he'd felt after Aiden disappeared? Worse still, would he have to live with the regret of not making up with Kate?

Aiden threw his hands in the air. "You're doing it again. You're giving your side of the story from the perspective of a child. You've never stopped to ask questions or find out what happened between Mom and Dad."

It was a painful part of his life he didn't want to relive. "What happened between them wasn't my concern." He had cared only about how his parents as individuals had treated him and Aiden. In this case, it wasn't well.

"Would it surprise you to learn that Mom and Dad fought hard and viciously to get custody of us? Dad dragged Mom's name through the mud during the custody battle to make sure she couldn't take us away. Mom borrowed a great deal of money and put herself in deep debt to hire lawyers to fight for us, for all the good it did."

His father had never spoken about what had happened between him and his wife. What Aiden described of their father hurting their mother fit what Connor knew of him. "Mom and Dad fought for custody of us?" Both their parents had wanted them. That knowledge lightened and softened the darkest, most hardened place of his soul.

Aiden nodded. "Dad had reasons to be angry with her. Mom had an affair and she openly admits it was wrong. She tried to explain it to me, the why and the how, but mostly she feels sorry for what it did to us and our family."

Their mother's affair was news to Connor. He wanted to hear what else Aiden knew.

"When Dad found out Mom was cheating on him, he filed for divorce and for sole custody of us. Mom fought it, but Dad had more money and more resources. When she lost us, she returned to England. She said her heart was broken and she had no reason to stay," Aiden said.

"She never called. Or wrote."

"She says she did for a while, but Dad wouldn't let the calls or letters through. By the time we were adults, you wouldn't speak to her even when she reached out."

Twice. His mother had tried to contact him twice during adulthood. "Why did Dad want us if he hated us?"

"He doesn't hate us. He never hated us." Aiden looked at the ground. "He didn't know how to be a single parent and how to deal with the stress. I know as the older brother you took most of the beatings. You put yourself in the way so that I was spared. You antagonized Dad to keep him away from me. I didn't realize how bad it was for you. Now that I look back, I carry a tremendous amount of guilt, knowing what you did for me and what it cost you."

"I didn't do any of it to make you feel guilty," Connor said.

"I know that. But you took on more than a child should. Dad was an alcoholic, and he was angry and depressed, and he needed help. He didn't know how to deal with life, and being a single father was terrifying for him. He acted out when he was frustrated, which was most of the time."

"That's not an excuse," Connor said.

"No, it's not. But it's an explanation. It wasn't the childhood I wanted, but it was a childhood that made me strong. It made me the man I am today."

Connor had never heard Aiden speak like this. Usually carefree and lighthearted, his younger brother went along with what Connor wanted and said. Though he'd contradicted him, Connor liked this side of Aiden, even if what he was saying made Connor uncomfortable.

Connor questioned his choices regarding his family. Why had he refused to allow their mother in his life? Why was he cold and distant with his father over hurt that had ended decades before? Why was he so quick to cut people—Kate, most recently—out of his life?

It didn't take weeks of therapy to draw a conclusion. Connor sealed people out because he didn't want to be hurt. But by isolating himself from the potential to be hurt, he was isolating himself from the people who loved him. Connor stood and reached for his brother. He drew him into an awkward hug.

Aiden responded by putting his arms around his brother and hugging him back. "I missed you, big brother."

Though they had both gotten misty, they cleared their throats and patted each other's backs and released each other.

"I made a mistake with Kate." And perhaps with their mother and father, too.

Aiden shrugged. "Find a way to make it right. We will get Ariana and Kate out. And when we do, you'll have the chance to tell her how you feel."

Connor scrubbed a hand across his face. "Do you think she knows I'm coming for them? She needs me now. She needs me to find her."

Aiden twisted his mouth in thought. "We're both going to find them. No arguments about that. Kate and Ariana may know we're trying. I don't know how much about the prison break they know. Regardless, I doubt they're sitting around waiting. They're capable women. They could find a way out on their own. They're fighters."

"Like you found a way out on your own?" Connor asked drily.

Aiden laughed. "Time would have told. I was close to getting out. If it wasn't for this bum leg, I would have climbed out."

Connor grinned at his brother. "If that's what you need to tell yourself to preserve your rep, we'll go with that story."

The sound of female laughter drew them both to their feet. Who had entered their bungalow? Finn and Hyde were keeping watch in shifts. Connor and Aiden moved to the front door, prepared to face a slew of Sphere agents.

Finn and Hyde were alone in the room.

"I heard a woman," Connor said, looking around.

Hyde stood from the chair. "Surprise." A distinctly feminine voice.

Aiden inclined his head. "You're a woman?"

She grinned. "Finally figure that out?"

Connor stared. Her petite features and smaller frame should have been clues. "Why were you in La Sabaneta?" From what he knew, it was a male-only prison. He shuddered to think about the abuse a woman would face inside.

"I was captured during a government raid of an AR camp, just like Aiden. I pretended to be a man. I thought I would fare better. It wasn't the first time I've pretended to be male, but it was the most challenging," Hyde said.

Connor stared at her for a long moment and recognition dawned. "I hadn't made the connection. You're Alexandra Hyde."

Alexandra Hyde was a female mercenary, one of the few with an esteemed reputation in their field. She had been off the grid for some time, which wasn't unusual for a mercenary.

"It's a pleasure to meet you," she said and nodded toward him.

"I should have known," Connor said. "Although your stature doesn't live up to the legend."

Hyde laughed. "My reputation has served me well. I've already thanked Finn for his role in my unplanned escape. Thank you, as well. I owe you one."

Connor knew exactly how he wanted to cash in the favor. "Glad to hear you say that. We're working on a second jailbreak."

Hyde lifted one brow. "Not at La Sabaneta."

"No. At the palace of *el presidente* outside Carvalo City," Connor said.

Hyde and Finn exchanged looks. Hyde shrugged. "I'm in. I have a bone to pick with that man. Might as well clear my debt to you while taking care of some personal business." She cracked her knuckles.

"We need to rescue two women being held against their will," Connor said.

Hyde's eyes narrowed. "I have a soft spot for that very cause. Point me at him and I'll charge in with guns blazing."

"The only open problem is who gets first shot at him," Connor said. If *el presidente* had hurt Kate in any way, he would die at Connor's hands.

"Guess it depends," Aiden said.

"On what?" Hyde asked.

"On who gets to that SOB first," Aiden said.

It wasn't as bad as the prison, but the holding cell at *el presidente*'s palace was without television, computer, clock or phone. The windows were high on the wall, covered in dark cloth and narrow. Too narrow for either Kate or Ariana to slip through.

Kate was facing extradition to the United States on treason charges. Or the Tumaran government would kill her and Ariana. She guessed they weren't killed on the spot because *el presidente* would make an example of them to show the rest of the country what happened to traitors and revolutionaries.

How much time had passed? She and Ariana had taken turns sleeping and keeping watch. They hadn't been fed and had been given only a small amount of water. Weakness wrapped its tentacles around Kate more with every moment that passed. No air moved through the room and the hours were endless.

"They want to break us," Ariana said again. For being trapped in a small room with little chance of escape, Ariana had maintained a positive attitude. "Once we're hungry and tired, their mind games will work better."

Kate rested her head against the door. It would be easy to play games with her. She didn't know what had happened to Connor, Finn and Aiden. The last she had heard, the helicopter had descended into the prison yard. Had Connor heard Marcus's demand that he come to *el presidente*'s palace? If he hadn't, he wouldn't know where she and Ariana were.

When Kate and Ariana hadn't shown at the rendezvous point, assuming that the trio of men had made it, they had to know something was wrong. A huge missing chunk of information existed between what she knew and what she longed to know. Had they rescued Aiden? Was Connor safe?

Would Connor figure out that Marcus had sold out to *el presidente* and given up everything he knew about Kate Swiss?

She had asked Marcus about Connor. She had asked the men who had delivered the water about him. She had asked in English, in Portuguese and in Spanish. No one would answer her.

Kate had left her relationship with Connor in a bad place. He had been angry with her, and though that anger had taken a backseat to Aiden's rescue, it bothered her to think about it and all she had was time to think. She hadn't meant to betray Connor or Aiden. Withholding information from Connor had been a mistake. He wanted brutal honesty. She could give him that. If she had a chance in the future, if she saw him again and if he forgave her, she would do better.

Questions and lack of basic necessities were driving her to a bad mental place. "How did you survive those months not knowing how Aiden was or where he was?" Kate asked.

Ariana gave her a small smile. "Day by day, minute by minute, I devoted myself to the AR. I told myself that I would change Tumara and I would find and free Aiden. I would get rid of *el presidente* and put someone in power who would be good for our country and who would give our citizens a chance at success and happiness, like my brother Bruno."

"You didn't know if Aiden was alive or not," Kate said, hating to speak the harsh words, but wondering about Connor. The ache in her chest was so strong, she wanted to cry. And Kate never cried. It was a sign of weakness and another of the thousand ways that she tried to blend with the men around her. She wouldn't sob. It wouldn't help and she had no hydration or energy to spare.

"I always believed he was alive. Just as I believe it now. Don't let them break you. Don't let them make you think Connor is dead. He and Aiden are coming for us. I know they are," Ariana said.

Soft, sad words. Kate focused on thinking about Connor and picturing him coming to her rescue. He had been angry with her. Was he angry enough to leave her in *el presidente*'s palace? Aiden would come for Ariana. How would Kate feel if Aiden showed up sans Connor?

Her heart would break all over again. "Connor and I had a disagreement the night before the jailbreak."

"And now you think he will forget about you?" Ariana asked.

"Connor isn't like Aiden. His trust is on a hair trigger."

Ariana straightened. "Aiden talked about Connor from time to time." She paused as if considering whether she should say more. "Connor and Aiden didn't have the easiest childhood, but they have good hearts. I don't think Connor would leave you here over a quarrel."

A quarrel that had struck close to the heart of Connor's trust issue. "When I fell in love with him, I knew what I was risking. I knew he was closed off. I just hoped I could get through to him and he would see that I could be trusted. I never intended to hurt him. I wanted him to see that we are meant to be together." When he'd finally told her he loved her and trusted her, she had taken a machete to the sentiment.

"You'll have plenty of time to explain yourself and come to an understanding when we get out of here," Ariana said.

That was where she needed to focus her effort: on getting out of this place. Kate would wait and she would get the opportunity. When she did, she would grab it and run.

She pictured Connor's face and hands, his soft touch and his strong body. She remembered how she'd felt when he'd kissed her for the first time, the excitement when they had made love and the wonderfulness of the word *love* on his lips. He would come for her. She wouldn't question it. Trust went both ways and trust was only real when tested.

Connor had to turn himself in to *el presidente*. For Kate's life, he didn't have a choice. He, Finn, Aiden and Hyde had discussed the options. They had planned and changed plans and reworked plans. In the end, the best they could do was to surrender. Connor couldn't talk Aiden out of coming with him. In Connor's current physical state, with his leg weakened and without weapons or resources, he couldn't fight off the army of men *el presidente* surrounded himself with at his palace.

He and Aiden walked to the gates of the palace. The past three days—three long, intense days of gathering resources and information and preparing in every way they could—had led to this moment.

"Do you realize this is the first time we've worked a mission together?" Aiden asked. "I always wanted to be in the field with the legendary Connor West."

"You'll give me a big ego if you keep that up," Connor said.

Aiden laughed. "Okay, no more compliments. You ready to face the music?"

Connor shrugged. "Ready as I can be."

They stood outside the gates, and within moments, they were apprehended by six guards. Aiden and Connor didn't waste energy struggling. They were dragged inside the house and they were patted down. One of the guards took the gun Connor had hidden at his ankle.

"Did you think we would allow you near *el presidente* with this?" the guard asked, holding it up.

He hadn't. It had been worth a shot. Though they had

chosen this path to save the women they loved and get them to safety as soon as possible, they weren't fools. *El presidente* was not an honorable man. His palace was opulent, painted in gold with thick velvet-and-satin draperies over the windows and shiny marble on the floor. He lived in luxury while his countrymen suffered and scrambled to have enough to eat. That alone spoke to his character.

Connor and Aiden were brought before *el presidente*. The dictator sat behind a mahogany desk. He smiled when Connor and Aiden were brought in.

"You've decided to be reasonable and turn yourselves in," *el presidente* said.

General Alva stood at his side, smirking. Though Connor had met the man only once, his dislike of him was potent.

"You have Kate and Ariana. What choice did we have but to come here?" Connor asked.

El presidente rose to his feet and circled the desk. He stood in front of Connor and Aiden. Their arms were secured by two guards each. The other two guards had taken a post by the door. Connor wanted to whip the man across his smug face, but he controlled his temper. This mission was intensely personal and required more control. Quick responses fueled by volatile emotions were catastrophic.

El presidente struck Connor across the face. Connor didn't avoid the blow and he didn't fight back. Outnumbered and weaponless, his struggle would be futile, and he wouldn't give *el presidente* the satisfaction of seeing him fight and fail.

All he cared about was seeing Kate and Ariana and knowing they hadn't been harmed.

"You are trusting men," *el presidente* said.

He could not have been more off target about Connor. "I did what I needed to do," Connor said. "You asked me to come and I did."

Aiden remained silent.

El presidente walked to stand in front of Aiden. "And you. You escaped the most dangerous prison in our country. You'll find the accommodations there are better than where you're going."

Aiden stared blankly and Connor knew he was controlling himself for Ariana. "Since I'm guessing I'll be six feet under, I guess you're right."

El presidente seemed gleeful with Aiden's words. "If you're lucky we'll bury your body. More likely, I'll throw it in the street for the dogs to make an example of what happens to people who interfere in my country and who betray me. You're an American traitor. Your country doesn't want you returned. They would rather see you dead at my hands. Works to my advantage since that's the outcome I prefer, as well."

Connor saw the anger light in Aiden's face and Aiden looked at the ground to hide it. *El presidente* was wrong. The American people wouldn't stand for an American to be treated as a rabid animal and violently killed, but Sphere would. *El presidente* knew that Sphere liked for messes to be cleaned up, and death was the surest way to keep their secrets and tie off loose ends.

"Release Kate Squire and Ariana Feliz," Connor said.

El presidente laughed. "You're in no position to make demands."

"Let them go. You have Aiden and me. You have what you wanted," Connor said.

El presidente shook his head. "I only expected one traitor to turn himself in. Lucky to get you both on some misplaced sense of honor. I have what I want. The four people who have caused me complications. Ms. Feliz has caused problems for me. She and her dimwit brother are leading the rebellion against me. I can't let her return to her terrorist network. She's the fuel on their fire. Ms. Squire knows too much. I can't stand for that. I will find and punish everyone who's assisted you. I will kill them. I will break the spirit of the rebellion, and peace will rule the land."

El presidente wasn't planning to release Kate or Ariana, and he had no plans for peace. No amount of money would sway him, no exchange of lives and no bargaining. The four of them were condemned to die.

Connor glanced at the clock on the far wall. It was two minutes until eight o'clock in the evening. Connor asked again for their lives. "Don't kill the women. You don't want their blood on your hands."

El presidente lifted a brow as if surprised Connor had responded. "I won't get any blood on my hands. That's why I have General Alva and my guards. They take care of uncivilized tasks."

If he'd had a sliver of respect for *el presidente,* Connor would have lost it then. A leader who forced others to do his dirty work, just as Sphere did, was cowardly and weak.

The sound of chanting drifted in through the closed windows. *El presidente* turned to General Alva. "What is that?"

Connor inclined his head and feigned momentary

confusion. "Oh, that noise? That's the ten thousand people we invited along tonight to make sure you kept your word. Clearly, we made the right choice, seeing as you have every intention of killing my brother and me and Kate and Ariana. Turns out Bruno Feliz likes his sister and the AR wants her alive. And Kate? I've never known anyone who has more friends online and around the world prepared to help her with almost no notice." That and the boost of support from Kate's sister, Elise. As an A-list Hollywood actress, she held sway over newspapers and society. Once she'd begun speaking out about her sister being held against her will in Tumara, support for them had tumbled in, wave after wave of it.

El presidente paled.

"They'll break down every door in this building until they find you. They will find and release Ariana and Kate. Your only hope is that the women are not injured, because if they are, perhaps your death will not be merciful," Connor said, relishing every word.

El presidente appeared terrified. He turned to General Alva. "Don't let anyone in here. Seal the gates and call for the National Emergency Reserves." General Alva and the two guards at the door raced out of the room to do *el presidente*'s bidding.

The chanting grew stronger and the sound of C4 explosions boomed. Hyde had scrounged up some explosives to help with the night's plans. Gates and doors would not keep out an angry mob.

Connor looked at Aiden. "How are you feeling, brother?" he asked.

Aiden grinned. "My arms are numb. I think it's time to put my boot in someone's backside."

At the same moment, Connor and Aiden sprang into action. They had the element of surprise. Connor freed his hands and disarmed the men on either side of him, while Aiden did the same. He took their weapons, arming himself. He raced to the windows and opened them. Aiden joined him. Every window and door they opened made it easier for their reinforcements to get inside.

At the front window overlooking the entrance to the palace, Connor caught sight of the crowd coming to their aid. The view stirred his pride in the goodness of people and strengthened his new belief that, deep down, people wanted to help. Ten thousand people from Tumara and around the world had taken up the cause of the Armed Revolutionaries. They raced across the grounds, barreling through gardens, shoving guards out of the way. They arrived at the open windows and cheered.

Finn and Hyde were first to reach Aiden and Connor. Hyde handed Connor some C4. "As promised." She grinned. "This is the most fun I have had in months. Let's pound some dictator scum into nothing."

"Did you find Kate and Ariana?" Finn asked.

"Not yet," Connor said. "We will."

As more people piled into the room, Connor noticed *el presidente* had fled. He couldn't get far with the throngs of people forming a barrier around the palace, and Connor wouldn't give chase. Not now. Kate came first.

He and Aiden raced through the halls, calling Kate's and Ariana's names. The chanting of "Power to the people!" was overwhelming. A dictator would be overthrown tonight and the history of Tumara forever changed.

Social media wasn't Connor's cup of tea, but he had

newfound respect for it. He didn't understand how it worked or why complete strangers got on board with the plans Aiden had posted to a website the AR ran. Though the messages were cryptic, Aiden had spread the word about what was happening at *el presidente*'s palace and people had arrived to lend a hand. Once Connor caught on about how to use it, he had spent hours at the keyboard, generating support for the release of Kate and Ariana and the overthrow of *el presidente*.

Supporters had flown, driven and walked, spurred by patriotic messages of democracy and freedom and eager to end the rule of a tyrant.

"If you were hiding two women, where would you put them?" Aiden asked.

"The basement?" Connor asked.

Connor and Aiden took the stairs down. Connor grabbed a guard who was standing in the hallway, watching people rush by and appearing bewildered. Connor took both his guns, handed them to Aiden and held him by the collar of his shirt. "Tell me where you are holding the women."

The man's eyes grew wide. "*El presidente* will kill me."

Connor shook his head. "You see these people? You think *el presidente* has a chance of surviving the night here? Think again. Do a favor for me, tell me where to find them, and I'll spare your life when this is over."

The man trembled from head to toe. "They are on the lower level. I will take you." Perhaps the man assumed he was safer with Connor than braving the crowd alone.

The basement was dark, cold and damp. Anger

stormed through Connor thinking of Kate and Ariana in these conditions. The guard led them to a locked steel door.

"Do you have a key?" Connor asked.

The man shook his head.

Connor kicked at the handle with his good leg and shouted to Kate and Ariana.

"Kate, are you and Ariana okay?" Connor asked.

"Connor! Yes, we're okay." The sound of Kate's voice triggered relief, love and joy in Connor's veins. She was alive. As long as he could hold her in his arms, everything would be okay.

"Stand back from the door. Cover your face and your ears. I'm blowing this door open." Connor took a small amount of C4 and set it in the lock of the door and ignited it.

"Run!" he said to his brother.

They took cover, and the door blew clear off, slamming into the wall across the hall.

"You're a crazy son of—" Aiden said.

His voice was lost as Kate appeared through the cloud of debris, stumbling over the rubble toward him. "Connor."

They ran for each other and Connor took her in his arms. "Kate, are you okay? Let me look at you. Let me see if you're okay."

"What about you? What happened? Is Aiden with you?"

Connor turned her to see Ariana and Aiden locked in a passionate embrace.

"We got him," Connor said.

"What is that chanting?" Kate asked.

"Ten thousand people storming the gates," Connor said.

"Ten thousand people? What are you talking about?" Kate asked.

"I'm talking about the power of social media and your sister."

"My sister? You mean Elise is involved in this?"

"She sure is," Connor said. "She was devastated to learn you were here, and she put her A-list weight behind this effort."

"I don't know what's more surprising—that she cared enough to speak out for me or that you used social media. You interacted with people online?" Kate asked.

He had. More in the past few days than in the rest of his life combined. "A man can change. This man has done a lot of changing. I made a mistake, Kate. I overreacted when you told me about Aiden and what happened when he went missing. I let one small thing get in the way of our future."

Kate's eyes welled with tears. "Then we have a future?"

"I hope we do. If you can forgive me."

"Of course I can. I love you, Connor. That will never change."

"I love you, too," Connor said.

Connor kissed her lightly on the lips and let his forehead fall against hers. With Kate in the circle of his arms, his world felt good and right.

find a headquarters and recruit his staff. His first hire had been Kate as his chief technology officer. He was bent on running the company with ethics and integrity that had gone missing at Sphere.

"Do you know my mother had dinner with my father the other night?" Connor asked.

"She told me," Kate said, holding up a paint swatch against the white primer on Connor's new office walls. He wouldn't be spending much time behind a desk, but the head of the United States' premier security consulting firm should have an office that suited the position.

"What do you think it means?" Connor asked.

Kate turned to face him. "I think it means that after being angry for too long, two people are willing to be friends for the sake of their children."

"Maybe they want to show up to Aiden and Ariana's wedding on good terms," Connor said. "After all, a brawl at the Tumaran president's sister's wedding is the kind of publicity the new president is trying to avoid."

"Could be. But I think the best gift for Aiden is to see the three of you getting along. Every time we talk about it, he swears I'm telling him stories."

Connor's relationship with his parents had improved since Kate had become part of his life. She had insisted on meeting them, and once she had, her regular calls and visits to his father had begun to heal some of the hurt Connor had carried all his life. Getting in touch with his mother had also been Kate's idea. His mother had been so happy to hear from her long-lost son's future wife, she had moved to Colorado to be near him.

Kate's gratitude to Elise for what she had done while Kate was held prisoner in Tumara had opened lines of communication between them. Kate had had dinner with her sister for the first time in years.

"I have another story I want to tell him very soon," Connor said, putting his arms around the woman he loved. "It involves you and me and a wedding and a dozen babies."

Kate arched a brow. "A dozen babies? Let's start with one and see how that goes."

"Is that a yes?"

"Was that a proposal?"

Connor withdrew a ring from his pocket and held it out to her. She extended her hand and he slipped the ring onto it.

"Yes, it's a most definite yes," Kate said.

The healing power of love had touched them all.

* * * * *

REQUEST YOUR FREE BOOKS!
2 FREE NOVELS PLUS 2 FREE GIFTS!

ROMANTIC suspense

Sparked by danger, fueled by passion

YES! Please send me 2 FREE Harlequin® Romantic Suspense novels and my 2 FREE gifts (gifts are worth about $10). After receiving them, if I don't wish to receive any more books, I can return the shipping statement marked "cancel." If I don't cancel, I will receive 4 brand-new novels every month and be billed just $4.74 per book in the U.S. or $5.24 per book in Canada. That's a savings of at least 14% off the cover price! It's quite a bargain! Shipping and handling is just 50¢ per book in the U.S. and 75¢ per book in Canada.* I understand that accepting the 2 free books and gifts places me under no obligation to buy anything. I can always return a shipment and cancel at any time. Even if I never buy another book, the two free books and gifts are mine to keep forever.

240/340 HDN F45N

Name	(PLEASE PRINT)	

Address		Apt. #

City	State/Prov.	Zip/Postal Code

Signature (if under 18, a parent or guardian must sign)

Mail to the Harlequin® Reader Service:
IN U.S.A.: P.O. Box 1867, Buffalo, NY 14240-1867
IN CANADA: P.O. Box 609, Fort Erie, Ontario L2A 5X3

Want to try two free books from another line?
Call 1-800-873-8635 or visit www.ReaderService.com.

* Terms and prices subject to change without notice. Prices do not include applicable taxes. Sales tax applicable in N.Y. Canadian residents will be charged applicable taxes. Offer not valid in Quebec. This offer is limited to one order per household. Not valid for current subscribers to Harlequin Romantic Suspense books. All orders subject to credit approval. Credit or debit balances in a customer's account(s) may be offset by any other outstanding balance owed by or to the customer. Please allow 4 to 6 weeks for delivery. Offer available while quantities last.

Your Privacy—The Harlequin® Reader Service is committed to protecting your privacy. Our Privacy Policy is available online at www.ReaderService.com or upon request from the Harlequin Reader Service.

We make a portion of our mailing list available to reputable third parties that offer products we believe may interest you. If you prefer that we not exchange your name with third parties, or if you wish to clarify or modify your communication preferences, please visit us at www.ReaderService.com/consumerschoice or write to us at Harlequin Reader Service Preference Service, P.O. Box 9062, Buffalo, NY 14269. Include your complete name and address.

SPECIAL EXCERPT FROM

H HARLEQUIN®

ROMANTIC suspense

When Drew offers to marry his brother's widow and care
for her son, he never expects to fall for Alyssa. But when the
child is kidnapped, Drew will do whatever it takes to make
his family whole again.

Read on for a sneak peek at

OPERATION UNLEASHED

by Justine Davis, available June 2014 from
Harlequin® Romantic Suspense.

"We did this."

Her voice was soft, almost a whisper from behind him.
He spun around. She'd gone up with Luke to get him warm
and dry, and set him up with his current favorite book. He
was already reading well for his age, on to third-grade level
readers, and Drew knew that was thanks to Alyssa. "Yes," he
said, his voice nearly as quiet as hers. "We did."

"It has to stop, Drew."

"Yes."

"What can I do to make that easier?"

God, he hated this. She was being so reasonable, so
understanding. And he felt like a fool because the only answer
he had was "Stop loving my brother."

"I'm not Luke," he said, not quite snapping. "Don't treat
me like a six-year-old."

"Luke," she said sweetly, "is leaving temper tantrums
behind."

He drew back sharply. Opened his mouth, ready to truly snap this time. And stopped.

"Okay," he said after a moment, "I had that one coming."

"Yes."

In an odd way, her dig pleased him. Not because it was accurate, he sheepishly admitted, but because she felt confident enough to do it. She'd been so weak, sick and scared when he'd found her four years ago, going toe-to-toe with him like this would have been impossible. But she was strong now, poised and self-assured. And he took a tiny bit of credit for that.

"You've come a long way," he said quietly.

"Because I don't cower anymore?"

He frowned. "I never made you cower."

For an instant she looked startled. "I never said you did. You saved us, Drew, don't think I don't know that, or will ever forget it. I have come a long way, and it's in large part because you made it possible."

It was a pretty little speech, a sentiment she'd expressed more than once. And not so long ago it had been enough. More than enough. It had told him he'd done exactly what he'd intended. That he'd accomplished his goal. That she was stable now, strong, and he'd had a hand in that.

And it wasn't her fault that wasn't enough for him anymore.

**Don't miss
OPERATION UNLEASHED
by Justine Davis,
available June 2014 from
Harlequin® Romantic Suspense.**

HARLEQUIN®

ROMANTIC suspense

SPECIAL OPS RENDEZVOUS
by Karen Anders

The Adair Legacy

Heartstopping danger, breathtaking
passion, conspiracy and intrigue.
The Adair Legacy has it all.

After surviving torture, soldier Sam Winston
sees threats everywhere. But when his politician
mother is almost killed, he teams up with his
psychiatrist, the mysterious Olivia, to find the
assassin. Except Olivia is keeping a secret....

Look for *SPECIAL OPS RENDEZVOUS* by
Karen Anders in June 2014. Available wherever
books and ebooks are sold.

Don't miss other titles from
The Adair Legacy miniseries:
HIS SECRET, HER DUTY by Carla Cassidy
EXECUTIVE PROTECTION by Jennifer Morey

Heart-racing romance, high-stakes suspense!

www.Harlequin.com

HRS27874